THE LEGEND OF
SEÑORITA SCORPION

Les Savage, Jr.

GUNSMOKE

This hardback edition 2003
by BBC Audiobooks Ltd
by arrangement with
Golden West Literary Agency

ISBN 0 7540 8249 0

British Library Cataloguing in Publication Data available.

Printed and bound in Great Britain by
Antony Rowe Ltd., Chippenham, Wiltshire

EDITOR'S NOTE

An earlier version of this Western novel concerned with the legend of the Douglas family and the legend of Señorita Scorpion appeared in three installments in *Action Stories*. This magazine did not feature serials, so breaking the narrative into installments was an editorial necessity. It was, however, the author's intention to combine them eventually into a novel. This first book edition is based on the author's original typescripts and appears now with the title and in the form the author intended.

TABLE OF CONTENTS

SEÑORITA SCORPION

I

Chisos Owens stepped down off his horse in front of Anse Hawkman's big frame hotel, and the creak of his Porter saddle was the only sound in the strange hush that hung over Boquillos. He dropped his reins over the animal's head and onto the sagging cottonwood hitch rack and stood there for a moment, feeling the physical weight of the silence press in on him.

A hawk-faced Apache stood barefooted between two adobe hovels, hands hitched into the big silver *conchas* of his Navajo belt. As Owens watched, a pair of gaudily garbed Mexicans trotted dusty horses in from the north end of the border town. They slowed to a walk going by the Apache. For a moment their sombrero-shadowed faces turned toward him, and a glance passed between the three men. The door of the *cantina* across the street opened to omit a drunken peon. Owens caught the noise of the usual Saturday afternoon revelry from within. Then the door closed again, and once more there was that silence. The two riders had halted their horses without dismounting. One spoke softly to the other, glanced toward Owens. Another horseman appeared at the opposite end of the street, halted there. He wore a fancy suit too.

Suddenly Owens shrugged and walked around the hitch rack to the hotel porch. He bent forward slightly in his sure-footed stride, like a man who might be hard to stop, and his blue denim jumper was carried away from the square ungiving block of

1

his torso. Beneath a Texas-creased Stetson, his eyes had the slitted, wind-wrinkled look that comes to a man spending his life in the open. The long ride had grimed the flat strong planes of his face with dust and thinned his lips with a weariness, but his chin held a certain stubborn tenacity in its bull-dog jut.

Bick Bickford had been waiting on the porch, a man taller than Chisos, heavy about the waist. The boards creaked beneath his weight as he moved forward, big freckled hands tucked into a cartridge belt.

"Began to think you weren't coming, Chisos."

"What," asked Owens in his deliberate voice, "is the matter with this town?"

"Same thing that's wrong with the whole border around the Big Bend," said Bick heavily. "Same thing Anse Hawkman brought you down here for."

Owens's lips twisted down at the name as if he had tasted rotten *frijoles*. He hadn't thought he would ever be coming back to this border town—much less be working for Anse Hawkman.

He spat. "Let's go in."

The door creaked on dry hinges and closed behind them. They crossed a faded flowered carpet in front of the desk. A bow-legged man in slick apron chaps blocked their way to the stairs, his rope-scarred hand slipping to his Colt.

"It's all right," said Bick. "Chisos Owens."

The man stood aside and watched Bick and Chisos all the way up the stairs. At the head of the banister on the second floor was a Mexican *vaquero* wearing the tails of his white cotton shirt outside his buckskin leggin's and a pair of Forty-Fives buckled around outside that. He turned his head sharply.

"Chisos!"

"Don't tell me you're working for Anse too,

2

Ramón," said Owens.

Something sullen crept into the boy's face. "You been away four years, Chisos. Everybody down this way works for Anse now."

Chisos followed Bick on past Ramón Delcazar and down the hall and, when they were out of earshot, he asked the big man: "Anse has enough gunnies around to start a small war. Somebody finally catch up with the old buzzard?"

Bick didn't answer. He stopped before number three and opened the door, indicating Chisos should precede him in. It was a shabby room with a cheap white pitcher reflecting itself in the cracked mirror above a rickety washstand. Springs squeaked as Anse Hawkman rose swiftly from one of his own beds. He was a tall man, gray beginning to show at his bony temples. His cold blue eyes were set deeply beneath craggy brows, and they wanted all the land and all the cattle they had ever seen, and his great questing beak of a nose was always looking for more. The black frock coat, though, hung loosely from his shoulders, as if he had lost weight, and there was a haggard, almost haunted look to his face. Owens had never been one to hide his feelings. Hawkman saw the first momentary expression slide over his features and spoke a little warily.

"Four years, Chisos. I didn't think you'd still hold the Smoky Blue against me."

"Why not?" asked Owens, a heavy bitterness in his tone. "It was my land, and you forced me out. I can't help the way I feel."

"Can't you understand, the Big Bend isn't a place for small spreads," said Hawkman. "I did it legally."

"You always do it legal," said Owens. "A man like you don't have to step outside the law. But I didn't come down here to talk about that. I made two

3

or three false starts after the Smoky Blue, and I'm just low enough and broke enough to swallow what pride I have left and come to you for the job. When Bick found me up Santa Helena way, he said there was a thousand dollars in it. What is it?"

Hawkman's face paled visibly. "The Scorpion."

"The Scorpion?" muttered Owens. "What or who is he?"

"A woman," said Hawkman swiftly. "The Mexicans call her *Señorita* Scorpion. She's a devil. They say she's lightning with a knife or a whip or a gun. Tall, blonde, rides like fury. She's. . . ."

Anse stopped, breathing heavily. Chisos waited, watching him get control over himself. Finally, Hawkman spoke again, holding himself in like a man bunching his reins tight on a spooked horse.

"If it keeps up much longer, Chisos, I'll go crazy. I've been robbed and rustled and threatened and shot by that blonde witch till I don't know which way my saddle's on. Every trail herd I try to shape up this *Señorita* Scorpion stampedes. My line camps in the Chisos and the San Vincentes have been raided and burned to the ground. She held up my bank at Santa Helena last week and cleaned it out. Nothing in the Big Bend is safe from her. You saw the town when you came in . . . dead as boothill, doors all shut, nobody on the streets."

"A woman," mused Owens. "How did you get hold of her spread, Anse?"

"It isn't anything like that, Chisos. I swear, I never saw the girl in my life. . . ." He cut off and began to pace back and forth. Owens's eyes were drawn to his deep, painful limp. Hawkman saw the glance and snapped: "I told you she threatened to kill me. That's why I met you here instead of in my own house. She hit my home spread two weeks ago,

4

burned the barn, ran off the saddle stock. I was lucky to escape with a slug through the leg."

"Why bring me in?"

"Why bring you in?" asked Hawkman. "Why bring in Chisos Owens? Because that's where she's holed up, Chisos, somewhere up in your mountains, the Chisos, the Rosillos. You were born and raised there. You know the land better than anyone else, know the people. I've tried to follow her. I've set traps for her. Bick can tell you. He followed her farthest."

"After she took Anse's bank in Santa Helena," said Bick heavily, "I got some Comanche trackers and tailed her as far as the Dead Horses. You know what kind of country that is. They lost the trail, and they gave up finally, even the Indians."

"The Dead Horses," mused Owens. "Ain't the Lost Santiago supposed to be somewhere in those mountains?"

"I'm not interested in mines," snapped Hawkman.

"For over two hundred years," persisted Owens, "nobody's been able to find the Lost Santiago. And now nobody can find this blonde bandit. Sort of harnesses up like a matched buggy team."

The veined hand that Anse Hawkman gripped onto the iron bedstead was made to grab what he wanted and hold on with all the bitter, grasping, greedy strength in him. He stood that way, face pale, mouth thin with control.

"Will you forget the mine, Chisos," he said tensely. "It's just another wild story like the Lost Adams Diggings or the Tayopa. All I care about is the girl. I'll give you a thousand dollars to bring her in . . . dead or alive!"

"Hell, Anse," said Owens, "a man can't go gunning after a woman like that. . . ."

5

"What does it matter whether it's a man or a woman?" snarled Anse, spinning around. "She's a cattle rustler. You catch a man running off stock and you string him up. Why should it be any different with a woman?"

His voice cut off suddenly, anger-fired eyes sweeping past Chisos Owens to the sound of running feet coming down the hall outside. Bick stepped away from the door, turned, pulled it open. Ramón Delcazar stopped there, panting.

"She's here," he gasped. "*Señorita* Scorpion!"

Through the window Owens heard the sharp flat sound of shots in the street below. Someone shouted. Chisos shoved out past Bick and knocked Ramón partly aside to run down the hall. The stairs splintered and popped beneath his boots, and behind him he heard Bick's heavy stride.

In the moment he took to run out across the hotel porch and down the steps into the dusty street, the whole blurred picture appeared before him. The Apache still stood between the two adobe houses on the same side as the hotel, his bare feet spread a little wider. His dark hands were no longer hitched into the big silver *conchas* of his Navajo belt. They held a gleaming Winchester. Farther down the pair of Mexicans still forked their mounts, and they had guns out. And in front of the *cantina* a sharp-faced *hombre*, a blue serape draped over a shoulder, stood holding two horses—a palomino stallion and a huge bronze-and-white pinto that kept lunging on the reins.

Then Owens was in the street, and he could see the girl. She was backing from the *cantina*'s open door. In one hand she held a big Army Model Colt, firing backward into the Mexican saloon with it. In the other hand, by each of its four corners, she

6

gripped a blue bandanna bulging with gold pieces and greenbacks. The tall slim roundness of her body was accentuated by her tight yellow blouse caught in a broad red sash and her clinging leggin's of buckskin with bright flowers sewn down the seams.

At the sound of Owens's pounding boots she turned her head sharply, and he could see a flash of blue eyes behind a narrow black mask and her long blonde hair cascading around, shimmering in the sun, stunning and unbelievable against the high color of her face. Bick had reached the porch behind Chisos then, and he shouted.

"That's her, that's the Scorpion . . . !"

The girl's Colt was already coming up. Owens tried to halt his headlong run and throw himself aside. He didn't think of her as a woman when he went for his gun, because if he had, he wouldn't have pulled it. But his .44 was no more than half out of leather when he saw the girl's rich red mouth twist with the upward jar of the big Army Model in her hand, and he felt the bullet smash his fingers off the butt of his gun.

Without a weapon now he didn't try to halt his lurching sideways motion, and he fell and rolled in the dust, beneath the line of fire. Bick was shooting from the hotel porch. Owens saw the man's first slug kick adobe out of the *cantina*'s wall a foot from the girl's head.

Then the Apache stepped from between the buildings on the same side as the hotel and, holding his Winchester across the silver *conchas* of his Navajo belt, he shot through the supports of the porch railing, and Bick Bickford fell forward down the steps, a plank collapsing beneath his great weight.

Ramón must have gone down the back stairs of

7

Anse Hawkman's frame building. He appeared suddenly from the opposite corner of the porch, the bow-legged man in slick apron chaps with him.

The Apache moved on out into the street and drove a couple of shots toward Ramón, and the two Mexicans began throwing lead, and Ramón and the bow-legged man ducked back around the hotel. While this was happening, Owens had risen to his hands and knees, clawing with his good hand for the Bisley .44 he had dropped. But already the girl was swinging into the saddle of her great palomino. Slung in front of the pommel were Mexican saddle bags, and she leaned forward and stuffed the bandanna full of money into one pocket of these *morrales*, digging spurs into her horse at the same time. With a reckless grin the man who had held the two horses swung onto his own paint stallion and pounded down the street after the Scorpion. Blinded by that dust, choking in it, Owens lurched to his feet and raised the Bisley left handed.

Then he lowered it without firing. They were already gone, the Apache, the gaudy riders, all of them. And coming back warped on the breeze was *Señorita* Scorpion's laugh, as feminine as a cat screaming through the swamp on a moonless night, as wild as the howl of a wolf signaling its kill. . . .

Now that it was over, Owens felt the knifing pain in his bullet-smashed fingers. He holstered his gun awkwardly. Bick Bickford had twisted around on the steps and was trying to sit up. His face was bleeding where he had fallen on it, but apparently his only real wound was the bullet hole in his thick upper leg. Owens's buckskin had run half way northward along the street, spooked by the gunfire.

"General," called Owens, almost angrily.

The buckskin turned, cocked an ear, then trotted

8

back hesitantly, reins trailing. The hotel door squeaked, and Anse Hawkman limped out. Only then did Chisos Owens realize how swiftly the whole thing had taken place—all in the time it had taken Anse to limp from the upstairs room to the porch. Maybe he hadn't hurried. His haggard face was flushed angrily. There was something in it besides anger. His voice was harsh, yet it held a tremor he couldn't hide.

"That was fine," he said acridly. "Fine. You had her right on the end of your guns, and you let her get away."

"She had her gunnies spotted all over town," spat Bick. "You can't just walk out and rope that wildcat like you'd dally a buggy mare, Anse."

Hawkman's voice had a shrill note. "Don't you think I know that . . . by now?"

Ramón had come from around the side of the hotel, white shirt tails flopping around his buckskin leggin's. His dark face was angry, sullen. A fat Mexican dealer in a green eyeshade and striped shirt sleeves came from the *cantina*. He stood in the doorway a moment then walked swiftly across the street. One by one others followed him out the door. There were a dozen Mexican cowhands in flapping pantaloons or buckskin ducking britches, a girl with black pumps and a short skirt, a scattering of tall-hatted Texans. They spread into the street, some following the dealer over.

"Well, Faro . . . ?" said Anse Hawkman thinly.

"Nobody hurt," said the dealer. "The Scorpion threw a lot of lead but just to keep us beneath the tables."

"I wasn't talking about that," snapped Anse.

"If you mean the take, she got it all," said Faro. "Cleaned out the cash-boxes . . . monte table, chusa,

9

roulette. She's out for your hide, Anse."

Chisos glanced sharply at Anse. "What's your hide got to do with the local *cantina*?"

Anse didn't answer. Chisos turned back to Faro. The fat Mexican dealer wouldn't meet his eyes. The other men began shifting uncomfortably. Owens took a weary breath.

"Don't tell me you own that, too."

Anse shrugged. "Why not? My cattle practically built this town, the hotel, the barns. . . ."

"And the bank in Santa Helena, and the wells up in the Smoky Blue," said Chisos harshly. "You've spread out since I left, Anse."

"What's that got to do with it?" snapped Anse suddenly. "Will you take my offer now?"

Chisos looked away, lips twisting down. If he had realized how much dislike for Anse was still in him, he wouldn't have come down here. Yet there were other emotions, now, beneath that dislike for Anse, emotions he couldn't explain or name. It seemed he could still hear the blonde girl's laugh, taunting, challenging.

"I'll take it," he said deliberately. "One thousand dollars for bringing her back. . . ."

"Dead or alive," finished Anse Hawkman.

II

There were some *viejos* among the Mexicans who declared the Chisos Mountains derived their name from the Comanche word for echo, and then there were others who held the derivation was from the Apache name for ghostly. Born and raised in those mountains, Chisos Owens always leaned toward the latter—for they did look ghostly, somehow, rearing

10

up darkly red or blue or yellow, like bizarre spirits cloaked mysteriously by the pale atmospheric haze that hung over them most of the time.

A week's riding was behind Chisos Owens as he dropped down through the talus toward the valley of the Smoky Blue Creek below him. He had traveled westward from Boquillos, through Chilicoatl Basin, hunting out the peons who had been his friends and from them trying to get a lead on the blonde girl. So far, he had gotten nothing but vague rumors. Either the peons didn't know, or they weren't telling. They gave him nothing.

The General's buckskin-colored hide was whitened with the alkali of the basin, and the scabbard of the .45-90 Winchester tucked beneath the left stirrup leather was turned dark with sweat. Owens sat humped forward in his saddle, free-bitting his horse as a weary man will, one rope-scarred hand holding the reins and resting on the pommel, the other hitched in his old apron chaps slung around the horn. From somewhere below him came the creak of a windmill, and it was almost a pain to hear it.

Six years ago people in the Big Bend had identified the Smoky Blue with Chisos Owens. He had built himself a house at the headwaters of the stream, was running a sizable herd of Angus in the valley below, and had plans for a future. But already Anse Hawkman was spreading his grasping hands over the Big Bend, and he had seen the Smoky Blue, and that was enough for him.

When the Smoky Blue began to dry up, Owens saw the beginning of the end. For two years he fought. He tried to raise the capital to dig wells, but the men who would have lent it gladly to him suddenly decided it was a bad investment, and

Owens knew Hawkman had brought pressure to bear on them. Finally there was no more water in the creek, and Owens sold his herd, and even that didn't bring him the required cash for the wells.

Chisos shrugged suddenly. It was over now. He had finally been forced to sell, at Anse's own price practically, and Anse had turned around and sunk the wells, and the valley was now a line camp for his two year olds. Owens knew he had no cause for bitterness, really. But a man became close to his land, and it was his feeling for the Smoky Blue that had drawn him back here, though it was a detour in his search for the Scorpion. Riding down the slope this way toward the two-room cottonwood cabin he had built, Owens felt a growing nostalgia.

General slid down through some slick rock, shoes striking sparks. Then they were into the first clumps of gramma grass on the lower slopes. He could see the windmill now, creaking, pumping water up for the A H cattle. He struck the first bunch of cows a little beyond it and stopped his buckskin suddenly. A steer raised its head to look at him with bovine indifference. He rode closer, saddle creaking as he bent forward, eyes slitted with the sudden eerie feeling that had come over him.

For twenty-thirty years now the cattlemen had been breeding out the old scalawag string-beefed longhorn strain and breeding in the sleek fat shorthorned Herefords and Angus. Yet these cattle all had the huge curving scimitar-like spreads of the old longhorns, and it was like meeting a memory out of the past.

Frowning, Owens quartered in closer to squint at the brand. A heifer bawled at him; then he caught the mark. It was like none he had ever seen before— a fancy-tailed ⑤ inside a big circle. He rubbed his stubble-bearded jaw, neck-reining General to ride off a way and look the cattle over from there. The whole thing just didn't make sense, somehow. Cattle like this hadn't run the Chisos since he was a kid.

At last he turned the buckskin up toward the cottonwood cabin that Anse had turned into his line-camp shack. He passed another bunch of cattle on the way, but they were fat white faces with the A H big and bold on their flanks. In front of the house, in the dappled shadows cast beneath the cottonwoods by the late afternoon sun, sat a pair of horsemen, one of them Ramón Delcazar.

He greeted Chisos Owens without a smile. "Hawkman sent me over ahead of you to ride extra guard on these two year olds. The Scorpion's hit his line camp over by Crown Mountain. She hasn't been here yet. He thinks it'll be soon now."

Owens climbed stiffly off General, turned to the old man who had been standing beside the two riders. "Ain't you glad to see me again, Delcazar?"

Pedro Delcazar was Ramón's father, a bent old Mexican in buckskin *chaparejos* that had seen better days, rawhide *huaraches* on his feet. He wouldn't meet Owens's eyes. He snuffled, wiped at his nose.

"Sure, Chisos, sure, I'm glad to see you. Like the old days, eh?"

Owens began untying his latigo, wondering at the old man's strange withdrawal. "Not exactly like the old days, Del. You didn't work for Anse then."

Ramón wheeled his horse with a sudden vicious jerk on the Spanish bit, spitting his words out. "Anse Hawkman got our spread up Rosillos way. What else did you expect? And what else could we do but work for him? You're working for him, I notice. I'm nighthawking the herd. I'll see you in the morning."

He spurred his animal off in a hard, angry gallop,

13

the other rider following. Owens looked after them, then he turned and slipped his freed latigo from the cinch ring.

"Sorry to hear you lost Rosillos," he said softly.

Delcazar didn't answer. He was scuffling about, gathering wood for the fire. He had aged since Owens had seen him last, hair pure white now, veined hands trembling a little once in a while.

"Where'd you get those Circle S longhorns down the valley, Del?" asked Owens, heaving the double-rigged, sweat-soaked Porter from his horse. "Anse taken up the sticky loop?"

"You know Anse don't have to rustle his cattle," mumbled the old man. "It's a loco thing about those longhorns, though. About four months ago some peon named Natividad came to Anse down in Boquillos. He was a go-between for one *hombre* named Douglas who wanted to sell Anse a big herd of beef. Anse made arrangements with this Natividad to have Douglas drive his cattle here to the Smoky Blue. Anse and Bick came up the night they were supposed to arrive. We were all down by the cabin. There was a shot up on the ridge. Before we could get our horses, there came a whole herd of longhorns stampeding down the valley, no point rider, no swing, nobody. We finally stopped the cattle down below. This Douglas never showed up. Nobody else never showed up. It leaves Anse with a bunch of steers that shouldn't even be alive, and he has no bill of sale. He doesn't know what to do with them."

Owens slipped off his bridle. "I didn't think there were any critters like that left this side of cow heaven. How about the brand?"

The silence before Delcazar answered was noticeable. He glanced almost sullenly at Owens

14

from beneath shaggy white brows. "The *Circulo* S was registered in the county book about fifteen years ago by Douglas. Nobody knows where his spread is. The brand itself looks like the old Mexican brands that date back to the Moorish *rúbricas*."

Owens nodded meditatively. "Ever see it before?"

The old man set a coffee pot deliberately on two stones over the fire. He took his time about stirring up a pan of *frijoles*. Owens stepped around his horse.

"What's the matter, Del? Why're you being like this?"

Delcazar stood suddenly, turned toward him, eyes accusing. "Ramón told me you were up this way, and why you had come, Chisos. I wouldn't believe him until I saw you riding down from the ridge. I wouldn't believe you're the kind to go gunning after a woman."

Owens's face relaxed. He grinned faintly. Using his rawhide dally for a hackamore, he led his horse around beside the cabin, staked it there, then came back toward the fire.

"So that's it," he said. "I should have guessed the peons were pulling for this *Señorita* Scorpion."

"If I was ten years younger," said Delcazar tensely, "I'd be riding with her against Hawkman myself. You're a fool to go out after her for that thousand dollars. Before you get much farther, some peon will shoot you and save her the trouble. But I guess you'll go ahead. You were always such a stubborn *burro*."

He broke off, shaggy white head raising a little as he turned to gaze past Owens, mouth opening slightly with the concentration of listening. Chisos could hear it then—a familiar sound on the border. In their half-breed bits many of the *vaqueros* put metal crickets set to emit a singular eerie clicking

15

sound when the horse spun it with his tongue, the noise magnified by big hollow *conchas* on the outside of the bit itself. The two men stood there, hearing that noise a long time before horse and rider appeared, looming up like somber shadows from beneath the stunted cottonwoods banding the dry Smoky Blue.

The animal was a pinto, white and tan. The rider sat a silver-plated, cactus-tree saddle with a jaguar skin slung on behind for show, and the reins and headstall dripped red tassels of horse hair. The pinto was five gaited, and the horsebacker put it through all five as he turned around the fire and stopped without using the reins or his feet or saying a word. Chisos Owens knew he had seen an exhibition.

"*Buenas noches, señores*," said the man, dismounting and bowing low to remove his glazed sombrero with a flourish. "I am Don Veneno Castellano Porveara del Santiago Morrow, and I am at your service."

His black spade beard and small mustache accentuated the chalky white of his teeth. His sombrero was of black *vicuña* skin with a band of gold *pesos*, and his leggin's were slick and shiny. Owens was trying to remember where he had seen the horse before.

"Santiago," he said. "Any connections with the Lost Santiago?"

"*Señor*," said the man grandiloquently, "I am a direct descendant of Don Simeón Santiago who discovered the Santiago Mine in Sixteen Eighty-One!"

"I've heard all the versions," said Owens, "but never a *hombre* who claimed to be a direct descendant."

Sudden anger flared into Santiago's sharp face,

16

flushing it, and his hard bright eyes dilated as he stepped forward jerkily, spitting words at Owens. "You doubt me, *señor*? That is an insult. You insult the House of Santiago!"

"Please, *señores*, please," begged Delcazar, coming between them, turning to the don. "I'm sure Chisos did not mean the insult, Don Santiago. It is rare we have such a *caballero* as you in this country any more, such a gentleman of the old school. We are honored by your presence."

The flush left Santiago's cheeks. With a startling change of mood, he smiled, teeth flashing white. "Chisos? Chisos did you say? Not the man who is hunting the Scorpion?"

"You seem to know," said Owens.

Don Santiago chuckled, a strange, secretive chuckle that irritated Owens suddenly. Delcazar had taken the jaguar skin from the horse, and he spread it out beside the fire.

"Word gets around, *Señor* Owens," he said softly. "I heard it from more than one peon. So you really think you can find the Scorpion when so many others have failed?"

Owens shrugged, hunkered down across the fire from the man. The coffee made a soft gurgle, boiling in the blackened pot. Santiago looked out past Owens into the falling dusk. Delcazar caught the glance.

"The nighthawks have already eaten, Don Santiago," he said respectfully. "They will not be back in."

Santiago's sibilant voice might have held a different meaning than Delcazar had put into the words. "No. No, they will not be back in."

From under sun-bleached eyebrows Owens had been studying the man, the horse, now looked at the don again. Where had he seen them before? Santiago caught his eyes on him and began to chuckle in that secretive way again, voice mocking.

"Chisos. Chisos Owens. A thousand dollars for the Scorpion, dead or alive."

Owens felt that irritation again. His voice was harsh with it. "Is my story any funnier than yours?"

Santiago stopped laughing, and that change of mood swept him once more. He leaned forward, blood rising darkly into his face. His eyes dilated. For a moment his mouth worked around words that wouldn't come out. Finally he closed his lips into a thin line and sat there, fighting to control his hot anger.

"You don't believe in the Lost Santiago?" he said at last.

"I didn't say that," said Owens.

Santiago eyed him hotly. Delcazar stood to one side, eyes going in a fascinated way from Santiago to Owens. Then, sensing that whatever was going on between the two men was not for him, he withdrew to the far side of the fire. For the moment the coffee pot was the only sound, boiling a little higher.

"More than two hundred years ago," began Santiago finally, his voice heavy with control, "my ancestor, Don Simeón Santiago, held the title of *adelantado* and was entrusted with the visitation of mines in New Spain. Spain was having trouble with England during those times, you will remember, and one of Don Simeón's slaves was an English freebooter who had been captured while raiding our plate galleons in the Caribbean. Before turning to piracy, this Englishman had spent some time in the tin mines of Cornwall, and Don Santiago often took him along when he needed a man to help construct tunnels or sink mine shafts. In Sixteen Eighty-One rumor of a mine somewhere north of the Rio Grande came to Don Simeón and, leaving his only son to oversee their *rancho*, he took the Englishman and other retainers and set off northward into what is now Texas."

As he spoke, Don Veneno Santiago's breath came faster, and the excited dilation of his eyes was more pronounced. He looked out past Chisos Owens again, and Owens got the impression he was waiting for something.

"My ancestor discovered the mine," went on Santiago, "and sent back a *mozo* with an order for his son to send him a hundred peons, a herd of his own cattle to feed them, and all the necessary equipment to dig. It is a matter of record that for six months Don Simeón shipped out of the Santiago Mine an average of two hundred and fifty thousand *reales* a month. Can you imagine, *señores*, how fabulously rich those diggings were? *Naturalmente*, the king got his royal fifth, and he granted Don Simeón all the land between the Rio Grande and his mine. But the politics of New Spain at that time were so rotten that Don Simeón would have lost the Santiago had he not kept its location in the utmost secrecy. None of the peons were allowed to leave, once they got there. And the chosen few who took the shipments south every month were sworn to secrecy, returning as soon as the gold reached the proper authorities. Then, suddenly, the shipments ceased, and the Santiago disappeared from sight of man as completely as if the earth had swallowed it."

It was just beyond the veil of memory for Owens now, and vainly he studied Santiago's face for the clue that would tell him where he had seen the man before. "The Englishman's a detail I never heard of."

"I suppose you don't believe it, either," hissed

19

Santiago. "George Douglas was his name, a huge yellow-haired man. He was there at the mine along with Don Santiago when the shipments ceased. Neither of them was seen again. The don's son searched, of course, but he hadn't seen his father since the old man set out to find the mine. To this day the Santiago has not been found. I can tell you that . . . I've devoted my life to hunting it."

"Douglas," almost whispered Delcazar. "That was the name of the *hombre* who was supposed to bring those *Circulo* S longhorns down here."

"Probably the same man," said Owens. "Must be a right spry *diablo* by now."

Santiago jerked forward. "*Señor* . . . !"

Lips still twisted over the hot word, Santiago looked out past Owens. First, Owens thought, it was the plunk of boiling coffee. Then he realized it was the dull thunder of hoofs somewhere lower down in the Smoky Blue. As he recognized the sound, he remembered where he had seen that pinto before, and where he had seen the man in shiny leggin's. He had never been good at hiding his thoughts. The realization must have shown hard on his face, because Santiago's glance was suddenly drawn to him, and Santiago began to chuckle in that sly, secretive way.

"You have been trying to recall me ever since I first appeared," he said softly, "and now it has come to you, has it not? *Sí, Señor* Chisos Owens, it was I holding those two horses in front of the *cantina* in Boquillos, and one of them was mine, and the other was the Scorpion's palomino, and that is she out there now!"

20

Santiago's gloved hand was stiffened above the ivory butt of his Navy revolver, and for that moment the three men were suspended there.

"She sent me up here to hold the old man," said Santiago, his breath beginning to come faster. "She didn't know you were here, *Señor* Owens. In the old days a Santiago would have spitted you on his blade for the way you insulted me. The only reason I controlled myself was to let her get those cattle running. They are going now, *señor*, hear them? I don't have to wait any longer. Make your play, Chisos Owens, because you insulted the House of Santiago, and I'm not going to leave you here alive!"

He leaned forward, face twisting like a man whipped, gloved hand trembling above his gun. Delcazar drew in a small, hissing breath. Owens kept his right hand well above his .44 as he turned it so the firelight revealed the bandage across the bullet-smashed fingers.

"With this?" he asked.

"With that or nothing, and right now!" Santiago almost screamed, all the anger he had held quivering within him suddenly exploding in his upward leap, his hand a blur that dipped for his Navy in the swiftest smoothest slap-leather draw Owens had ever seen.

Without rising from where he sat, Owens shot his right leg out. His boot slammed into the fire and beneath the coffee pot, and he kicked violently upward, scattering the burning wood in every direction.

"¡*Diablo*!" shouted Santiago, and his shot went wild because he was lurching backward with the pot

21

flying up at him and the scalding liquid casting its black spread across his face and upthrust arm.

The pot clanged off his shoulder. Then Owens was across the fire and on the man. One of his rope-scarred hands drove flat against Santiago's chest where the fancy braided jacket was soaked with coffee, and his hurtling weight carried Santiago over backward. Owens jumped on across the falling Mexican, going for the pinto which had taken a startled step away. He caught the ground-hitched reins and slapped a palm onto the big cactus-tree pommel and, carrying the reins back over the horse's head, he vaulted into the saddle. His slamming into the leather like that caused the paint to wheel and break into a headlong gallop.

With stirrups snapping the scattered mesquite, Owens bent low and whipped from side to side with the reins. Santiago's shots were a futile volley, passing into the night around him. Owens cut through the cottonwoods and down the outbank into the bed of the Smoky Blue, sand spurting from beneath the mount's pounding hoofs. Splashing through the thin trickle of brackish water that was all that remained of the creek, he urged the beast up the other bank and past the ghostly bulk of a creaking windmill. The Scorpion had gathered the herd on the side and was pointing them down the valley, and he struck the drag after a long, hard run.

Those mysterious *Circulo* S *ladinos* were all mixed in with the white faces, longhorns rising like huge, gleaming scimitars above the stubby spreads on Hawkman's steers. One of the girl's *vaqueros* was riding swing, popping his sombrero against his buckskin pants, whooping in Spanish. Owens bent over on the off-side of the pinto as he went by the man, hidden but for his leg.

22

"¡*Viva* Santiago!" shouted the *vaquero*.

The pinto had run its heart out down the valley for Chisos Owens, and it was beginning to stumble beneath him when he sighted the girl. Once more he saw the blonde glory of her hair shimmering that way in the moonlight and the slim tall roundness of her body, swaying to the gallop of her Morgan.

They threw a sixty-foot *lazo* down below the border, and Santiago's rope was lashed to his silver-mounted cactus tree. Owens freed it and whipped the pinto into a final burst of speed. Then he slipped the hondo down the *lazo* until he had a community loop swinging in the air above his head. His target was that shining blonde hair, and he made his toss with a grunt.

With the *lazo* settling about her tall slim body, the girl stiffened. Owens yanked backward. The hondo slid swiftly down until she was pinioned. Her hands still held the reins, and she sawed at her bit, bringing her Morgan to a rearing stop to keep from being pulled off. Owens skillfully walked his hands down the rope, nursing his quivering pinto along until he was up to her, the loop still tight around her braided *charro* vest. The cattle continued to thunder on by, a rider passing in a cloud of dust. Owens was close enough then to see the flash of her blue eyes.

"You!" she exclaimed.

He grinned faintly. "*Buenas noches, Señorita* Scorpion."

He had kept the rope taut, expecting her to try automatically to free herself by pulling away. She suddenly stood up in her stirrups and leaped out of her saddle directly at him.

Desperately he tried to send another loop across the sudden short slack and snag her sideways so she wouldn't carry him off the pinto. But she hit him

23

before he could do it, her body soft and warm against him for that moment; then both of them went on over the horse.

The ground jarred hard into him, and the girl's weight came down on top. With the breath knocked from his body, he was dimly aware of her straddling up on him, fighting out of the rope. He lurched up after her, hands clawing around her slim waist. She fought savagely, striking, biting, kicking. One of her hard boot heels caught him in the chin. He slammed back against the ground, stunned for that instant.

Finally he groped to his hands and knees. She was already mounting the pinto, urging it into a jaded trot toward her Morgan. Shaking his head groggily, Owens lurched to his feet, took a few stumbling steps after her. Then he stopped, cursing the futility of that. The herd had passed and was nothing but dull thunder down the valley. A rider clattered past through the settling dust somewhere on Owens's left. He saw the girl change from Santiago's horse to her Morgan out there in the night, a dim blur of movement. Then she disappeared, leading the pinto, and the last thing he heard was that laugh, triumphant, wild, taunting.

Hiking back to the cabin took him an hour. On the way he found two of the nighthawks tied to an aspen where the Scorpion had taken them by surprise. Farther on was Ramón. He had managed resistance and had a slug through the shoulder for his trouble, and his horse had been run off along with all the others. The four men crossed the river bed and walked glumly through the cottonwoods and came up to the cabin from the lower side. Owens's buckskin was gone and his big Porter saddle. Santiago had undoubtedly taken the horse; perhaps that last rider clattering after the herd had been he. Owens was the first to walk around the corner of the cabin. He stopped suddenly, and his blocky, rope-scarred hands closed into grief-tight fists.

"Ramón," he called. "You might as well come now as later."

Ramón Delcazar came around the corner, holding his shoulder. He stopped abruptly beside Chisos. For a long time he was silent. Then the grief crept into his face, and he closed his eyes.

"*Padre*," he said. "Father."

The two men stood there a long time in the silent darkness, looking at the sprawled dead body of Pedro Delcazar.

IV

Often, in the dry desolate badlands north and west of the Chisos Mountains, the only source of water was the occasional natural sink formed in the rocks to catch rain and hold it there. It was high on the rugged slope of the Rosillos, above one of these, that Chisos Owens hunkered in the meager shadow of a big boulder. A month had passed since the Scorpion's raid on the Smoky Blue. Cannily she had run off every one of the horses that night, and it had taken Owens three days to hike to Hawkman's Crown Mountain line camp and get a remount. By that time the girl had sold her wet cattle in Mexico and had disappeared.

It was useless to try and get anything from the peons. Their sympathies lay with the blonde *bandida* and, if they did know anything, they weren't telling. Thus Owens had turned to the *tinajas*. No matter how wild and nebulous the Scorpion was, she and her *vaqueros* would have to obtain water somewhere in these mountains. Owens had worked his way north up the ancient Comanche Trail, scouting out each rocky water hole as he came to it, patiently, stubbornly. Most of the tracks he found around the *tinajas* were those of wild animals. The few human prints were made by the bare feet of peons who had the *jacales* nearby. Then, at the end of the fourth week, he had come across the *tinaja* below him now.

About it were the usual prints, the trail of an ocelot that had come down to the ridges to drink, the old marks of driven cattle. Then, across the face of rock that formed one side of the sink, he had caught the numerous scars made by shod hoofs. Some of them had been old, indicating they were made by horses that had drunk there more than once; some were fresh, indicating the animals had passed recently. And where a narrow strip of sand spilled across the granite into the water were the distinct prints of more than one pair of high-heeled boots.

He had been waiting up here on the slope for two days, hidden from below by the uplift of granite in front of him and by the scraggly growth of scrub oak. It had been a long weary search, through all the cruel heat of midsummer that lay over the badlands. He showed the effects of the pursuit. The weight had melted from him, and his ragged jumper fitted loosely about a torso that had lost some of its solid squareness. His face had a haggard, driven look, and his eyes burned deeply in their sockets like those of a man with a fever. *Well, maybe it was a kind of fever*, he thought heavily.

At first he hadn't been sure why he had gone out after the girl. He'd made so many false starts after the Smoky Blue, and a thousand dollars could set a man up once more. But he knew now it had never

26

been that. No money could have driven him through all the hell of hunger and thirst and heat and exhaustion of the last weeks. He couldn't have said exactly whether it was the sight of her blonde hair shimmering in the moonlight, or the feel of her body warm against him when she knocked him off the paint horse, or the wild feminine taunt in her laughter. He only knew it was one of those things or, maybe, all of them.

Behind him the stocky dun he had borrowed from the Crown Mountain camp cropped idly at some prickly pear. It was saddled and bridled and, sitting there like a dusty statue, Owens could afford this last Indian patience. Few white men passed by here. The chances were in his favor.

The sun was low when he sighted the first spread of rising dust in the valley below him. His hands tightened in their clasp around his knees. It was the only sign he gave. From beneath the dust they appeared, a line of riders forcing flagging mounts. The blaze of the sun caught for a moment on the blonde head of their leader.

Owens remained motionless, watching them stop at the *tinaja*. He had made the same mistake twice before now, trying to get the girl. He wasn't going to make it again. He saw them allow their horses a short drink then jerk their heads up to avoid foundering them. They were too far away to recognize individually. The only thing that marked the girl was her hair. Chisos saw one of the men suddenly stoop and hunker down, apparently studying the ground. He stood up finally, and another man came to him, and they seemed to be talking. Finally all of them mounted, rode toward a cut that led westward through the Rosillos, and disappeared.

27

Unhurriedly Owens stood and mounted the dun. He slid down through the talus and turned eastward into the cut. With night falling, he followed them through the mountains and out into the Rosillos Basin. Across the empty flats he kept out of sight behind them, following their fresh tracks by moonlight. Dawn was spreading its pink haze across the basin when Owens reached the first jagged uplift of the *Sierra del Caballo Muerto*. The Dead Horse Mountains. The range received its name from a party of Spaniards who had mistakenly tried to penetrate its vastness and whose horses had all died from lack of water. Anse Hawkman owned much of the spread in and around the Dead Horses, but the land was patently useless to cattle, and he had never seen it, and none of his line riders could be hired to go deeper than the first foothills after strays. Bick Bickford's Comanche trackers had quit on him when they reached these mountains on the trail out of Santa Helena.

Owens sat his sweat-caked dun there a moment and looked up at the dark bulk of mountains, rising infinitely desolate and mysterious ahead. Then a stubborn line thinned his mouth, and a dogged hump came into his shoulders, as he leaned forward in the saddle to put a boot against the dun's flank. Reluctantly the horse moved into the rising slope of the *Sierra del Caballo Muerto*. Already the horse was groaning beneath him with thirst, and Owens's tongue was swelling in his mouth. He knew the chance he took, following the riders any farther. Ahead of him lay the wildest, least known section of the Big Bend.

They were nightmare mountains, human in their malignancy, where giant buzzards circled on waiting wings above Owens as he rode over ridge after ridge that was covered with gaunt skeleton trees and dropped into valleys with river beds that had been bone dry before Texas was called Amichel. Finally he turned into a narrow cañon with walls of red rock so tall the sun reached its sandy bottom only at midday. It twisted and turned like a writhing snake, and Owens lost all sense of direction. Then rattling mesquite and prickly pear began growing in scattered clumps, and farther on the brush became thicker, and finally it choked the cañon from one wall to the other.

Catclaw ripping at his Levi's, nopal raking his face, he fought his way through. The stirrups on the dun had no *tapaderos*, and it was a constant battle to keep his boots from being torn out. His old apron chaps had been slung on the Porter saddle Santiago had taken, and a thousand times he cursed the don for that.

The sand became covered with a thick mat of dried brush that had piled up there through the ages, and Owens lost the trail he had been following. But there was no way they could have gone except ahead, so he plunged on through the almost impenetrable thickets. Suddenly the jaded, thirst-crazed dun balked, and Owens was jerked forward in the saddle. For a moment he stared unbelievingly at the cañon wall rising in front of him. He realized then that this was a box cañon, and that he had come to the end.

Desperately he wheeled his horse, hunting for some sign of the riders he had trailed in here. He came into an open patch finally, and to his left some black chaparral grew up the cañon wall, intertwined with mesquite to form a dark, forbidding thicket. A lot of branches had been knocked to the ground, and the bush itself looked as if someone had tried to ride

29

his horse through it, and there were even hoofprints all around the base. Owens couldn't understand why anyone would try to get through the thicket when all they would meet on the other side was the rock wall.

He had stopped the dun there and was looking blankly at the brush when the shot crashed out, its sound magnified to deafening thunder by the narrow cañon. The horse leaped forward in a startled way and screamed with mortal agony. With the animal twisting sideways and going down beneath him, Owens kicked his boots free of the stirrups and jumped.

He hit running and took two or three steps and then dove into the brush, rolling over and over beneath the thickets, knocking clumps of mesquite berries off, and before he stopped his Bisley was in his hand. He lay there like that with the sweat clammy on him, the gnats beginning to settle on his face and hands, and blood from the rips and scratches drying on his skin. He turned his head carefully so he could see the horse, lying on its side in the clearing, dead. His hat was dangling a foot off the ground on a nopal branch, caught there when he had taken the dive.

There was no sound but the maddening buzz of gnats and the mournful sigh of an afternoon breeze down the cañon. He tried to lick his lips, but there was no moisture in his mouth or on his swollen tongue, and he began to feel his terrible thirst. A last mesquite berry dropped off on his face. The wind stopped, and utter silence settled down. He lay motionless, knowing that was the way it would have to be.

The man was an Indian. He made no noise coming through the brush. He walked into the opening with a Winchester held in dark hands across his spare belly. He stopped suddenly, head turned sharply toward the dead horse, surprise sliding into his face for that instant.

"That was the hoss screaming, not me," said Owens, "and, if you don't want to get shot out of your silver *conchas*, you better drop the rifle before you turn around."

The Winchester made a soft crackling sound against the carpet of brush that had piled up there through the centuries. Then the Indian turned to look through the mesquite to where Chisos Owens still lay on his back, Bisley .44 leveled across his belly. Owens rose. He got his hat from the nopal and picked up the rifle, and all the time he kept the man covered. The Indian was barefooted, and the *conchas* he would have been shot out of if he hadn't dropped his gun were sewn into a Navajo belt. For the first time Owens realized it was the same Apache who had been between those two hovels in Boquillos when the Scorpion had raided and who had stepped out to put a Winchester slug through Bick Bickford's thick leg.

Owens leaned forward slightly, his feverish eyes holding the Apache's glittering gaze while he spoke, and his slow deliberate voice held a grim threat. "You better take me to the blonde gal now, or I'll wait till the sun goes down before I kill you."

The belief that a man who died at night would lose his soul eternally in hell was prevalent among most tribes, and the effect of Owens's words showed in the tightening of the Apache's skin across his high cheekbones, the flick of his eyes.

"Chisos Owens?" he asked.

"Chisos Owens."

The Indian shrugged, turned, and headed straight for the black chaparral where it grew up against the

31

rock wall. Owens followed him, slipping his Bisley into leather, putting both hands around the Winchester. The Indian plunged into the thicket and, wondering what the hell, Owens went on in behind, jamming the rifle up against the man's back. The Apache shoved a springy branch out ahead of him; then he ducked beneath it and let it go suddenly. Owens tried to dodge, but it slapped across his face, stinging, blinding.

He went forward with the rifle held out in front of him. Instead of hitting the Indian or crashing into the rock wall, Owens burst through the last growth of chaparral and staggered on into empty blackness. He heard the Indian running ahead of him, and he lurched on forward, staggering two or three more paces before he regained his balance. His boots made a solid thudding pound against the soft earth, and directly ahead of him he could hear the panting Apache. Dropping the rifle, he threw himself on the man.

They went rolling to the ground. Owens slugged blindly where he thought the back of the man's neck would be, and his fist hit flesh and bone with a solid meaty sound, and the struggling body beneath him collapsed suddenly. Sprawled across the man that way, with his left hand out on the ground to brace him, Owens felt a scattering of what seemed to be kindling wood beneath his fingers. With his knee in the small of the Apache's back, he picked one of the objects up, fishing for a match in the hip pocket of his Levi's. The flare of light showed him to be holding an *entraña*—the buckthorn cactus torch used by the peons below the borders for centuries. This one had been burned almost to its butt end, and he lit it with difficulty. Holding the torch high, he saw scattered around him more of the *entrañas*, the charred ends of them turned whitish as if they had been burned a long time ago.

Then the torchlight revealed the huge, hand-hewn rafters above his head. There was another farther down, and another, and each beam was supported by vertical timbers on either side. The Apache groaned and stirred.

"What is this?" asked Owens, and already he knew.

"That thicket of chaparral covers the mouth of it," said the Apache sullenly. "We, *señor*, are in the Lost Santiago Mine."

V

Chisos Owens found the Winchester where he had dropped it and drove the Indian ahead of him through the ancient diggings. He had seen many examples of how the arid atmosphere of the southwest preserved things, but it gave him an eerie feeling to realize that, if this were actually the Lost Santiago, then these charred *entrañas* were the torches Simeón Santiago's peons had used to light the workings over two hundred years before.

He gathered up half a dozen of the buckthorn torch butts, and the light lasted them through the long tunnel, leading deeper and deeper into the mountain. Finally they came to a caved-in portion so narrow it would barely allow the passage of a horse. Beyond this daylight began to filter in, and Owens snuffed out his *entraña*. They passed a vertical shaft, sunk to one side of the tunnel, the tops of a rawhide-lashed *piñon* ladder poking over its crumbled lip.

"That is the shaft George Douglas was in when the Indians raided," said the Apache.

"Douglas?"

"The Englishman Santiago brought up with him to engineer the workings."

"Close your *boca*," said Owens, realizing how loud the man was talking.

The Apache led on out, the silver *conchas* on his belt gleaming suddenly as he stepped into the sun. Owens waited a moment then moved after him, Winchester gripped in blocky fists. He stood there, blinking his eyes for a moment at the large valley sweeping down the slope beneath him. The Dead Horse Mountains rose high and jagged and forbidding in a circle that enclosed the place completely. Juniper and scrub pine grew on the slope at Owens's feet, down to where shadowy *bosques* of cottonwoods marked a stream bed. He realized this valley was not as dry as the rest of the Dead Horses. It would support cattle. Then there was a faint movement above that half turned him and a thin voice he knew well enough.

"Now that you have had your look at the Santiago Valley, did you think we wouldn't guard the entrance to it, *Señor* Chisos Owens?"

Owens realized then why the Apache had talked so loudly by that vertical shaft, and there wasn't much surprise in his voice as he turned around. "Santiago."

Don Veneno Santiago's shiny leggin's were scarred and dusty with the long ride behind him, and his *charro* jacket was white with alkali from the Rosillos Basin. He smiled thinly as he waved the ivory-butted Navy slightly.

"Give the rifle back to Gitano."

Owens handed the Winchester back to the Apache named Gitano. A dull flush crept into Santiago's sharp cheeks, and he looked on past

34

Owens to the Indian, something acrid in his voice.

"You *pendejo*, I told you, if it was Chisos Owens, you'd better make the first shot good!"

The Apache rubbed his rifle, face turned down. "I heard the scream and saw him go out of his saddle. What would you have thought?"

"Stupid *burro*!" spat Santiago disgustedly, then he turned back to Owens. "You saw our tracks around the *tinaja*?"

"It took me a long time to find the sink you'd been using."

"Unfortunately, in reading our sign about the *tinaja*, you left some of your own and didn't succeed in blotting it all out," said Santiago. "When Gitano spotted the fresh prints, I supposed it was you. Nobody else would have gotten even that far. If you weren't such an insistent devil, *Señor* Owens, you wouldn't be dying now."

"Nobody's dying now, Santiago," said a *vaquero* who had come out of the juniper trees above the mouth of the mine.

Don Santiago jerked around toward him in a surprised way. He spoke hotly. "Address your betters correctly, Natividad, you *paisano*. I am Don Santiago, hear, *Don* Santiago."

Natividad wore a suit of soft red buckskin, and he had a gun too, and the big single-action hammer was eared back under his thumb. He had jet black hair, and the angular cast of his face looked Mexican, yet his eyes were distinctly blue.

"The Scorpion wouldn't want the *hombre* killed," he said. "We'll take him to her."

Santiago's eyes began to dilate. Owens looking down the black bore of the Navy, and he saw Santiago's finger tremble against its trigger. Sweat broke out on Owens's palms, but the Don wasn't unaware of Natividad's cocked gun. He drew in a hissing breath, speaking carefully.

"Listen, Natividad, this is *Señor* Chisos Owens. Anse Hawkman offered him a thousand dollars to bring back the Scorpion dead or alive, and he is just the kind of *hombre* to do it. You see how much farther than any of the others he has gotten. He is too dangerous to play with."

"I know he is Chisos Owens, and I know Hawkman offered him a thousand dollars for her, and I know he is dangerous," said Natividad. "But that isn't why you want him dead. You want to kill him because he kicked the coffee pot in your face back there on the Smoky Blue and because he almost ran that pinto of yours to death chasing the Scorpion."

"Just a show hoss," grunted Owens.

Santiago's head jerked back to him sharply. "What do you know about horses? That *caballo* of yours wasn't fit to skin for its dirty hide."

"You did take General then," said Owens, anger creeping into his voice. "And it was you killed Delcazar."

"You mean the old man?" shrugged Santiago. "He got in the way."

"You didn't need to kill him," said Owens.

Santiago bent forward, and his finger began trembling against the trigger again. "He got in my way, I tell you, just as you're in my way. . . ."

"You didn't need to kill him," repeated Owens with a dull bitterness.

"Gitano," said Natividad impatiently, "get us horses. And you, Santiago, put the *pistola* away."

"Don Santiago, you *pelado*," snarled Santiago, whirling back to him. Then he stopped, and that startling change of mood swept him, and suddenly

36

he was smiling and chuckling. "*Por supuesto*, Natividad. You are right. We are all equals here in the valley. And we will take *Señor* Owens to the Scorpion. *Sí*, of course."

Gitano had gone up the slope to what was evidently the camp of the mine guard. He came back through the trees with three horses, one of them the pinto. Owens mounted and neck-reined the sorrel they had given him down the slope between Santiago and Natividad, leaving the Apache to stand there watching them go. They came into an open meadow where several heifers browsed in the curly red gramma. Their horns were huge and majestic and on their flanks was that *Circulo* S brand. Santiago caught Owens's look, and his smile was mocking.

"*Sí*, those longhorns you saw down in the Smoky Blue came from this valley," he said. "The *Circulo* S is the ancient brand of the Santiagos, dating back to the time the Moors stamped *rúbricas* with their signet rings. These longhorn *ladinos* are a pure strain, descended directly from the steers Don Simeón Santiago brought into this valley from his *rancho* to feed the peons working in the mine in Sixteen Eighty-One."

"And the Scorpion . . . ?"

"Also a pure strain," said Santiago. "Descended directly from the English freebooter, George Douglas, who was here with Don Simeón when the South Plains Indians came down the Comanche Trail in that year and raided this valley. That is how the mine disappeared, *señor*. You saw the caved-in portion of the tunnel? The Comanches and Apaches swept in here and committed their massacre and burned all the buildings and ran the cattle and horses off through the mine. On their way out, they pulled

37

down a whole section of supporting timbers so the mine would cave in after them. But they had not killed quite everyone. Go head, Natividad, tell him the rest of it."

"You passed that vertical shaft on this side of the caved-in part," said Natividad. "George Douglas sunk that shaft. You must remember that in the old days the women worked alongside the men in the fields and the mines. Douglas and a peon woman were in the very bottom level of that vertical shaft when the Indians raided. The Comanches missed them and, when they came up, they found Simeón Santiago and all the others dead and the mine caved in, cutting them off completely from the outside world. There were a few cattle and sheep and a horse or two left in draws on the upper slopes where the Indians hadn't taken the time to look. From these Douglas and the woman made their start."

Owens rubbed his chin, speaking slowly. "And you mean to say . . . ?"

"That for two hundred years George Douglas and his descendants have lived in the Santiago Valley, cut off from the world," said Santiago impatiently. "They tried to dig out, naturally. But they had only crude tools, and you saw how long that cave-in extended. It was like trying to dig through the mountain all over again. Only fifteen years ago did they finally succeed."

"Delcazar said the *Circulo* S was registered about that long ago," said Owens.

"We kept the only Santiago brand, the Circle S," said Natividad. "My father was the Douglas who finally dug through. It didn't take him long to learn how you register your brands and how you have to file a claim on property. He filed, and we have a deed, and our cattle are legal beef. But you had a

38

deed too, *Señor* Owens, and yet Anse Hawkman got your land. That's why we've kept the valley a secret, even after digging out. Hawkman's all around us. We're the last small spread in the Big Bend he hasn't seized."

"And the mine?"

They dropped down the slope past a split-rail corral, and Owens saw his double-rigged Porter slung over the opera seat and inside among other horses was the buckskin hide of General. Natividad shrugged.

"George Douglas was the only miner, and his knowledge died with him," he said. "Anyway, what good would gold have done us? What good would it do us now? All we want is to live here as we have been living here, left alone by men like Anse Hawkman."

Owens looked at him squint eyed. "Natividad ... ?"

"Is a Spanish name," said Natividad, reining his jughead around the corner of a sprawling adobe ranch house they had been approaching. "The woman George Douglas took was a Mexican peon, remember? We are of those two bloods, yet you couldn't call us half-breeds in the strictest sense. There have been so many generations in between that first union we are a race apart, really. There are about two dozen of us in the valley now, young and old all the same strain, all descended from George Douglas."

Natividad and Santiago dismounted before the long portals that stretched across the whole front of the house, forming a roof for the flagstone porch. Owens swung his leg over the cantle and stepped down. He was still standing with his face turned toward the horse that way and his back to the porch when he heard the light tap of boots across the flagstones. For a moment he was almost afraid to turn around. He had only those two glimpses of her in Boquillos and on the Smoky Blue, and this would almost be like seeing her for the first time, and he had come so far for it and fought through so much. With a sudden jerky motion he turned.

She had removed her braided jacket. The pleated cotton camisa she wore beneath it was tucked into her tight leggin's. The big Army Model Colt still hung heavily on her hip, cartridge belt hooked up to the last notch around the slim span of her waist. Chisos hadn't realized a woman's lips could be so red—like the scarlet of nopal after a spring rain. And the size of her blue eyes made him dizzy. Then he saw the hate in them.

"I might have known it would be you," she said bitterly, "Anse Hawkman's man!"

He felt his face flushing beneath the grime of dust. Then his shoulders humped forward a little, because he knew he should have expected it this way.

"Santiago and Gitano tried to kill Chisos Owens," said Natividad.

"I almost wish Gitano had succeeded," she said. "But I guess it would take more than that Apache to kill a man like this . . . this . . . ?"

"*Maldito*?" asked Santiago mockingly.

"From what Owens said, I gather Santiago killed the old man named Delcazar down on the Smoky Blue," said Natividad.

The girl turned sharply to Santiago. "Veneno, I told you not to, I told you! I only sent you up there to keep the *viejo* from getting into trouble. He worked for Hawkman, but he wasn't Hawkman's man, like Bick Bickford or Chisos Owens."

"You seem to have something against Anse," said

40

Owens.

Her blonde hair shimmered as she whirled back to him, and for a moment she seemed surprised. "Are you trying to tell me you don't know?"

Owens shrugged. She studied him for a moment, biting her lip, eyes clouded now, puzzled. Finally she turned toward the door.

"I can't believe you don't know," she said. "But come with me anyway. I want you to see it!"

The living room covered the length of the house, thick wooden shutters open to let the afternoon light in through the few windows. It came to Owens that the ponderous oak center table and the crude chairs set against the adobe wall might have been pegged together by George Douglas two hundred years before, and the blackened *vigas* forming the rafters over the fireplace at one end had been hewn by the great yellow-haired Englishman with the few ancient tools he had salvaged from the Indian raid.

The girl was going through the door into a hallway. She stopped suddenly, stepping back as a man lurched by her. His sandy hair was rumpled, his eyes bloodshot and bleary in a puffy, discolored face. He wore a dusty, tattered clawhammer coat over a soiled pin-striped vest. Putting one hand on the table to keep from falling, he raised his head with difficulty, taking a moment to focus his gaze on Chisos Owens.

"Ah," he said, "another hapless creature from the outer world. Pray, sir, what did they bring you in here for?"

"Go back to your room, Doctor Farris," said the girl stiffly.

The doctor's bloodshot eyes opened wider, shining with a sudden wild look as he saw Santiago behind Owens. He lurched away from the table,

41

clutched at the lapels of Owens's jumper.

"You've got to get me out of here, please, got to," he babbled hysterically. "They brought me up to operate on the old man. Said they'd let me go if I was successful. But they'll kill me either way. I know. Nobody ever gets out of this valley, see? Help me, please, for . . . !"

Veneno Santiago took a swift step forward, one of his gloved hands closing around Farris's arm. The doctor winced, struggled feebly. Santiago whirled him sharply and shoved him abruptly through the opposite door into the hall. The girl followed and, going in after her, Owens could hear Natividad's boots behind him. Santiago turned Farris down the hall, but the girl went straight across into a large bedroom.

She walked to the bottom end of the big bed and stood there watching Owens with white-lipped intensity, her hands gripping the wooden-pegged bedstead desperately. The gaunt, still figure of an old man lay beneath the covers of coarsely-woven lamb's wool, and the cast of his face bore the same wild aristocracy as the girl's, with its finely planed forehead, its aquiline nose.

"Your father?" Owens asked.

"Yes," she said bitterly. "John Douglas. Completely paralyzed since Anse Hawkman put a bullet through his back four months ago."

Owens turned sharply toward her. "Anse . . . ?"

"It's the way Hawkman works, isn't it?" she flared. "Our herds of *Circulo* S beef had grown so large the valley's browse wouldn't support them any longer. We'd kept the Santiago a secret from Hawkman up to then. That's why Dad made the deal to drive the steers down the Smoky Blue. It happened on the ridge above Hawkman's line camp.

Dad was riding point on the herd when Anse and his men started the stampede and shot him in the back. He would have been killed by the cattle except for Santiago."

"Oh," said Owens. "Santiago."

Natividad nodded. "Santiago came across us driving the beef down the Comanche Trail. He was going south anyway, and he and Gitano helped us with the beef."

"Gitano's his man?"

"Did you think he was a Douglas?" snapped Natividad. "I was riding drag below the ridge when I heard the first shot. By the time I galloped up to where Dad had been pointing the herd, there was more firing, and the cattle were stampeding. I found Santiago off his pinto, pulling Dad out of the cattle's path, shooting off down the ridge. He said Hawkman had his whole crew out, and we didn't have a chance."

"You hadn't seen Santiago before he met you driving the beef down the Comanche?" asked Owens.

"No," said Natividad. "He helped us bring Father back here. When he saw this was the Lost Santiago of his ancestor, he said he'd stay and help us fight Hawkman."

"Doesn't sound like Santiago . . . helping someone," muttered Owens. "Doesn't sound like Anse, either. He never had to do anything like that before when he wanted something."

"Don't you see?" said the girl hotly. "Somehow Hawkman found out about our valley squatting right in the middle of his holdings, the last piece of land in this section of the Big Bend that isn't his. He shot my father, I tell you . . . !"

"We tried to get a doctor," said Natividad. "We

43

didn't have any money, and we got desperate finally and brought Farris in from Marathon at the point of a gun. You saw him. He said he wouldn't even attempt that kind of operation under ordinary circumstances, said it was a job for a specialist. We made him try anyway, but his hands shook so much we were afraid he'd kill Dad."

"The next doctor's hands won't shake," said the girl. "When we bring him in, he'll be paid hard cash and won't know it's different from any other operation. Farris said there was a specialist in San Antone."

"Specialists cost real *dinero*," said Owens.

"Why do you think I've been running off Anse Hawkman's cattle and the cattle he stole from us and selling them wet?" she asked. "Why do you think I've robbed his bank and *cantinas*? He's the one who shot my father. He's the one who's paying. I swear, if I ever meet him face to face again, it won't be his leg my slug hits."

"Too bad you didn't wait a minute longer in Boquillos."

"He was there?"

"You missed him by a hoss hair," said Owens.

"*Dios*, if I'd only known," she almost whispered. Then she straightened, eyes flashing, "And you . . . I should have done more than shoot you in the hand that day. It would have saved me this. Really, I don't know what to do with you, Chisos Owens. You claim you didn't know that Hawkman shot my father. Would you have come after me if you had known?"

"Do you really think I came all this way for Anse Hawkman's thousand dollars?" he asked her.

Some of the anger left her eyes, and once more that puzzled shadow darkened them. "I don't know what to think. I'm confused, puzzled. Hawkman made the same offer to other men, men who were stubborn or patient or who knew the country. They all gave up sooner of later."

"The kind of gun money Anse Hawkman offered carries a *hombre* so far, no farther," Owens said. "It takes something more to drive a man through country like the Big Bend for months on end, hunting for what he isn't even sure is there."

"Then, what drove you?" she asked. "You don't look like a mining man."

"I didn't care about the Lost Santiago," he said, "and I guess from the first I didn't care about that thousand dollars. After I saw you in Boquillos, I would have come whether Anse asked me to or not. Maybe this isn't the right time to say it, but maybe it's the only time I'll get. I won't even try to tell you that you're the first one. There was a woman in San Antone, but I didn't stay there long, and I wouldn't have followed her through hell just because I saw the moon shining on her hair one night down in the Smoky Blue. There were others, and I would have followed them. I followed you. That's how it is."

Her mouth opened slightly, revealing the shadowed line of her white teeth. Light from the window fell softly across the rich curve of her underlip. For a moment the spell held them like that, and Chisos saw a certain understanding begin to grow in her blue eyes. Then Santiago broke it, coming in through the door past Natividad with Doctor Farris. Farris had his black bag. His clawhammer was off, and his shirtsleeves were rolled to the elbow.

"I've sobered him up," said Santiago. "He's going to try once more, aren't you, Doctor?"

The girl turned sharply to him. "No, Santiago. I

45

told you we were getting one from San Antone. I have the money."

Santiago glanced at the doctor, waved a gloved hand imperiously. Farris pulled the lamb's wool covers hesitantly down and began unwrapping a cotton bandage from about John Douglas's gaunt waist. Reluctantly he turned the paralyzed man over on his belly.

"Santiago!" cried the girl. "Please! Wait till we can get to San Antone. Anything but this stupid fool, anything!"

Chisos Owens took a step forward, half turning to Santiago. The don's gloved hand slid down till it hung above the ivory butt of his Navy .36.

"At the moment *Señor* Owens," he said softly, "I wouldn't say you were in a position to interfere, would you?"

Owens met his bright gaze, then he looked at Natividad. The Scorpion's blue-eyed brother was watching Santiago, and Chisos couldn't read the glance. He shrugged, feeling the knotty tension across his stomach relax. The girl's breath came heavier as the doctor opened his bag, took out a scalpel. He bent over Douglas. Owens saw the girl's eyes widen; her chin quivered. Then the doctor's hand began to shake.

"Stop it!" screamed the girl, lurching around toward him. "Stop!"

Owens had seen something there on the strip of bandage still caught beneath John Douglas. He was around the doctor before the girl, and his rope-scarred hand closed over the small piece of lead, wet with the old man's blood.

"Must have lodged against his spine close to the surface," mumbled Farris. "I've seen bullets work free like that before. It was what paralyzed him, I

46

guess."

"Anse Hawkman's bullet," half choked the girl.

"Anse Hawkman packs a Forty-Four," said Owens, wiping blood from the slug. "And none of his crew pack anything smaller in caliber. This bullet came from a gun you don't see much of nowadays. It came from a Navy Thirty-Six."

VI

As one, every person in the room turned to Santiago. He stood with his back to the open window, and hanging above the ivory butt of his Navy that way there was infinitely more threat in his gloved hand than if it had actually held the cocked gun. They all knew his unbelievable skill with that .36, and for a moment it held them.

"You told me . . . Hawkman," breathed the girl.

Chisos Owens's lips thinned then, and he began settling his weight forward, and his shoulders humped into a solid, dogged line. Santiago took a step backward. He spoke to the girl, but he watched Owens.

"Of course I told you Hawkman," said the don. "Did you think I'd let you know it was my bullet that paralyzed John Douglas?"

He took another step backward, toward the open window, hand stiffening. Owens took a slow breath. Santiago's eyes dilated suddenly, and he laughed.

"Go ahead, Chisos Owens. There isn't any coffee pot to kick in my face now. Go ahead and do it."

He took a third step backward, and Chisos Owens did it. He crouched and dove and drew with a hard-driving grunt. Before his gun was half out of leather, he saw Santiago slip the Navy clear with that blinding speed, and he knew he was bested. Santiago's slug caught Owens in the right shoulder and spun him back against the wall with his unfired Bisley clattering to the floor.

But it had given them their chance. Natividad fired from the hip almost before his gun was drawn, and the girl's Army was leaping out of its holster. Santiago made a difficult target in that half-dark room. With Natividad's wild lead plonking into the earth floor at his feet, the don jumped on backward and fired a last snap shot their way as he put his free hand on the window sill and vaulted backward out through the open window.

It had taken Owens that long to get his gun, staggering away from the wall and scooping it up with his good hand. The girl caught at him, her weight dragging for a moment.

"You're wounded, Chisos," she panted. "You can't go out after him that way. He's loco. I never realized it before, but that's why he gets so excited talking about the mine. He's loco and he's a *diablo* with that gun, and you can't go after him left handed."

"I never was so fast on the draw," said Owens, breaking free of her. "That part's over now."

He went through the window head first with his .44 held out in front of him and his finger whitened on the trigger ready to blast anything in the way. Santiago was already running upslope toward the corral. Another of the Douglas clan came from around behind the house. Santiago fired twice before the man went down and slid on his face in the dirt.

The don glanced over his shoulder and saw Owens coming up after him in that dogged, forward-leaning stride. Santiago turned and broke into a run again, bent over his gun, reloading. Natividad was behind Chisos, and farther back was the lighter sound of the girl's boots.

Santiago stopped at the corral a moment, fumbled with one of the bars. Owens closed the gap between them. He threw a shot at Santiago, and the man quit trying to let down the bar and turned uphill.

The afternoon sun was low, and it cast long shadows of the split-rail corral across Owens as he ran past. General whinnied at him; he grinned thinly and stumbled on. He was breathing heavily now. The pain in his shoulder had turned to a dull throbbing. His right arm swung at his side with each jerky step, useless.

Gitano had been left at the entrance to the mine, and the shots brought him out of the stunted trees above the tunnel mouth.

"Cut around through the junipers," shouted Owens. "Gitano has that rifle."

The girl quartered toward the motte of scrub oak and juniper, disappearing in their shadows. Gitano levered his Winchester, threw a shot at Owens. It kicked dirt in his face. Then the girl and Natividad showed in the trees, and their fire drove Gitano back until he no longer commanded the section Owens would have to cross following Santiago. The don halted and turned in front of the tunnel.

"Do you think you can get me in my own mine, you stinking *ladrón*?" he shouted crazily back at Owens.

Chisos didn't answer. His boots made a steady, insistent pounding, coming on. With a shrill yell Santiago whirled and disappeared into the black maw. Halting there at the entrance a few moments later, Owens could hear him running farther in. Bisley gripped tight, Chisos followed. He ran by the vertical shaft George Douglas had been in when the Indians raided. He stumbled across an ancient fallen *soporte*. Daylight passed behind, and for a few

49

minutes it was utterly dark. Then a ghostly yellow glow flared up ahead, and Don Veneno Santiago laughed in a cracked, panting way.

"See, Chisos Owens, that's an *entraña*, a torch. I've stuck it in the wall. You'll have to come through the light to get me. I'll be behind it, in the dark. Did you think you could get me in my own Santiago?"

Owens halted, still in the dark portion, taking a deep breath. "Why'd you shoot Douglas, Santiago?"

"When I came across John Douglas driving those old longhorns down the Comanche Trail and saw the ancient Santiago brand on them, I knew I'd found a clue to the Lost Santiago," shouted the don. "It didn't take me long to find out Douglas was going to sell the valley to Hawkman as well as the cattle. The old fool had his deed and a bill of sale already signed by him, and all it needed was the buyer's signature . . . ," he cut off, and another light flared beyond the first. "There you are, *Señor* Chisos Owens, a second *entraña* for you to come past."

Owens gathered himself and rushed into the light of the first torch.

"*¡Borrachón!*" screamed Santiago, and his gun blared.

With the slug thudding into the wall at his side, Owens threw himself forward and knocked the blazing buckthorn *entraña* down, rolling over on it and snuffing it out with his own body. He lay there in darkness for a moment. Finally Santiago's voice came, mockingly.

"Are you there, *señor*?"

"You didn't finish about Douglas," said Owens grimly, rising to his knees and looking at that next blazing torch.

"Ah, I missed you *Señor* Chisos Owens, how

unfortunate," called Santiago. "And Douglas? I told you he was going to sell the valley. Do you think I'd let him do that? Do you think I'd ever see my mine if Anse Hawkman got his hands on this valley? We were on the ridge above the Smoky Blue when I tried to force the deed and bill of sale from Douglas. He wheeled his horse and galloped away. I shot him, and the noise started the stampede. I wasn't pulling him from its path when Natividad found us. I was searching for the deed and bill of sale, and he didn't have them on him—ah, there you are, *señor*, another torch."

It flared up beyond that second burning *entraña*, and again there were two spots of light Owens would have to go through, and Santiago was backing on into the cave, laughing. Chisos rose to his feet and moved into the weird glow, running hard.

"¡*Maldito*!" screamed Santiago and shot and shot again.

Owens heard the first slug whine past him. The second one hit him in the thigh like the kick of a mule. As he went down with his leg knocked from beneath him, he grabbed desperately at the torch ahead and knocked it out of the wall. It fell to the floor and sputtered and died.

In the darkness once more Owens crawled to the wall of the cave and twisted around so he could sit up, biting back pain. "Why bother with telling the Scorpion that Hawkman shot John Douglas and riding along on her raids that way? Seems to me your style would be more shooting them all in the back and being done with it."

"*Dios*, what a stubborn *burro* you are!" shouted Santiago, a touch of hysteria entering his voice. "I told you I wanted the deed and that bill of sale already signed by the old man. When a *hombre* starts working a mine as rich as the Santiago, he has to have legal possession of the property, even up in this *malpais*. I was just as anxious to get a doctor for John Douglas as Elgera Doulgas was. The old man couldn't exactly tell me where he'd hidden the deed as long as he was paralyzed, could he?"

Owens could hear him fumbling to light another torch. There was only one spot of light now, only one *entraña* burning. Chisos knew it was the last one he could reach. He was finished if the don got another lit. He dug his hands into the wall, clawed up till he was standing, then he lurched away from the wall.

Every time he took a step, his staggering, lurching weight almost went down on the side of his wounded leg, and he grunted sickly with each dull pound of his boot into the ground. Then the solid blocky squareness of his figure burst into that last light, and the sudden racket of Santiago's Navy was all the sound in the world to him. He felt a slug burn across his ribs. Another clipped at his flapping denim jumper. He slammed into the wall, grabbing at the torch stuck there.

"Go down, you stubborn *patata*, go down!" screamed Santiago, and his gun drowned his voice.

With the same hand that held his Bisley, Owens tore the blazing *entraña* from the earthen wall and half knocked, half threw it out ahead of him. For that moment its light flared across the whole tunnel, flickering over Santiago. He was backing up with his face flushed excitedly and his eyes dilating, and he jerked his smoking Navy up to fire again.

Owens held his .44 out, and the light burned long enough for him to see his single deliberate shot take Santiago squarely in the chest. Chisos leaned up against the wall with his weight over on his good leg, feeling dully for the wound in his ribs, knowing he would fall over if he moved. Then he heard them moving down the cave behind him.

"Chisos . . . ?"

"Back here," he called. "It's all over. Back here."

"*Dios*," said Natividad, stumbling through the darkness, "that Gitano was a tough *hombre* to smoke out. You got Santiago?"

"Did you think he wouldn't?" asked the girl.

They were helping him back out, then, and with one arm across Natividad's shoulder he spoke wearily: "Santiago said your dad had a deed and a signed bill of sale all ready for Anse."

"I should have known that was what Santiago wanted," muttered Natividad. "Before Santiago cut our trail on the Comanche, I found out Dad was selling the valley, and I took the deed and bill from him. I have them now."

"Natividad!" flamed Elgera. "Dad would never sell our valley."

"He was an old man," said Natividad heavily, "and, during the fifteen years we had been in contact with the outside, he saw all the small *rancheros* lose their land to Hawkman, no matter how bitterly they fought him. He didn't want to cause us the pain and bloodshed and heartbreak that would come with bucking Anse Hawkman. He hadn't brought himself to telling us about it yet when he left with the cattle."

"Santiago may have been loco," said Owens, "but he'd been hunting mines all his life. It seems to me he'd be able to tell one with yellow in it when he saw it. If the Santiago's as rich as he claimed, you won't have to worry about bucking Hawkman. You can buy and sell him every month."

"There'll still be some trouble," said the girl.

53

"The only one killed in my raids was Delcazar, and Santiago did that. But I ran off a lot of Anse's cattle, and robbed his bank, and clipped him and some of his crew."

"When you get your diggings going good, you can ride down to Boquillos and pay Anse a visit, and I reckon the kind of man he is, he will be right glad to forget any worry you caused him when you plunk down a pack saddle full of solid gold bars in repayment," said Owens. Then he took his arm off Natividad's shoulder and turned to the girl. "Why did you try to stop me down at the house?"

"Because I saw you going out after Santiago with your wounded shoulder and your gun left handed, and I suddenly realized how I felt about you," she said, and it was natural for her arms to slip around him. "Remember how you tried to explain it to me . . . all about the woman in San Antone you wouldn't have followed and the other women you didn't follow, and me you followed because you saw the moon shining on my hair down in the Smoky Blue. That's how it hit me, Chisos, just as fast. You came a long way to find me. Will you stay?"

Chisos's head raised sharply, and he could feel his hands tighten on her suddenly.

"What would I be," he asked her with an effort, "if I did stay? A foreman in your mine maybe, or ramrod for your spread, or one of your waddies."

She looked up at him, and in semi-gloom he could see the darkness creep into her eyes. Perhaps she was beginning to understand.

"You wouldn't have to . . . ," she began.

"Then what?" he said. "If I didn't work for you, I'd just stay and live off you, is that it? I couldn't do it either way, you know that. I couldn't take a job from you. I didn't come in here to be your ramrod or your waddy. And I couldn't let you keep me. Call it pride, call it whatever you like, it just doesn't seem right. When a man comes to a woman feeling the way I do about you, he doesn't come asking her for a job, asking her for anything. He should come with something to offer. But I haven't even that. And still, I'd almost ask you to come away with me. . . ."

"This is my valley, Chisos," she said. "I couldn't go away now. The trouble with Hawkman isn't over. The mine has to be worked, whether we want to work it or not, if we're to keep the valley. Dad has to be taken care of. . . ."

She trailed off, and Owens stood there, half supported by her, breathing heavily. He could see there was no use in further argument. He was too proud to stay and take anything from her that way. She was too stubborn to go. A man had no right, anyway, asking a woman to give up what the Santiago had to offer. He shrugged and turned to throw his arm again across Natividad's shoulder, and the three of them stumbled out into the open.

Ⓥ   Ⓥ   Ⓥ

A week later two of them rode silently up through the shadowy *bosques* of juniper to the mouth of the cave. They halted there, saddles creaking as each turned to look at the other.

"Once more," almost whispered the girl, "won't you stay?"

"Once more," he said heavily, "won't you come with me?"

She shook her head, lips thinning.

"All right," he said. "It's *adiós* for now. But don't think this ends it. The Big Bend's my country as much as yours. I'll give you odds we meet again."

55

Then Chisos Owens neck-reined General into the maw of the cave, and the darkness closed around him. He knew he would never forget the picture of her sitting the Morgan there with her blue eyes glistening and the sun shining on the blonde glory of her hair.

THE BRAND
OF
SEÑORITA SCORPION

I

The snort of a horse outside brought Elgera
Douglas up out of her wooden-pegged chair by the
stone fireplace. Texas sunlight streamed in through
the west windows of the big room and caught the
momentary shimmer of her blonde hair when she
turned nervously toward the creak of leather that
was men dismounting. She was a tall girl, a pleated
white camisa serving her for a blouse, tucked into
Mexican *charro* leggin's of reddish buckskin with
big silver bosses down their seams. Her full red lips
compressed as she heard the pound of boots across
the flagstone porch, and she wondered for the
hundredth time that day if she had made a mistake,
trusting an outsider with this thing.

Then the heavy oak door was shoved open, and
the first man entered with a swift, catty stride. His
eyes met Elgera's, and she drew a sharp breath with
the sense of a staggering physical impact. They were
set deeply beneath a heavy black brow, those eyes,
and a savage violence seemed to emanate from the
brilliant little lights flaring and dying again in their
jet black depths. A feeling of suffocation crept over
Elgera as she was held there. Then the man's white
teeth flashed in his swarthy face, and he bent
forward in a bow. The inclination of his dark head
took his eyes away. It snapped the spell.

Elgera realized she had been unconsciously
holding her breath. She expelled it with a small
hissing sound, only then becoming aware of the

other two men who had entered. One was her brother, Natividad Douglas, lean and young in the same reddish *charro* leggin's as worn by Elgera. His angular face was burned deeply by the sun. He removed his flat-topped Stetson, introducing the men.

"Elgera, this is *Señor* Ignacio Avarillo, the mining engineer," he said, indicating the swarthy man with the strange eyes. "And this is *Señor* Thomas. Gentlemen, my sister, Elgera Douglas."

Thomas was skinny and dour; his face seemed like an ancient satchel. With one claw-like hand he clutched a briefcase of brown leather up against his dusty tail-coat. Elgera was drawn again to the swarthy man. *Señor* Avarillo wore a *cabriolé* of blue broadcloth, the short Spanish cape still affected by some men in this border country—but even its loose folds failed to hide the hulk of his great shoulders. He was looking around the large room with its *viga* poles for rafters, blackened by the smoke of generations above the fireplace. His glance stopped at the rawhide-rigged saddle that hung from a peg to one side of the door, its hand-stamped skirt marked with the Circle ⑤ brand which had been used by the Douglases ever since they had come to the Santiago Valley.

"Ah yes," said Avarillo, and his voice held a deep vibrancy. "The *Circulo* S, the mark of the fabled Lost Santiago Mine. You can imagine how I must feel, *Señorita* Douglas, after hearing the thousand legends of the mine, to be standing here in your house in this lost valley, knowing I have at last found what men have hunted for two centuries. And those Dead Horse Mountains . . . *Santa Maria*! I can well understand why no one has ever discovered the mine before this. Without your brother to guide us in from Alpine, *Señor* Thomas and I would be buzzard bait right now."

His faint smile suddenly disturbed Elgera. She was surprised at the impatience in her own voice. "You brought your papers?"

"*Naturalmente*," he said, inclining his head toward the dour man. "If you please, *Señor* Thomas."

Thomas glanced around the room, chose the ponderous, wooden-pegged table by the far adobe wall. He set the cheap oil lamp to one side, put the briefcase on the sleazy, fringed satin cloth. Elgera saw the gilt letter A inscribed on the flap before he unlocked and opened it.

"I don't want to seem rude, rushing it this way," said the girl. "But you understand why I want to be so sure of you."

"Your brother told me about some trouble with this Hawkman," said Avarillo. "He owns all the land around you, I understand, and is trying to get yours away from you."

The girl spoke bitterly. "The only reason we're still here is that Hawkman hasn't been able to find us yet. He owns land in these Dead Horses, but he's never seen most of it, never been able to hire men who would ride in and survey it for him. It's the worst badlands in the Big Bend. Our valley is the only spot capable of supporting cattle. The Indians have avoided these mountains ever since they began passing them in their raids down the Comanche Trail into Mexico. Few white men have penetrated beyond the first ridges and lived. Even if it weren't for the mine, though, Hawkman would still go to any lengths for our spread."

"What a boundless greed the man must have," murmured Avarillo. "*Sí*, what a boundless greed."

59

Thomas glanced at him sharply then went on taking papers from the case. A shadow entered Elgera's blue eyes. She looked from one man to the other.

"What I can't understand," said Avarillo, "is why you didn't develop the Santiago Mine before."

Natividad answered. "That tunnel by which we entered the valley is the original mine shaft. It leads right through the mountains from the outside and is the only way in or out. It was the mine that brought Don Simeón Santiago and George Douglas here in the first place. They had worked it about six months when the Comanches and Apaches raided. The Indians killed Santiago and all the others except Douglas and a woman who hid in the bottom level of the diggings. When the Indians left, they caved in a portion of the tunnel behind them, leaving Douglas trapped on the inside. We are the descendants of that George Douglas, *señor*, and it was only fifteen years ago that we succeeded in digging back out."

"There were some of us who wanted to stay cut off, to have the peace we had known," said the girl. "Others wanted to begin working the mine again. It has been a continual argument among us. But Hawkman has been closing in, and our hand is forced. The mine is all we can fight him with. If we can get it working before he discovers our whereabouts. . . ."

"*Sí*," murmured Avarillo, and his voice held a sibilance. "Before he discovers your whereabouts. *Ahora*, my papers. You have the diploma from the *Escuela de las Minas* in *Méjico* City, the sheepskin from Columbia School of Mines, letter of recommendation from the Apex in Colorado, letter of introduction from *Señor* Hopwell at Alpine, and so on . . . you see them, they are all there."

Elgera glanced perfunctorily at the gilt-edged diplomas with their fancy scrolls. She picked up the letter of introduction from Hopwell's land office in Alpine. They had been reluctant about trusting even him, though he had run the office there for many years. But they had to trust someone, and Natividad had asked Hopwell to recommend a competent, trustworthy mining engineer. Hopwell had communicated with Avarillo in Colorado. When the man arrived at Alpine, Natividad had gone up to meet him and bring him back to the Santiago.

"And now," said Avarillo, "if everything is in order, might I presume and ask to see your papers."

"My papers?" asked Elgera.

"Legal aspects," muttered Thomas in his dry voice. "Deeds, will, mortgages, anything you have. That's why Avarillo brought me. After all, he doesn't want to start digging on any mine unless he's sure you own it."

Elgera frowned, hesitating, and Avarillo spoke softly. "Of course, if you have nothing here, we could check on the county records. *Pues* that would take time. And Anse Hawkman. . . ."

The name goaded Elgera. She turned toward the fireplace. "I have papers."

She drew a heavy stone from its place, took a packet wrapped in greased buckskin from the cavity. She handed it to Thomas. He unwrapped the soft hide, rustled through the papers.

"Last will and testament," he muttered, waving one.

Avarillo turned to the girl. "Your father?"

"Made out before we took him to the hospital at Alpine," said the girl. "He. . . ."

"Ah, sick, how unfortunate," broke in Avarillo, something impatient in his voice. "Did you hear that,

Thomas? The old gentleman is sick."

Thomas held up another document. "Quit-claim."

"Is it what we want?" asked Avarillo quickly.

"'This indenture, made the . . . ,'"—Thomas paused in his reading—"no date. We can fix that. 'This indenture, made the blank day of the blank month, Eighteen Hundred and Ninety-Two, between John Coates Douglas, cattleman, Santiago Valley, Brewster County, Texas, party of the first part, and'"—he paused again—"no name there either. We might as well see to it all right now."

He drew a bottle of ink and a quill pen from the briefcase bending over the table. Elgera heard the scratch of pen on paper and stepped forward.

"What are you doing?"

"You," said Avarillo, and his eyes caught her, "you must realize how dangerous that deed might be in Hawkman's hands."

"My father made it out," she said. "No matter how hard the small *rancheros* fought Hawkman, no matter what they did, Hawkman got their land sooner or later. Dad saw him closing in around us like that with nothing stopping him and thought it would be useless to fight. He wanted to spare us the pain and bloodshed and loss the others had suffered. He made arrangements to meet Anse down at the Smoky Blue line camp, had the quit-claim drawn up. My brother found it before he left and stopped him."

"Hawkman, then, might know about this deed?"

The girl shrugged. "Dad might have told him he'd have it. What does it matter?"

Thomas straightened, clearing his throat. "How does it sound now? 'This indenture, made the fifteenth day of March, Eighteen Hundred and Ninety-Two, between John Coates Douglas, cattleman' . . . so on, so on . . . 'party of the first part, and Anse Herald Hawkman, Boquillos, Brewster County, Texas, party of the second part. Witnesseth: that said party of the first part, in consideration of twenty thousand dollars' . . . I made it a tidy sum, you see? . . . 'twenty thousand dollars lawful money of the United States, paid by the party of the second part, do hereby grant and release unto said party of the second part, heirs and assigns, forever, the land lying between Dead Horse Peak. . . . '"

"Never mind the rest," snapped Avarillo. "That do the job?"

"It does," said Thomas. "I made the date as of today, you see. We can register the transfer when we get back to Alpine."

The girl was looking from one man to the other, trying to grasp what she had just heard. It was simple enough. Yet she couldn't believe it. Her voice was faint.

"You. . . . you signed Hawkman's name?"

"You're sure it's legal now?" said Avarillo swiftly to Thomas. "You can put Hawkman's handle to it like that?"

"I have power of attorney," said Thomas. "If no one contests this, it's as good as the gold in the Santiago Mine. And that's your job, Valeur, to see that no one contests it."

It must have taken Natividad that long to understand. His boots made a sharp rasp on the earthen floor as he stepped forward, hand slipping to the butt of his old-fashioned Remington.

"Valeur?" he said.

The swarthy man's hand slid upward to the lapel of his coat, and he smiled. "*Sí*, Jan Valeur. . . ."

The pound of someone's feet across the flagstone porch turned them toward the door. It burst open,

63

and Elgera's younger brother, Juanito, stumbled in, white cotton shirt tails flapping around his buckskin *chivarras*.

"Elgera," he gasped. "It's Bickford. He must have trailed Natividad and Avarillo in when they came. He was waiting in the mine with Hawkman's *vaqueros*."

"Juanito," cried Elgera, taking a step toward him and reaching out to keep him from falling.

Bick Bickford's huge form was skylighted for a moment in the doorway as he came through after the boy. Juanito Douglas was still stumbling forward when Bickford caught up with him and slugged him behind the neck with a big black .44.

The boy fell against Elgera without a sound, hands clawing down her leggin's as he slumped to the floor. Her horrified eyes rose slowly from the still form at her feet to Bick Bickford, standing there with his thick legs straddled one on either side of the kid he had struck down. The round bore of his gun covered the room.

The swarthy man's voice startled Elgera, coming in harsh anger from behind her. "You fool, Bickford. I told you not to show till we gave you the high sign!"

He was a big bull of a man, Bickford, with a heavy-boned forehead that lowered over close set eyes, a week's stubble of yellow beard on his ugly, bulging jaw. He tucked his freckled left hand into a cartridge belt that was pushed down low beneath the sag of a growing paunch.

"This kid heard us waiting in the cave," he growled to the man behind Elgera. "I tried to cut him off, but he got away. No use staying after that, was there? Did you get the quit-claim?"

The girl turned to Natividad. His face was white

and twisted. He opened his mouth helplessly, closed it again. She whirled back to Bickford.

"You . . . !" she choked.

"Yes," he said without smiling. "Me. Did you think Anse wasn't going to find you sooner or later? Everybody in the Big Bend knew he's been hunting for this valley, knew how much he'd pay for any information about it. Hopwell kept his mouth closed, but he had to get in touch with Avarillo by mail, and he made the mistake of sending his Mex handyman to the stage with the letter. The Mex guessed it had something to do with the Santiago. He'd seen Natividad in the land office. The letter went to Avarillo all right, but we found out what was in it before we sent it on."

The girl's pale face turned slowly back to the swarthy man.

Bick went on heavily. "You knew me and the rest of Anse's boys. The only one you didn't know was Thomas. We brought Valeur, here, in from New Orleans to do the job. He made a right nice Avarillo from the looks of things."

"Yes," said Thomas dryly, crackling the deed. "A very successful deception. Too bad you didn't see what the real Avarillo looked like, though, Bick."

"We got his papers, didn't we?" said Bick. "That's all we needed."

"And left him running around free as air," snapped the swarthy man whose real name seemed to be Valeur. "You were a fool to jump him at night like that. And not even getting a look at him before he vamoosed, that was the payoff."

"Let's not quarrel," said Thomas. "It's done now, and we have what we want. We found the way to the valley, and the Santiago belongs to Anse now."

The girl heard her own choked sob. Yes, the

Santiago belonged to Anse Hawkman. She couldn't believe she had just stood there and let them take it away like that. Yet what could she have done? How could she have known? Fists clenched, she looked at Natividad again. He held his hand out in a small, helpless gesture, eyes blank and stunned. And how could he have known?

The girl shuddered suddenly with a wave of terrible impotent anger. She whirled back toward Bick, taking a jerky step toward him. The man snapped his .44 up.

"Hold it, Elgera," he said. "Valeur, you better take care of this girl right now."

Elgera felt the insistent pound of a little pulse in her throat. Her body was still rigid with the impotent rage. But the first sense of her utter defeat began to creep through the anger. She looked from Bick to Valeur, and suddenly she wanted to cry very badly.

"We'll take care of all the Douglases right now," smiled the swarthy man. "You leave it to me. Especially the girl."

It was an odd thing that came to Elgera's mind then. Yet, not so odd, in a way. A certain man had helped her once before. Through all her anger and fear and stunned surprise, the name began to take form. It was a singular name Bickford would know or Hawkman. Chisos Owens.

II

The Del Norte Mountains cast purple afternoon shadows into Alpine, huddled at the base of their western slope. The town had been founded twelve years before with the coming of the railroad. The Southern Pacific's brick depot and loading platforms fronted on the tracks at the north end of the main street. The Alpine Lodge took up half of the first block, a paint-peeled frame hotel with a sprawling porch that looked across toward the dilapidated row of business houses on the other side. The Mescal Saloon squatted forlornly on the southwest corner of the next block, the blank windows to the assayer's office staring from its second floor. Beneath the warped overhang of the pine oak lounged a dusty idler, leaning against an unpainted *soporte* to one side of the saloon's batwings.

His Texas-creased Stetson cast a shadow across blue eyes holding the narrowed wind-wrinkled look that comes to a man spending most of his time on the range. He was rolling a wheatstraw with a deftness that seemed odd, somehow, for his blocky, rope-scarred hands. He finished with the cigarette and lowered his free hand to tuck a thumb inside the cartridge belt of his oak-handled Bisley, its scarred holster slung indifferently against his brass-studded Levi's.

Three horsemen had just turned in past the depot and were cantering toward the Mescal. The man in front of the saloon glanced at them disinterestedly. He could already see that none of the three was the girl, and he found himself wondering if she would ever come riding in that way. Then he took an impatient puff on his wheatstraw.

Chisos Owens, he told himself, *you are a fool.*

He allowed gray smoke to stream from his nostrils. All right, so he was a fool. That was the only reason he kept drifting back to Alpine, though, because of the girl. She would be opening the mine about now; rumors of it had already reached this far north. And Alpine was where her ore would come for assaying. It was in the back of his mind always, the hope of seeing her again.

The first dry gritty feel of dust raised by the riders came to Owens, blown by a vagrant gust of wind. He took small notice of it. He was still thinking of Elgera Douglas.

It seemed a long time ago that he had followed her into the Santiago. Yet it was only a few months. He was sorry now that he had ever left the valley. He knew it was only his stubborn pride that prevented his return. Even when he had discovered she was heiress to the Santiago, he still had asked her to leave with him. And she had asked him to stay. But it just hadn't seemed right, somehow, for a man to live off a woman when he felt that way about her. It still didn't seem right. Staying there, or taking her away, he should have something to offer. And he had nothing. . . .

"Hell!" It was but a whisper.

Owens shrugged, dropping his cigarette to grind it out with a scarred heel of his Justin. The three horsebackers had passed him and were pulling up at the hitch rack farther down where a covered stairway went up the rear of the saloon to the assayer's office on the second floor. Chisos couldn't help marking the size of the man who forked the chestnut mare. It wasn't so much his height, though he must have stood over six feet without his patent leather boots. It was the tremendous bulk of his chest and shoulders that not even the loose hanging folds of his short blue cape could hide. In a land where most men were as lean and drawn as a rawhide dally from spending all their time in the saddle, this man stood out like a Brahman bull in a bunch of range-gaunted Mexican *ladinos*.

He pulled the chestnut to a halt and swung down, alighting with an easy grace that was surprising in such a large man. He spoke swiftly to the other riders. The tall, dour one in a dusty frock coat climbed off his nag stiffly. The plank walk groaned as he stepped up onto it, popped beneath his boots as he turned southward toward the newly erected municipal building. He held a brown briefcase under one arm.

Slung across the chestnut's withers were leather *alforjas*. The man in the blue cape slipped one arm beneath the high pockets of the Mexican saddle bags and bent in under, heaving them off onto his shoulder. Their weight was evident in the way he leaned forward when he stepped to the walk and disappeared up the stairs. Owens got the impression that few other men would have been able to carry the *alforjas* without help.

The third man was dismounted now, and he stood there with his sharp face turning nervously up and down the street. Owens was about to look away when something on the man's horse caught his eye. It was a blocky dun, flanks caked with sweat and dust of a long ride. On its heavy rump was a very evident Circle ⑤ brand.

"Ees a strange mark to see in the Big Bend, no?" said a soft voice at Owens's elbow.

Chisos turned sharply. He hadn't heard the man come up. He was Mexican, and he couldn't have measured much more than five feet tall, or much less than five feet around. His moon face was the color of a coffee bean, and his big, sad, bloodshot eyes reminded Owens of a hound dog's. Providing striking contrast to his English riding boots and gray whipcords was the broad sash of a violent red bound around his singularly prodigious girth.

"What's so strange about it?" asked Owens warily.

69

The Mexican took a *cigarro* from the pocket of his white silk shirt, bit off the end, spat it out. "The *Circulo* S. A very ancient brand. Used by the House of Santiago in Mexico. It was Don Simeón Santiago, was it not, who discovered the Santiago Mine, and who subsequently disappeared along with that mine."

"Are you asking me?"

The man lit his *cigarro*, chuckled.

"Maybe I should ask you. I think you could probably tell me things about the Santiago no other men in the Big Bend know. Then, again, maybe I could tell you things about the Santiago which even you don't know. Monclava was the old capital of the combined provinces of Tejas and Coahuila when Spain held this country. Simeón Santiago was *adelantado*, entrusted with the visitation of the mines in New Spain, when he discovered the Lost Santiago. The church at Monclava still has the official documents. I have had access to those documents. They contain things which would be interesting. . . . even to you." He cut off as Owens glanced at him sharply then chuckled. He took a complacent puff on his cigar before speaking. "Chisos Owens, isn't it?" he asked, then: "*Señor* Chisos Owens who owned the Smoky Blue until the creek dried up and one Anse Hawkman forced you out. *Señor* Chisos Owens who might know what it could mean to see a man like our friend out in the street riding a horse with the ancient *Circulo* S brand, which hasn't been seen in existence since the House of Santiago was confiscated during Santa Anna's time in the old country."

"You seem to have a fund of information," said Owens.

"Upon discreet inquiry by me the barkeep in the

70

Mescal was glad to oblige. He seemed to think you were the only man who had bucked Hawkman and stayed around to talk about it."

"I don't talk about it," said Owens. "Two things generally happen to *hombres* who buck Hawkman. Most of them give up and go to work for him, sooner or later. Hawkman has a man named Bickford who takes care of those that don't give up, in a permanent way, sooner or later."

"*Sí*," grinned the Mexican, "only you are the exception which proves the rule. That *hombre* standing by the horses? He strikes me as being a stranger here. Perhaps brought in by somebody for something . . . ah, special . . . as it were."

The man by the dun had his gray vest buttoned up tightly about a skinny chest. Owens hadn't missed the way he slung his gun around low in front, because there were always men in such towns as Alpine who wore their guns in that manner. He might, as the Mexican said, have been brought in by somebody for something special. Men of his type had reasons for coming and invariably had even better ones for leaving. Chisos shook his head.

"I'd say he isn't a native."

"And not being a native, he wouldn't know you, perhaps?"

"No," said Owens. "I don't think he'd know me."

"*Excelente*," laughed the Mexican, and suddenly he held a pack of tattered cards in one pudgy hand. "Now, *Señor* Chisos Owens, has it ever struck you what a big majority of men who, shall we say, have a certain skill with their guns which they use in a professional way also have an irresistible passion for gambling? You couldn't say that almost every gambler was a gunman, *pues* you could say with a reasonable certainty that almost every gunman was a

71

gambler. No . . . ? *Sí.*"

While talking, he had begun to do tricks with the deck, turning slightly so his manipulations would be visible to the man in the street. Black *cigarro* in his mouth he flipped the cards back and forth between his fat fingers, made them leap from one hand to the other as if alive. His voice became louder than before.

"*Dios*, what a dull *día* this is. No *compadres* in the *cantina*, no friends to play cards with. I would give my right *brazo* for another *hombre* or two. A man's money can only stay in his pocket a little while before it begins burning holes. . . ."

Chisos caught the small shift of the skinny man in the gray vest; something intent came into the tilt of his head. The Mexican went on talking, moving toward the saloon door.

"What could be more enjoyable after a long dusty ride than a bottle of mescal, a *compañero* or two, and a deck of cards, eh?

"What's the game?" Owens asked, and he wasn't talking about the cards.

"Anything you like, *amigo*, keno, chusa, poker," said the fat man in a tone still loud enough to reach the man in the street; then he had reached the batwing doors, and he lowered his voice. "Many men have heard the rumors that the Lost Santiago had been found again, *Señor* Owens. But who was beside the quaking asp on Saltillo Peak when it whispered to the wind that Anse Hawkman had branched out of the cattle business into mining? Eh, *señor* . . . who?"

Still playing with the cards, he shoved through the doors. They creaked shut behind him. Owens could hear his bland chuckle diminishing inside.

The three of them sat around a scarred deal table

72

at the rear of the Mescal. Chisos Owens had been the first to follow the Mexican in. The skinny man held out a few moments then swung through the door almost defiantly. He went to the bar first, had a drink beside the other two men there. But the light slap of cards drew him irresistibly, and now he was sitting across from Owens, gray vest still buttoned tightly. The Mexican leaned back in his chair, grinning expansively.

"What shall we call you, *señor*," he chuckled, "what shall we call such a good *compadre* who has come to drink with us and play with us and win all our money?"

The thin man glanced nervously toward the door. "Hoke. My handle's Hoke. You?"

"Me," chuckled the Mexican. "*Por supuesto*, you could call me Felipe, and that would be my name, or Juan, or Amole, and those would be my names too, and yet none of them would quite be my name entirely, if you understand what I mean."

Hoke seemed to appreciate that. He laughed shortly. "Yeah, I understand. You?"

His glance swung to Owens inquiringly. Chisos shoved the cards to him.

"No thanks," he said. "You deal."

Hoke looked at him sharply then down at the cards. He grinned, shrugged, took up the deck. As he began to shuffle, the Mexican looked at Owens and laughed softly. Chisos shifted uneasily in his chair. He knew he had been drawn into this by the Mexican who sat calmly smoking the cigar and wondered just how much he knew about the Santiago Valley and the *Circulo* S and Anse Hawkman.

Owens hadn't much skill with the cards and wasn't surprised when Hoke took the first pot. He got the impression, though, that the Mexican did possess a skill and that he had let Hoke win deliberately. Hoke seemed to relax a little. He took a long pull at the clay jug of mescal. It was growing dark outside, and the bald-headed barkeep dragged a chair beneath the single overhead light, climbing up to turn the lamp high.

It was stud—two down and three up—and by the third hand Hoke was showing his liquor. Trying to focus his eyes, he put down a pair of aces and turned up the two kings on the table. Felipe slapped his cards into the center disgustedly.

"Santiago!"

Hoke jerked up. "Whassat?"

"Santiago," said Felipe with a bland grin. "An expression. A war cry, really. Originated when the Spanish were trying to rid Spain of the Moors, you understand. *Santiago y cierra España*, they would cry, Saint James and clear out of Spain."

"Oh," said Hoke, and he seemed relieved. "Oh."

They went through another hand. Hoke finished the bottle. He was perspiring. His ratty eyes were dull. Felipe leaned back in his chair.

"*Por Dios*," he said. "My pockets are light again. My *dinero* is disappearing. And I have no mine to fall back on like you, Hoke."

"When those diggin's begin turning out yellow, I'll play cards every night and lose an *alforja* full of gold pieces every game and still be able to buy me a spread ten times the size of Hawkman's mangy pasture," hiccoughed the skinny man—then he raised his head with a jerk, suspicion flickering into his eyes. "How'd you know?"

The Mexican leaned forward, plunking a stack of yellow coins.

Hoke's glance fell on the stack of yellow coins.

74

"Yeah, yeah. I'll take this hand too."

Understanding what the Mexican was pointing at now, Owens dealt. He hadn't enough skill to plant the card. He knew the Mexican named Felipe would keep Hoke drinking and all the beans would spill out sooner or later.

The narrow-faced gunman bent over his cards, underlip slack. The Mexican perused his hand, grunted almost under his breath.

"You know, I'm not sure whether to believe these stories about the Santiago or not. I don't think Anse Hawkman has found it at all. Not when men have been hunting it for two hundred years."

"Who says Hawkman found it?" grunted Hoke, pawing for the empty jug. "Valeur did all the work. Those damn' Douglas coyotes would've rec'nized Hawkman or any of his riders. It was Valeur fooled the gal. It's him working the mine now."

Chisos Owens stiffened. The girl? Then he caught Felipe's eyes on him, a warning in them. He relaxed, allowing a heavy breath to slip from him, glancing dully at his cards. They were crumpled in his fist.

Felipe held up a fat finger for the barkeep, turned back to Hoke. "It seems to me a *hombre* of your caliber would ride a better horse than that crow-bait dun."

"My hoss went lame," muttered Hoke, looking blankly into the empty jug. "I was going to take the Douglas gal's palomino. Bick wouldn't let me, wouldn't even let me take any of the others in the Circle S remuda. Hell. Think I was gonna shove up my animal riding him up here lame? I snuck the dun out."

Felipe took the fresh bottle from the barkeep, shoved it to the center of the table. "There you are, Hoke, *compadre*, more paint remover, so to speak.

75

This Bickford must be a very uncooperative *hombre*. I'll bet he wanted the palomino himself."

"He didn't want the blondie," snarled Hoke thickly. "Bick's just spooked by this Chisos Owens, that's all . . . Bick and Thomas and Anse, the whole bunch of 'em. They said Chisos Owens was still around and might spot the palomino. They was even skeery of him seeing me forking any other Circle S animal."

He tipped the full bottle up and his Adam's apple bobbed when he drank. Felipe flourished his *cigarro*, knocked ashes from it, gave Chisos a sidelong glance.

"This Chisos Owens must be quite a *diablo* to have a man like Anse Hawkman afraid of him," he said.

"I dunno," said Hoke, head sinking toward the table. "Anse's getting old. Maybe he is afraid of Chisos Owens. He told us to finish Owens's tortillas for good if he showed at the valley. Seems Owens is sweet on the gal. He followed her in from the outside. The only one who knows where the valley is . . . at least he was the only one. Now, Valeur and me, yeah, Valeur and me. . . ."

His voice trailed off as his face pressed into the table. Felipe shoved the bottle into his hand again, smiling slyly at Owens.

"*Sí*, you and Valeur. And I'll bet you're the only one who isn't afraid of this Chisos Owens. I'll bet you're the one who gets him if he comes. No . . . ? *Sí*?"

"Bick's the one who knows him," said Hoke, trying to raise his head for another pull. "Valeur and me came in from New Orleans for the job. I don't see why they're all so skeery of one *hombre* like that anyway."

Felipe was still looking at Owens. "Neither do I. *Pues*, maybe Hawkman knows this Chisos Owens better than we do, Hoke."

He stopped, turning toward the sound of boots coming down the walk outside. Owens saw the batwings swing open suddenly, and the big, swarthy man in the blue *cabriolé* burst into the room. He came on in with that swift, rolling walk, like a savage jungle animal pacing its cage. For a moment his eyes swept to Chisos Owens and their glances locked.

Owens felt himself recoil as if he had been struck. The force of personality emanating from the man's eyes was almost physical. They were jet black but lacking the opaque quality of an Indian's eyes, and all the unbridled violence boiling inside the man seemed to burn in the brilliant little lights flashing through their depths.

When his glance left Owens and jumped to Hoke, it was like snapping a cord between them. Chisos straightened in his chair, realizing how tightly his hand gripped the table. The big man stopped beside Hoke, grabbing the edge of his vest in a hairy fist, jerking him up.

"Damn' fool, Hoke," he snarled. "I told you to stay clear of this place. I told you not to get drunk this time."

"'Sall right, Valeur," mumbled Hoke. "These *hombres* already knew Hawkman was working the Santiago."

His words ended with a gasp as Valeur's arm straightened, shoving him violently over backward. Even before Hoke hit the floor, Valeur was turning.

"You pumped him," he almost yelled, and his hand slipped beneath the blue cloak. "Nobody knew Hawkman had the Santiago. You got him drunk, and you pumped him."

Owens kicked his chair back from beneath him and tried to rise and draw. But before his hand touched his Bisley, he saw Valeur's fist flashing back out of his cloak, the butt of a gun gleaming between taut fingers.

Then a bulk was thrust in between Owens and Valeur. It took that instant for Chisos to realize Felipe had leaned over the table with his burning *cigarro* held outthrust in one pudgy hand.

The swift deftness of the Mexican's whole movement made it seem almost ludicrous. He jammed his *cigarro* against Valeur's gun hand. The big man bellowed with pain, hand pulling away spasmodically. His shot went wild into the ceiling instead of hitting Owens.

Valeur whirled toward Felipe, face twisted savagely. Chisos had his Bisley out by then. He drew down on Valeur. Someone shot out the light.

With the tinkling crash of the wrecked oil lamp following the thunderous shot, Owens fired blindly into the sudden darkness. The flame that stabbed out ahead of him might have been Valeur shooting at Felipe. Someone pounded in through the door.

"Valeur?" he shouted. "You in here, Valeur?"

Owens lurched forward, cocking his gun. He slammed into a man before the hammer was eared back. Anyone else would have been staggered by his hurtling weight. This man stopped him like a stone wall.

Chisos struck upward with the barrel of his gun, heard a pained curse. He threw out his hand to ward off the return blow. Then the man's arms were about him.

He felt the terrible driving surge of strength in that awful bear hug, knew his first shot had missed

Valeur, and knew who held him now. He tried to free his Bisley and strike again. His right arm was pinned. He twisted, jabbing in a left. He struck a belly like an oak plank and wondered if his hand was broken.

The scuffle of their feet was sharp and swift on the bare floor. Owens jabbed again with his left. He choked on the pain it caused him. They slammed into a table.

"Damn you!" gasped Valeur. "Damn you."

His arms flexed, and Owens felt himself levered backward. He fought for solid footing, breath exploding from him. Someone struck his head from behind.

With sound and smell and pain suddenly slipping from him, Owens sagged against Valeur. He heard a dull thud, and Valeur cried hoarsely. The man's arms relaxed. Owens went on down against him.

Hands slipped beneath Owens's armpits, jerking him free of Valeur. His boot struck the table leg as someone dragged him across the floor. A man groaned to his left. Hoke, maybe.

Owens's last coherent thought was to wonder who had hit him from behind like that. The man who had come running in shouting for Valeur hadn't had time to reach them. Hoke had been on the other side of the table. Felipe?

Ⓥ Ⓥ Ⓥ

Chisos Owens's first sensation upon regaining consciousness was the fetid, gagging smell of decaying food. He rose to an elbow and was very sick without opening his eyes. Then he looked and was sick again. It came to him finally that he was jammed down between two boxes of refuse in the alley behind the saloon. A month old *New York Sun*

79

poked moldering headlines in his face. Empty bottles clinked beneath him when he moved. Shoving the trash off, he got to his feet, staggered toward the rear door of the Mescal.

The barkeep was a pot-bellied little man with a fringe of reddish hair around his bald pate. He stood on a deal table in the center of the room, putting up a new oil lamp. Owens weaved to the bar.

"Who conked me last night, Irish?" he wanted to know.

Irish climbed down, circled behind the bar. He poured Owens two fingers, flipped the jigger across the scarred mahogany.

"Dunno, Chisos," he said. "I make it a practice to duck behind the bar when things like that begin. I do know those jaspers spent about an hour hunting you before they left."

"Somebody tucked me away for the night beneath a pile of your trash," mumbled Owens, tossing off the drink. "I don't wonder they couldn't find me. You tell 'em who I was?"

"The big gent in the blue *cabriolé* asked me your name," said Irish, "but I just couldn't seem to remember. That fat Mex had asked me about you earlier in the day, and I figured I'd blabbed enough to him. He has such a way of asking things, though, you don't know you've told 'em till they're out."

"That," said Chisos, fishing for a quarter, "is the truth."

He put the coin down and turned toward the door. His buckskin was standing at the rack. Owens unhitched a pair of old apron chaps from a tie string on his saddle skirt, slipped them on over his dusty Levi's. He would need them where he was headed. He didn't feel like breakfast. There was some coffee and flour in the fiber *morral* slung from his saddle horn that would do when he got over being sick. There was something decisive about the way he swung aboard the buckskin and turned it toward the brick depot. His destination was clear in his mind now, and he felt better than he had in a long time, somehow.

An early morning freight was halted by the loading platform. He rode by the puffing engine and on out across the tracks without looking back at the town.

In all Texas there was no more wild, rugged country than the Big Bend, and in all the Big Bend the wildest, least-known, most desolate section was the mysterious badlands encompassed by the *Sierra del Caballo Muerto*—the Dead Horse Mountains. White with alkali of the Rosillos Basin, Chisos Owens turned into the Dead Horses late the second afternoon out of Alpine. He had followed the ancient Comanche Trail through Persimmon Gap and hugged the western flank of the Santiagos for the better part of the day. Irish had said Valeur and the other two had left Alpine after their hour's search for him. Often now he could see their trail. Sometimes, too, he caught the sign of a fourth man's track. It was hard to tell whether he rode with Valeur, or alone, but Owens didn't need their sign to tell him the way.

He had a forward lean to his seat in the saddle that humped his shoulders into a dogged line, giving a stubborn quality to the weariness that lay in the sag of his blocky torso. Grinning mirthlessly, he urged the flagging buckskin up the first barren slope of the mountains.

Topping the ridge, he was struck by a wind that was dry and yet cold, a cutting wind that made him hunch deeper into his denim jumper and wish for a mackinaw. The gaunt *alamos* arched past him as he dropped down the opposite slope, their foliage sere and sparse. A hoot owl heralded the coming night.

Memory of his other trip into this lonely place served Owens now. Ridge after ridge lay behind him when he finally dropped down a shaly *barranca* into the bottom of a valley, turning northward along the dry course of a river. There was absolutely no water, and a man not knowing the way would face sure death, turning on into unknown land that way. Owens could already feel his cutting thirst as the valley narrowed, becoming a cañon. Brush began to thicken in the bottom, clawing at his apron chaps, ripping at his *tapaderos*. Finally the chaparral became practically impenetrable, and he dismounted, cursing the pop and snap of mesquite as he forced his way through. A hundred yards beyond he hitched the buckskin to a growth of nopal and began to move forward alone. He stopped finally, pulling out his gun, staying there a long time, listening.

It was a box cañon, and ahead of him the brush thinned out until an oblong clearing lay beneath the towering walls of red sandstone blocking off its end. The cliff here had more slope to it than the part behind Owens. He searched the hovering shadows formed by the boulders and uplifts until his eyes ached. Nothing moved up there. He shrugged. There was only one way in, and he would have to take it sooner or later. His figure made a square blot against the pale yellow parch of sand, moving out in a solid-footed stride.

Half way across he stopped abruptly. His head jerked upward toward the small scraping sound. His gun swung in a tightened fist when he saw the man on the rocks above him. Then it stopped its swift upward arc. Owens turned part way toward the other wall of the cañon, and he was too dog tired to feel his defeat very sharply.

There was another man across the way there—the noise he had made climbing down was what had stopped Owens. Both men had rifles that caught the moonlight in fitful metallic glints, and they were in a position to cut Owens down with a crossfire. He realized suddenly how confident they were to have allowed him that instinctive upward swing with his gun and still hold their lead. They didn't even ask him to drop his Bisley now. They moved down the steep wall, sliding from boulder to boulder.

One wore slick batwing chaps that made a faint slapping sound against his extremely bowed legs as he moved. A steeple sombrero cast his face into deep shadow. He seemed puzzled by Owens's dull acceptance of this. He tipped his head sideways and regarded Owens for a long moment.

"Think you could walk right in?" he said.

Owens shrugged, and the other man spoke from where he stood in the sand at the base of the cliff. "Got a handle?"

"Not one that sticks out," said Owens.

The man in batwings stiffened, motioning with his Winchester. "Don't act smart. Hand over that iron and tell us your name."

Apparently they didn't recognize him. That didn't mean they weren't Hawkman's men. Many of the *vaqueros* on the northern A H pastures knew Chisos Owens by name only. Owens handed the gun over, oak butt first. The man waited a moment, breath harsh.

"I'm Bick Bickford's brother," said Owens finally. "Anse sent me to tell Valeur everything's set."

The bow-legged man bent forward sharply. "Whaddaya mean, everything's set? What's set . . . ?"

He must have gotten it then. He broke off and took a vicious step forward, rifle bearing on Owens's belly. The other man made a move in the sand.

"Hold it, Pinky," he said. "You know what Valeur told us."

"Bickford's brother, hell!" spat Pinky disgustedly. "I say we dust him, Drexel. I said we should have dusted him first off."

Drexel was a big, lanky man, *chivarras* greasy on skinny legs. "I'll go get Valeur. Ventilate this *potro* before I get back, and you know what Valeur'll give you."

Pinky spat again. Drexel went to the thicket of black chaparral that climbed up the rock wall of the cañon. He pushed his way straight into the thicket. Pinky was watching Owens closely. Perhaps he expected surprise. Owens kept any expression from his dust-grimed face. He knew what lay behind the chaparral. Apparently anyone going in through it would meet the abrupt wall on the other side, but Owens had been through it himself once. It covered the mouth of the Lost Santiago Mine.

Evidently they had staked horses inside the shaft. Owens heard one snort, caught the creak of saddle leather. The dull thud of hoofs faded away, and there was silence. Owens's hand moved over to the makings in his jumper pocket.

"Keep 'em free," snapped Pinky.

Owens let his hand drop away from the cigarette papers. The other man sat cross-legged in the sand, facing him, rifle across his lap. Chisos must have dozed. He didn't know how much later it was when

84

the snap of bushes jerked his nodding head up.

The first man through the chaparral leading into the mine was Drexel. After him was Valeur, blue *cabriolé* swirling around his great shoulders. His teeth flashed white in his dark face when he saw Chisos Owens.

"Well, if it isn't our inquisitive card player," he laughed. "Or is it insistent, like your Mex *amigo*? Might've known you'd be trailing in."

Pinky stood up. "We kill 'im?"

"Why not?" said Valeur—then a strange sly expression crossed his face. He looked at Pinky, at Drexel, his smile growing. He looked at Owens and began to chuckle. It held a sibilant menace. "No," he said finally, "no, on second thought, no. I have a better idea." His chuckle grew. Pinky's boots made a soft sound shifting uncomfortably in the sand. Owens felt a sudden clammy sweat breaking out on his palms.

"Yes," laughed Valeur, "I have a much better idea."

III

Elgera Douglas sat on her bed, gazing absently at the weather cracks in the adobe wall of her bedroom. *They should be plastered again soon*, she thought dully. Then she shook her head, blonde hair shimmering. What was the use of torturing herself with thoughts like that. They wouldn't be plastering walls again, or bringing in the cattle from the outer draws again, or eating together in the living room. They wouldn't ever be doing the normal, happy things they had done. It belonged to Hawkman now. She looked up as sounds from the other part of the house reached her, the clink of dishes. A man's harsh laugh. Valeur had returned from Alpine that evening. He had taken a load of ore up in his *alforjas* to check on the assay. That wasn't his only business in the town, though. Thomas had registered the transfer of title. He had registered it with the same county clerk who had helped her father draw up that quitclaim and who had been expecting it to come in under Hawkman's signature like that. It had all been so simple. It gave Elgera a sick sense of utter defeat.

She straightened a little as the door opened. Ed Walker stood just outside, one of Valeur's men, tall and rawboned with a single galus holding up his tattered jeans. He spoke to the old woman who came in past him.

She carried a bullhide pail of water, and her shapeless shift of cotton flapped dismally about the torn rawhide *huaraches* on her feet. It might have been weathering that turned her seamed face the yellow tan color, or it might have been her great age. Maria Douglas was her name, but they all called her Granny. Valeur had kept her at the house to cook and serve for them. Elgera rose, helped her lift the bullhide pail to the white china crock on the crude side table.

"You've got to escape tonight," hissed the old woman, beneath the gurgle of water. "Thomas and Bickford left just as soon as Thomas and Valeur got back from Alpine. They've gone to Boquillos for Anse Hawkman. You know what that means."

"I can't leave you now," said the girl. "Even if I could get free, do you think I'd run away like that. It would be like. . . . like betraying you."

"Hurry up," snapped Walker from the door.

The old woman turned. "You've got to, Elgera. Chisos Owens is somewhere on the outside. He's

86

our last hope. The rest of us are helpless down there in the mine. If we don't do something before Hawkman gets back, we'll never be able to do it. You're the only one, Elgera. . . ."

The scuffle of boots at the door cut her off. Hoke had come down the short hall and was shoving past Walker, snarling at the man.

"You know Valeur told you not to let 'em talk like that, Ed. Get out of here, Granny, and next time you act funny, we'll put you down in the mine with the rest of 'em." He gave the old woman a backhand shove as she went past then turned to Elgera. "Valeur wants to see you."

Elgera rose slowly, fists clenching at her sides. There had been no trouble with Bick during the time Valeur had been at Alpine, perhaps because Bick was the older man, or because his heavy indifference to most things included women. Whatever it was, there had been no trouble. But Valeur was a different kind of man. And he was back now.

He sat at the big center table in the living room, leaning back a little in his chair. A scattering of empty plates lay before him, some cold pan bread left in one, a coffee pot beyond that. He turned as Elgera entered. During the first few days Valeur had stayed at the house, before he had left for Alpine, Elgera had learned that those strange little lights flickering through his eyes could reveal whatever emotion was passing through him at the moment. She had seen them blaze in anger at Hoke, or dance mockingly at Granny, or smolder with contempt for Bickford. And now she could see them kindle instantly with a certain cruel, hungry eagerness.

"Elgera," he said softly.

Hoke laughed shortly, sidled across the room. Walker stood yet behind the girl. Valeur rose, and she couldn't help mark the easy grace of his movement. Her own eyes narrowed, becoming opaque.

"Don't look like that," he laughed. "Bick said you were a wildcat, didn't he? Do you know how long we'll be here, now? Do you know how long we'll have to tame wildcats?"

Still laughing, he moved toward her. Valeur's boots made a soft noise against the earthen floor, coming on.

The knock on the door sounded like a thunderclap.

Valeur took a heavy breath, turned. "Yeah?"

Hoke opened the door, and a man took a step inside, blinking in the light. "Some *hombre* just showed at the cave."

"Who?" asked Valeur impatiently.

The man shrugged. "He gave us a line about being Bickford's brother. Pinky wanted to kill him. I thought you'd better know first."

"You didn't bring him on through?" asked Valeur, swinging around to get his *cabriolé* from the back of the chair.

"No," grunted the man. "But I don't see why. . . ."

"Too many *hombre*s know about the mine already. After that business up at Alpine, nobody even sees the shaft or this valley till I'm sure about them, understand? Hoke, you watch the girl"—Valeur stopped in front of Hoke, grabbed him by the vest, jerked him close—"and don't pull another botch like that at Alpine. I think I'd kill you if you did."

He glanced once more at Elgera, inclined his head toward Walker, went out the door. Walker followed. Hoke stood there a long moment, blood returning to his pale face slowly.

Elgera suddenly felt sick. The fingers of her right

88

hand twitched slightly, and she realized how tense she was. She forced herself to relax, moved toward the table. Then she became aware of Hoke watching her. She turned sharply toward him.

"I saw you," he said, his laugh shaky and forced. "Yeah. You woulda scratched Valeur's eyes out. I saw your hands. Like Bick said. Reg'lar wildcat."

There was something rat-like in his narrow face, his weak unshaven chin. It revolted her. Yet she continued to watch him, a speculation entering her blue eyes. Granny had been right, of course. Elgera knew she did her own people no good here. And Chisos Owens was on the outside somewhere, the man who had bucked Hawkman before. Elgera measured the weakness in Hoke carefully. The she rubbed her arm, shivering a little.

"It's cold," she said. "Why don't you light the fire?"

Hoke's smile was sly. "Think I'm gonna turn my back on you that way? Think you're smart? *You* light it."

She let her lips pout, turned toward the fireplace. Hunkering down on the hearth, she began to strip kindling from a length of jack pine. There was a poker lying beside the big kettle to one side of the hearth. She placed it in her mind without looking in that direction. She muffled her voice deliberately.

"What happened in Alpine?"

She heard Hoke's automatic movement toward her. "What?"

"I said, what happened in Alpine that made Valeur so angry."

"Nothing," he muttered. "I got high with a couple of *hombres* and talked a little."

She turned without rising. "Got a match?"

He fished in his hip pocket, came toward her with

89

several matches in his sinewy hand. Then he stopped suddenly, that sly smile revealing discolored teeth.

"Think I'd hand 'em to you," he laughed.

Still hunkered down that way with one hand flat on the hearthstones beside the kettle, she felt her lips twist with contempt. She held her other hand out.

"Oh, no, Hoke," she said, "you're very clever. I wouldn't think of trying to put anything over on you. Give me the match, please."

He stood two or three paces from her, boots shifting nervously. He laughed again and tossed her the matches. She moved while he was still bent forward slightly that way. With a savage little cry, she bent sideways and scooped up the fire iron and threw herself upward at him. Hoke's mouth opened, and he took one clumsy step to the rear, trying to drag at his gun. Elgera swung the poker viciously. It struck Hoke's right arm. He shouted hoarsely with the stunning pain of it. His gun clattered to the floor.

Still going forward, Elgera swung the iron out with a jerk and brought it in again at Hoke's head. The sound of the blow was dull and fleshy. He hit the table, slid down to the floor, and lay there.

Elgera stopped herself and stood above him a moment, panting, wiping a lock of blonde hair absently off her wet forehead. She dropped the poker finally and bent to pick up the six-shooter. It was a Smith & Wesson, and the black butt was smooth in her palm. The reaction to what she had done was coming now. She began to tremble. With a hoarse breath she stepped past the man toward the hall door. She was almost running by the time she reached it, and she turned right to the end of the south wing. The rear door was unlatched. Night enfolded her, dark and chill and protecting.

She headed toward the split-rail corral a hundred

90

yards behind the house, tore at the rawhide tie on the let-down bars. There was a whole remuda inside, but she wasted a precious moment getting a coiled dally from a peg and cutting out her own horse. It was a perfect palomino Morgan, hide the color of newly minted gold, mane as blonde and as silky as Elgera's own hair. She had trained it herself, and all it needed was the dally tossed across its back to stop it running the rail. She was moving toward it, looking for a saddle hanging from the rail, when Hoke appeared from the house in a weaving run that carried him from the black shadows thrown by the sprawling building into the yellow moonlight.

"The gal's got away," he shouted feebly, holding his head as he ran. "The gal's got away. Somebody stop her. . . ."

Knowing there would be no saddle now, Elgera hackamored the palomino with a swift half-hitch around its lower jaw. Holding the rest of the forty-foot dally coiled in her hand, she twined fingers in the creamy mane, swung her body with a leaping twist that carried her up and onto the horse.

Hit bareback like that, the palomino spooked and reared. She jerked the hackamore, forcing it out through the gate. She lay forward along the horse, feeling the breath heave through it as the hill steepened across a clearing of curly gramma. Ahead were the shadowy motes of juniper climbing up on either side of the mine. She could see the mouth of the tunnel, a dark blot in the upthrust of jagged hill. Hoke was yelling louder now.

"The gal," he shouted, "get the gal!"

There was a dim movement in the trees above the mouth of the mine. Another to the side. Elgera pleaded more speed from her animal as the first man showed between two junipers. The horse gathered

91

itself perceptibly, sweat beginning to warm its flanks beneath her legs. The second man scrambled down from over the cave.

"Hoke?" he shouted.

"That's not Hoke! Can't you see, that's the girl's horse?" yelled the other man as he quartered toward the cave, turning to call to Elgera. "Stop your animal. I don't want to shoot you. Don't make me do it!"

The moonlight glinted on his Winchester as he jerked it from the crook of his elbow. Elgera ducked low on the Morgan and let go a loop of the hackamore to give her slack, reaching for the Smith & Wesson in her waistband.

With the gun fisted, she caught up the loop again, bunching the rawhide tight on the horse. The men levered their Winchesters. One of them yelled again, then their shots made two flat detonations. Something tugged at the girl's leggin's, clipping off one of the bosses with a metallic ring. Holding hackamore and gun in the same hand, she threw her first wild shot. The rawhide was taut, and the buck of the gun jerked the horse's head around.

Elgera thundered straight for the first man. He tried to jump back and lever and shoot all at once. He tripped and went down with the gun exploding into the air. The other man yelled crazily and threw himself out of the way, dropping the rifle. The palomino's right front hoof struck his boot as it raced by. Elgera pounded into the blackness of the cave, the only way in or out of the Santiago Valley.

The palomino was heavy set, even for a Morgan, and not trained for bareback. It was all she could do to drive on through the Stygian gloom of the tunnel. Suddenly she heard a yell from ahead.

"Who is it?" shouted a man. "Don't come any

nearer. Who is it?"

She didn't answer. A gun began to thunder from ahead, then another. The palomino whinnied shrilly, squatted like a jackrabbit. Elgera was almost thrown off by the mount when it wheeled, heading back the other way.

The guards she had passed must have followed her in, because guns began to blaze from their direction. Screaming its fright, the Morgan slid to a halt again, lunged back around the other way. There were men on both sides of her, then, and she was trapped. Desperately she tried to drive the Morgan on. But the guns began pumping ahead of her again, throwing a veritable wall of viciously stabbing flame up in front of her, and she realized she couldn't hope to get through alive. Lead forming its high whine about her, she was swept with the reasonless panic of a cornered animal.

She leaned forward on the palomino, giving the terrified beast its head. The horse wheeled once more toward the mouth of the cave and broke into a wild gallop. The two guards began firing again, and the Morgan tried to slide onto its haunches.

But whatever happened, Elgera knew this was her last chance to break through, and she was determined not to be taken alive. Sobbing bitterly, she jerked the Morgan's head from side to side and drove spiked boot heels into its sweat-soaked flanks. The animal reacted instinctively, quit sliding, gathered itself, and plunged with a wild whinny back through the cave.

Elgera sensed the dim movement of men throwing themselves aside. She snapped a shot toward them. There was a yell, a last deafening gun thunder. Then the palomino crashed out through the mouth of the cave and back onto the moonlit slope.

Hoke was a dozen paces ahead. She turned the animal sharply, catching the surprise in his white face. Then she was clattering into the trees, low branches clawing at the camisa serving for a blouse.

Finally she broke into the open on the other side of the motte. Behind her she could still hear the men shouting to one another. She turned the palomino up the rise, fighting back her sobs, and she didn't know whether she was crying from that or from her utter failure to break through.

On the peak of the rise she turned the horse a moment, trying to quiet it, sitting there rigidly as she fought to control herself. Below her, past the trees, was the house, a dim U-shaped sprawl, *viga* poles thrust from its walls at rafter height and casting an uneven shadow pattern across pale adobe. Elgera caught movement in the corral, heard the faint nicker of a horse. They were saddling up to follow her by then.

She wheeled her palomino, looking at the forbidding ridges of the Dead Horses ahead. Another attempt to get through the cave was no good. The only other way to the outside was through the mountains themselves. More than one Douglas had been lost in those jagged uplifts, never to be seen again. It was a mysterious, unknown barrier that had kept outsiders from finding the Lost Santiago all these years, holding secrets no man had seen and lived to tell. Yet it was the only way.

She straightened a little on the horse and turned it down the other side of the rise and into the black shadows puddling the bottom of the draw. Then she rose again onto the moonlit slope opposite, heading straight into the *Sierra del Caballo Muerto.*

IV

94

Chisos Owens didn't know how many miles he had ridden through the mine shaft behind Valeur when the first two shots came to them, flat and muffled. Valeur leaned forward on his chestnut, cursing beneath his breath. Pinky sat a line-back mare behind Owens, carrying the buckthorn *entraña*, its weird light throwing their shadows black and monstrous across the ancient hand-hewn timbers forming the *soportes* and beams of the shaft. There were more shots. Valeur turned to Pinky.

"Hold this *hombre* here," he said. "Walker, come with me."

The rawboned man named Walker urged his horse into the blackness after Valeur. The last thing Owens saw of him was the buckle on his single galus, winking in the torchlight, then it disappeared. The buckskin snorted dismally beneath Chisos. There was no sound for a moment—then the noise of a running horse down there in the dark somewhere and Valeur's voice.

"Who is it? Don't come any nearer. Who is it?"

The pound of hoofs became louder. A sudden volley of shots stiffened Owens. A horse whinnied in high fear. The noise of galloping hoofs ceased abruptly. There was another crash of gun fire. Chisos couldn't help his instinctive forward move.

"Watch it," snapped Pinky, and the torchlight wavered.

The horse must have started back the other way, because it began running again, and the sound diminished swiftly. Owens caught a muffled yell, a final pair of gunshots. He barely heard the horse whinny this time. Then it was silent.

Finally Valeur's voice came, impatient. "Pinky.

Bring him on."

Thrown by the flickering light, Owens's shadow undulated across the rolling sides of the tunnel and the sagging timbers as they went around a turn. Valeur was waiting for them, dismounted.

"What happened?" asked Pinky.

"I don't know," snapped the swarthy man. "Some fool on a horse. Maybe one of the Douglas bunch got loose. When he saw he couldn't get by us, he turned around."

Valeur had put his gun back in the holster underneath his brown coat. He pulled the short *cabriolé* over that, lifting a foot to his chestnut's stirrup. He stopped that way. Someone was stumbling through the cave toward them. Hoke weaved into the circle of light, head raising at the sight of them. Valeur put his foot down again, turned a little.

Hoke took his hand away from a bloody weal that ran along the side of his head. He was looking at Valeur, and his face grew pale. He choked his words out.

"I couldn't help it, Val. She took me by surprise. You stopped her in here, though. She came back out the tunnel and scooted into the hills. I already put Smith and Tommy on her tail. . . ."

Valeur almost yelled it. "I told you what would happen if you pulled another botch like Alpine, Hoke!"

Hoke's mouth opened. He took a step backward, trying to say something. He must have seen it coming.

"Val, I couldn't help it . . . !"

Owens didn't see Valeur's hand when it moved. He only knew the big man took a vicious step forward, and the gun was suddenly in his hairy fist, bucking. The dust puffed out of Hoke's gray vest, and he stumbled on back with a hollow grunt. He fell over, clawing at the top of his empty holster.

Valeur's heavy breathing was the only sound for a moment. The flush faded slowly from his face. The revolver he held was a double-action .38. When he slipped it back beneath his cloak, it made no perceptible bulge. He turned and climbed onto his chestnut.

"Let's go," he said.

Face pale, Walker urged his mount after Valeur. He glanced momentarily at Hoke's body as he passed it then looked away quickly. Owens clucked his buckskin forward, lips compressing until the flesh around them was whitened. He had a sick, hollow feeling inside, and he didn't know whether it was from seeing Hoke killed that way, or from realizing fully, perhaps for the first time, just what kind of man Valeur really was.

A hundred feet back of where the tunnel opened out into the Santiago Valley they came to a railing of split juniper that surrounded a large vertical shaft, sunk to one side of the tunnel. The shaft itself was topped by a framework of fresh-cut timbers supporting a large winch. Suspended by a thick hemp rope from the spindle of the winch was a four-by-four platform that dangled over empty space. Valeur turned slightly in his saddle.

"Get on the elevator," he told Owens.

Chisos dismounted, moved toward the railing. He put a hand on the top bar and looked over it into the shaft. It fell away beneath him, bottomless as far as he could see. Pinky and Walker had dismounted. The bow-legged man thrust his *entraña* into the earthen wall then went with the other to the crank. Valeur's voice was sharp.

97

"Get on, I said."

Owens ducked beneath the rail, leaned out, and caught the rope. He had to pull the platform a little. When he stepped on, it swung back out and continued swinging, back and forth, like a pendulum.

The shriek of the winch startled him. He gripped the rope with a certain desperation as he began to go down. The last man he saw was Jan Valeur, sitting his chestnut behind the railing.

Their glances locked for that moment. In the brilliant lights that flared through his jet black eyes, Chisos Owens could see all the ruthless violence and unbridled savagery of the man's nature. Again, it gave him the sensation of a staggering physical impact. Then the lip of the shaft cut off his view, and he went on down into the darkness.

Spinning around and around in the black emptiness, swaying back and forth in that pendulum motion, bumping now and then against the earthen sides of the shaft, Owens lost all sense of time or distance. It might have taken an hour, or a day. It might have been a hundred feet they lowered him, or a thousand. His hand on the rope became cramped with the force of his grip.

Finally the downward motion seemed to cease. The swinging elevator knocked against something. A flare of light blinded Owens momentarily. Then he could make out a stationary platform built into the side of the shaft. From it led a tunnel, and in that stood a group of shifting, muttering people. The one holding the torch stepped out onto the boards.

"Chisos," he said sharply. "It's Chisos Owens."

There was defeat in the haggard lines of Natividad Douglas's angular face. His blue eyes regarded Owens dully. Raising the burning *entraña*, he reached out and helped Chisos onto the platform. Eddger Douglas was there too, Natividad's uncle, a tall, spare man with stringy gray hair and bony shoulders bent wearily beneath his torn shirt of homespun. Juanito Douglas had blood splotching the cotton bandage around his head, the dirt smeared on his cheeks as if he might have been crying. The women stood farther back among the other men; one of them let out a hopeless sob.

Natividad put a clumsy hand on Chisos's shoulder. "Somehow, we didn't think we'd see you . . . down here."

He trailed off, and Owens moved into the tunnel with them, not knowing what to say exactly, seeing how he had failed them. He tried to hide his own bitter sense of defeat, speaking gruffly.

"Hawkman?"

Natividad stuck the torch into the wall, nodding. He told Owens how it had happened.

"I know it sounds stupid, Chisos," he finished. "It was stupid. I'll never forgive myself. Hopwell sent for him, and I was to meet him at Alpine. When I met Valeur instead, with all Avarillo's papers and Hopwell's letter of introduction, how was I to know the difference?"

Eddger grasped his nephew's arm. "You couldn't know, Natividad. Don't blame yourself. We were all taken in. I'm as much to blame as you. I was up here at the mine with Juanito and should have stopped Bickford. . . ."

"It was the only way they could find the valley," said Juanito hotly. "Bick and his riders must have trailed Natividad when he brought Valeur back from Alpine. I guess they were supposed to wait in the cave until Thomas and Valeur had located the quit-claim."

"Hawkman knew about that, then?" grunted Chisos.

"He must have," said Natividad. "Either Dad told him he had it made out when he got in touch with Hawkman, or Hawkman found it out from the county clerk who helped Dad draw it up. Thomas had it witnessed and then transferred the title up at Alpine. I guess it went through without a hitch. There wasn't anybody to protest it."

For a long time Owens had been aware of the man standing slightly apart from the others, farther back in the cave. He had the feeling he should know him, yet couldn't remember anyone so small and fat in the Douglas clan. Now the crowd was shifting apart, and the torchlight fell across the pudgy figure fully. The man's legs were thick as post oaks and seemed to stretch his English riding boots to the bursting point. His white silk shirt and gray whipcords were turned incongruous by the broad sash of violent red bound about his imperious girth. In one side of his mouth he held a black *cigarro,* and his fat lips twisted around this to form an expansive grin.

"*Buenas noches*, *Señor* Chisos," he said. "You are late."

Ⓥ Ⓥ Ⓥ

A series of burning buckthorn *entrañas* thrust into the wall cast a weird red glow over the Douglases, picking at the sides of the tunnel with the tools Valeur had packed in. Owens stopped work for a moment, leaning wearily on the splintery handle of his pick-axe. There was no telling night from day down here, but it must have been sometime in mid-morning. After a fitful slumber he had been awakened with the others by Pinky and Walker, who

100

came down on the elevator with a breakfast of soggy pan bread and cold coffee.

Beside Chisos the fat Mexican named Felipe pried at the pay-streaks running down the tunnel. His white silk shirt was soaked with sweat, and it clung to his pudgy torso like skin, revealing a gross roll of fat that bulged over his tight red sash every time he bent forward. Owens reached automatically for the makings in his jumper pocket, opening the sack of Bull Durham with his teeth.

"No!" cried the Mexican, straightening, putting up a protesting hand. "*Dios* no, Chisos. Light a *cigarrillo* now and you blow us down to *el Diablo*. Can't you smell the gas?"

He sniffed loudly to emphasize his question. Chisos sniffed too. All morning he had been aware of the faint cloying odor in the tunnel. It was heavier now, gagging. He put the tobacco away.

Felipe flourished his cold cigar. "Gold forms along faults, understand, fissures that reach to a profound depth. In a volcanic formation like this, you are bound to find gas. It seeps up through faults. And where you have a fault, you have a possibility of a slide. No . . . ? *Sí*."

"Felipe," grunted Chisos, "who conked me on the head that night in Alpine?"

"I've seen cave-ins started by no less than a sneeze when there is such a fault," muttered the Mexican, glancing up at the ancient beams above them, puckering his lips. "And look at those shorings. Dry rot. Touch them with a horse feather and they collapse. *Pues*, I hope nobody makes a loud noise in here. I hope nobody sneezes."

"Was it you?" asked Chisos.

Felipe turned to him, chuckling. "¡*Caracoles*¡ What an insistent fellow you are. Maybe that is why

101

Hawkman fears you so, eh? Beware of the man with the single-track mind. Of course it was I who hit you on the head. Who else? I knew that fight wouldn't finish until everybody was dead. That's the kind of *hombres* you are, you and Valeur. Did I want everybody dead? *Dios*, no! Why do you think I seduced you and Hoke into the Mescal in the first place? He might have known what was going on down here, but we didn't. You might have known the way down here, but I didn't. And if you killed each other, I would have no one to follow down here, would I? No . . . ? *Sí*. I shot out the light. I tapped you on the *cabeza*. I had to tap Valeur to get you free. I hid you beneath the garbage in the back alley. When Valeur and his two *amigos* left, I was the sinister character trailing them."

"Why?" asked Chisos. "Who are you? What's your stake in the Santiago?"

"*Por Dios*, how can you ask that? What is any man's stake in the Santiago? Look at that bench gravel . . . ?"—the Mexican waved his *cigarro* at the streaks of yellow in the sides—"a thousand dollars to the ton at least. And not only the pay streaks. After all, think of what an achievement it is merely to find this fabled mine. Do you know how old these diggings are? It was originally worked by Indians for centuries before Santiago found it. In that shaft above I saw pieces of pottery bearing the distinct imprints of the paddle-and-anvil methods of thinning walls which were used in the Second Pueblo period."

"That isn't mining," said Chisos, grinning faintly.

"Did you think my accomplishments were limited to cards and gold?" said Felipe, waving his *cigarro* excitedly. "That is archeology. Upheavals thrust the Dead Horses up and around this valley sometime in

102

the Mezoziac era . . . and that is geology . . . cutting it off completely from the outside. Those Indians weren't deliberately trying to open the valley, understand, they were just following a vein through the mountain, that's all. Can you guess how many generations it must have taken them to drive the shaft in from the box cañon on the outside?"

Natividad was coming toward them, a leather strap around his head supporting the *zurrón* on his back—a bag of woven acopyune fiber of the same type the Indians used for centuries in which to carry their ore. He set the *zurrón* down, glanced backward. Farther down were more Douglases, a little group of three or four digging under each burning torch. Beyond them Owens could see Pinky and Walker.

"Chisos," said Natividad. "You've got to get out of here. Bickford has come with Hawkman!"

Chisos straightened, hearing the silence that had fallen over the tunnel farther on. His rope-scarred hands closed more tightly about the pick handle. He could hear Valeur talking from beyond Pinky and Walker.

"You'll have to pack the ore out on mules, Anse. There isn't any other way. The less men we bring in from the outside the safer it'll be. We might as well work these Douglas coyotes instead of importing any peons."

Anse Hawkman spoke in a harsh grating voice. "I didn't want it this way, Valeur. You know that. You can't just turn people into slaves this way. I always gave a man a chance to work for me. I never stepped outside of the law."

"You mean they never caught you stepping outside the law," snapped Valeur. "And you never did nothing this big Anse. You're in the Lost Santiago. Men have been hunting this place ever since they put an x in Texas. Maybe the Douglases didn't know what they had. I do. . . ." His voice trailed away.

They were coming into the light now. Hawkman, a tall spare man in a dusty frock coat, wore his gray trousers tucked into cavalry boots. A black Mormon cast his bony face into shadow, hiding its features, but there was something greedy in the way his sinewy hands hung at his sides, grasping fingers curled a little like talons.

"Chisos!" said Natividad. "You can't stay here. You know what'll happen if he recognizes you."

"You told me yourself this was a dead-end tunnel," said Chisos. "Where can we go? What's the use in running?"

"In *Méjico*, we call them *yalotis*," snorted Felipe. "Big birds what sit on a branch and let *hombres* come along to knock them off with a stick."

Anse was still talking. "I know, Valeur. But this . . . !"

"What else?" snarled Valeur suddenly. "I told you what you were putting your loop to when you started out to get this valley. Thomas got the deed on the legal side. Far as the law goes, you own this fair and square. That's as far as it does go. Any of these Douglases get out, and you'll have more troubles than you had in the big freeze. It's kill 'em or work 'em. Which'll you have?"

"Listen," growled Felipe, pulling at Chisos. "At least be moving when they kill you. I never did like to die standing still."

Anse stopped suddenly down there, stiffening. Valeur followed his gaze to Chisos Owens where he stood in the light of the torch, his square blocky figure humped forward a little, eyes gleaming from the gray mask of dust and sweat that was his face.

"That's the *hombre* I told you about," laughed Valeur. "I thought I might as well use him in the diggings. Maybe this is worse than a good quick slug through the brisket anyway."

"You fool!" yelled Anse, his voice cracking on the last word. "That's Chisos Owens! Bick. That's Chisos Owens!"

Bick Bickford lurched out from behind Anse Hawkman, his face expressionless as he pawed with a freckled hand at his gun. Chisos crouched in a jerky, instinctive way. Valeur's voice was high in surprise.

"Chisos Owens?" he yelled, and his mouth stayed open after the words were out.

Anse was pulling a six-gun from beneath the frock coat, but he threw himself backward at the same time, leaving Bick out in front. Owens already had the pick swinging upward in both hands. Bick's gun came out.

Owens grunted with the effort of heaving the pick. It struck Bickford full in the face. With a wild scream the heavy man staggered backward, dropping his gun, pawing at his smashed features. Felipe must have yanked the *entraña* out of the wall from above Owens. They were suddenly standing in darkness. Chisos felt the fat Mexican's pudgy hands pulling him. He had to turn to keep from falling.

"¡*Santiago* . . . !" cried Felipe lustily. "Saint James and clear out of Spain, you *ilegítimo* blackamoors!"

Out in the light the Douglases swarmed at Hawkman and Valeur, picks and stakes in their hands. Pinky and Walker clubbed viciously with their Winchesters. There was a shot. Eddgar Douglas fell away with a cry of pain. Valeur burst through two more men, face dark with rage. He came pounding down toward Owens, gun flaming.

The shots echoed, and the echoes multiplied, until the whole tunnel seemed to tremble and rock with the deafening sound.

"¡*Dios*!" howled Felipe, "and I was afraid of someone sneezing."

Stumbling through the blackness, trying to fight free of the Mexican's hands, Chisos heard a groaning, slipping noise, louder than the shots. He brought up suddenly against the resilient pudginess of Felipe's body, clawing at the thick shoulders to keep from falling. Then he knew why the man had stopped.

"There it goes," shouted Felipe.

Whatever else he said was silenced by the terrible all-enveloping wave of sound that covered Chisos Owens. Rocks and earth rained down on him in an ever-growing hail. He went to hands and knees beneath the crushing avalanche of dirt and *turfa*, head ringing, mouth filled. A rotten beam fell across his legs, pinning them. A *soporte* hit him over the ear. He reeled sideways, arms slipping from beneath him. He thought all the Dead Horses had fallen in on his body.

After a long time the terrifying sound began to die. A last chunk of rock thudded down somewhere to Chisos's left. There was a creaking groan. Then a silence that was worse than the noise had been. He tried to raise himself weakly. The beam held him helpless. He heard someone moving. Whoever it was kept on making small grunting sounds. Finally Felipe spoke.

"That's it, I guess," he said heavily. "The main portion of the cave-in was between us and the others out there. Maybe they didn't get it. We got it. We are trapped!"

106

V

Beneath the sun of mid-morning the Dead Horses lay cruel and empty and desolate around Elgera Douglas. Cenizo, the color of ashes, blotched the barren slopes; sickly gray-green pamilla squirmed feebly from cracks in the lava formation. The gun in Elgera's waistband pressed coldly against her stomach as she leaned forward wearily on her palomino. A rider could make it from the outside to the valley with a bare margin of safety, if he knew that route in through the narrow box cañon and the mine. But Elgera knew she had been wandering, and as yet she had found no water. She knew that it was the only thing that would save her now.

They were still behind her or on her flank. That was the way they had followed her—not by tracking, for that would have been next to impossible during dark, but by keeping her below them so they could see her whenever she crossed the open slopes and moonlit meadows.

She had tried to hide in timber where she wouldn't be visible from above. But she saw whenever she did that, they stopped and waited on some hogback, and she knew that whenever she chose to move again, they would spot her, and in desperation she had ridden on. The only thing that kept her ahead of them was the superiority of her Morgan. But the palomino was caked with lather and alkali now and was blowing most of the time.

She was nursing it through scattered prickly pear when something glinted in the sun on the ridge lying across her right flank. Her blonde hair shimmered as she turned sharply that way. It took her a moment to make out the rider quartering down the slope.

The muted crash of mesquite on her other side jerked her back. From the angle the second man was cutting toward her through the brush. This was it, then. They were riding the ridges. They were going to finish it.

She bent forward on the Morgan, plunking a boot into its flank. The horse responded sluggishly, broke into a flagging gallop. She heard the shout from her left. Then came the gunshot, flat and ugly across the dry air. Reddish sandstone kicked up a length in front of the Morgan. Bareback that way it would have been deadly to release either hand. Her control over the animal lay in the hackamore she kept bunched tightly in her right hand. If she released her grip on the mane with her left, a sudden turn would unhorse her. She shook out some slack to give her length enough for reaching the Smith & Wesson in her waistband. Then she caught up the loose rawhide till the dally was tight again. She turned toward the man on her left because he was the closest. Holding gun and hackamore in her right hand, she watched the rider come on in. He forked a blazed-face sorrel, and he had his gun out too. He let go another shot that went over Elgera's head before she fired.

Every time her Smith & Wesson bucked in her hand, the palomino shied to the right, head pulling that way to the jerk of the taut rope. On her third wild shot, Elgera saw the sorrel stumble and veer sharply. Instead of quartering in down the slope now, it was running parallel to her own mount. The man jammed his revolver back in leather and started jerking back and forth on his horse. Dust rose thickly around him. It was a moment before Elgera realized what was the matter. The sorrel was still going ahead, but its gallop was twisting and lurching. She had hit the animal. The rider was trying to kick free. His boot must have been caught, because he was still jerking wildly that way when Elgera heard his sharp cry and saw the running sorrel go down onto its face. Both horse and man disappeared in the cloud of dust they had raised.

Elgera cast a look behind her. The second man had cut too sharply down his side, evidently expecting the other rider to block her off. He was at the bottom of the slope now, far behind.

It gave Elgera a faint stab of hope. Their success in following her had depended on their team work, keeping her down in the draws and gullies by blocking off whatever attempts she made toward the ridges. Now there was only one of them. The palomino hadn't been trained for bare back. Any chance she had now to outride that second man lay in her getting a saddle. It was worth the few precious moments. She turned the Morgan into the prickly pear.

Hawkman's rider lay beneath the dead sorrel. Elgera couldn't tell whether he lived or not. She slid off the palomino, untied the latigo on the dead animal's saddle, then she jammed her dusty Hyer boot against the sorrel's barrel and tugged the broad hair cinches from beneath it. A moment more and she had the hull on her own horse, cinching up front and flank of the Texas rig with swift surety. The Smith & Wesson had one bullet left unfired. It was a .44 while the man who lay there packed a .45. She dropped Hoke's black-butted S.& W. into the sand, unstrapped the gun belt from around Hawkman's rider. She drew it around her slim waist to the last notch and still it hung far down her thigh.

When she mounted again, the man on the ground was stirring feebly. The palomino seemed to take out with more eagerness under saddle, and the leather was a relief to Elgera's sore, weary legs. She didn't have to fight the animal now, and she free-bitted it, cutting across the bottom of the valley, turning into a narrow cañon that cut through high sandstone cliffs. Behind her she could see the second rider halt his horse on the opposite slope, where the dead sorrel lay among the prickly pear. He dismounted and helped the other man to rise. She could see them standing there, ant-like figures that grew smaller in her vision as she rode on into the gunsight notch. Finally they mounted tandem on the remaining horse and turned after her.

She found a brackish sink hole of water a hundred yards on and had a hard time keeping the Morgan from foundering itself. She took a few careful sips herself, keeping an eye behind. When the men showed at the mouth of the notch, she mounted and went on.

The walls of the cañon rose steeply, and soon the sandy bottom of a dried-up water course was the only space between. At first she thought a cloud had swept over the sun. The cañon had darkened perceptibly about her. Then she felt the hot biting sensation in her lungs and saw that it was a haze, that darkness, a red haze that thickened as she rode forward. It gave her an eerie feeling.

She came to the end of the notch abruptly, finding herself looking out into a vast amphitheater over which the haze hung like a mysterious curtain, shredding here and there to reveal mountains on the opposite side, rising harshly and nakedly into the thin blue sky. Elgera turned sharply in the saddle. They were still behind her. She could see them making their way up through the cañon. There was no way to go but forward.

She gave the horse its head once more. The Morgan picked its way down a shelf of sandstone that crumbled incessantly beneath nervous hoofs. Finally they reached a gentler slope and dropped into a stretch of timber. Elgera recognized cottonwoods and aspens and a scattering of juniper, but none of the trees had foliage. Their branches reached out naked and gray, like malignant, clawing hands. When a slight wind sighed down from the rimrock, they rattled in hollow, mocking echo.

Elgera wiped a lock of blonde hair off her flushed forehead. It was damp with perspiration. The horse began to shy and snort. The girl felt the heat then, striking out at her in waves. Farther on it was like coming up against a solid wall of it. The palomino whinnied. Elgera jerked it around, out of the furnace blast, breathing swiftly. Filled with nameless apprehension, she wheeled her horse and trotted it through the trees a quarter mile to the north. Every time she tried to go back down, the wall of heat stopped her dead. Finally she brought up against a sheer cliff of sandstone and had to turn back. It was the same thing on the other side of the round valley. At any spot she chose, she could only ride so far into the haze-covered grove of seared trees, then the awful heat rose up impenetrably.

Cliffs on either side too sheer for the horse, the heat before her—Elgera realized the only way out was to go the way she had come. She turned the palomino uphill, panting with exhaustion.

Hawkman's men stood in the mouth of the notch. They must have been there all the time she had ridden back and forth down among the trees, must have sensed something had stopped her, must have realized how they had snared her. With a hoarse pant, she tried to keep the Morgan in its gallop

111

upslope like that, running it directly toward the men, savagely wanting it that way now. The horse might have been good for a level run. Uphill it was no use. It began to blow and stumble. Finally the gallop slowed to a walk, and nothing Elgera could do would speed it up again.

The wild, heady excitement of going at them full tilt faded from her. It was a different thing, walking into it that way. It was certain death. Dully she halted the wind-broken horse and slid off, stumbling to a pothole amidst the crazy cottonwoods, sinking into it. The men began to move down toward her.

All right, that was the way it would be. She cocked the .45 and shoved it over the lip of black rock forming her scant cover. The man who had ridden the sorrel showed first, working down through the trees. He was tall and skinny, greasy *chivarras* belted around his middle with a piece of mecate. He must have borrowed the other man's six-iron. He held it out before him, searching the red haze for Elgera. The second man came through the trees with his saddle gun. Brush crackled beneath his boots.

The man with the short gun saw Elgera then. She had waited that long, wanting it sure. Her full lips twisted, and her gun bucked hard with the shot. The man in *chivarras* jumped backward with a sharp cry, dropping his weapon.

She couldn't see him then. She could hear the brush rattle as he crawled away. The man with the rifle stayed out of range, shifting back and forth indecisively. Then he disappeared too. After a time they showed again above the haze, moving back toward the notch. The one with the saddle gun was helping the wounded man. She could barely see what they were doing. They seemed to stand by the

112

horse a moment, talking. Finally the wounded man mounted and turned the jaded animal back into the narrow cañon. The other one settled down on the limestone bank, rifle across his knees.

Elgera could guess well enough where the rider was going. Perhaps the two of them hadn't found the heart to face her gun that way. Half a dozen could finish it without too much risk. Half a dozen led by Valeur.

The one thing they hadn't wanted was to have a Douglas escape to the outside. She knew how far Valeur would go to protect what he had hold of. She sagged wearily into the pothole, rocks hard against her limp body. Her choked sob was small, somehow, in all the vast desolation of that weird place.

VI

It was silent in the mine shaft now. Chisos Owens lay where Felipe and Natividad had dragged him, after digging the earth off his back and prying the fallen timber off his legs. At first he had been numb from the knees down, but now a tingling pain was beginning to seep through. He hoped dully that it didn't mean his legs were smashed.

"The whole thing was caused by the fault," muttered Felipe, making small scratching noises in the darkness. "The gas had to leak in from somewhere. I was in a cave-in at Virginia City just like this. . . ." He broke off, sniffing. "*Sí*, just like this. We located the fissure by smelling for the gas. Then we followed the fissure out. There is a chance, a small chance."

"What's the use?" choked Natividad. "There's a dead end behind us and a million tons of earth in front. We're through."

"*Pues*, maybe not a million," chuckled Felipe, crawling around Owens, sniffing like a dog on the scent. "Ah, here it is. Chisos, over here."

Owens struggled across smashed timber. Felipe's body was hot and fetid beside him. He sniffed, choked. Natividad came crawling to them. Together they tore at a beam, clawed earth free. The smell of gas became stronger. The fat Mexican began to chuckle.

"The fault," he kept laughing. "We have struck the fault. They are caused by earlier displacements of earth, understand? It might lead down. It is the chance we take. The gas will asphyxiate us if we stay in it too long. I will go first. I am the bulbous one and, if I can get through, you most certainly can. May the gods of chance smile upon us this *día*, *compadres*. No . . . ? *Sí*."

His voice was muffled on the last words. Chisos crawled forward tentatively, found the narrow hole in the wall. The surface pressing into his belly was smooth and slick. He worked against an upward slant, clawing, digging, trying to hold his first breath as long as possible. Finally he had to empty his lungs and suck in the gas-laden air.

He buried his face into the earth for a terrible moment, fighting the paroxysm that threatened to sweep him. His ears began to ring, and there was a pounding in his head. He would never be able to remember the rest clearly. It was one hell of crawling a few feet, expelling air, drawing in another breath that had more gas than oxygen, fighting to keep from choking on it, crawling on. Once, as if in a nightmare, he heard Natividad coughing mutedly behind him. Then the sound stopped.

The earth began grumbling. The whole fault

shook and trembled. Chisos fought down a wave of panic. At the end of an interminable period he felt pudgy hands slipping beneath his armpits, drawing him out into a larger space that was filled with deliciously cool, fresh air. He lay on his belly for a long time, sucking in great gusts, sobbing. Finally he sat up. Behind he could still hear the ominous rumbling sound. The earth began to tremble beneath his legs.

"Felipe?" he said.

"*Sí,*" answered the Mexican weakly. "I think we have reached one of the old tunnels dug by the Indians. They must honeycomb these mountains. It has a definite slant feel. We take the upward way, and . . . ¡*Sacramento*! . . . we are out. *Pronto* now, before the whole *negocio* caves in on us."

"Natividad?" said Chisos.

No one answered. For a moment they sat there in the dark with the earth groaning and slipping all around them. Felipe let out a hissing breath.

"We cannot be *pendejos* now, *Señor* Chisos, we cannot be fools," he said swiftly. "We must look at it coldly. It would be better for two of us to live than all of us to die. It is the expedience, Chisos. It is hard, but it is the expedience."

Chisos made a small scraping sound crawling back toward the fault. The rumble grew louder. The tunnel rocked suddenly with a violent tremor. Owens took a great breath, jammed himself into the fault. He heard Felipe shout after him.

"You won't stand a chance. If the gas doesn't finish you, the whole Santiago Mine will cave in on you. Come back . . . !"

Again it was that crawling, fighting, digging madness, trying to breathe where there was no air, battling with a terrible panic and violent horror of

115

being buried alive, clawing at earth that shook and roared beneath his hands, squirming like a doomed slug deep down into its own grave.

Then he felt the limp body of the boy. Somehow he got twisted around so he could shove Natividad back out ahead of him. There was a shaking roar, drowning out the smaller groanings of earth. He kicked, clawed, drew in a spasmodic breath—and felt a horrible suffocation grip him.

Consciousness began to leave him for long moments at a time. He would come to, realizing his legs and arms were still working in a desperate instinctive effort of self-preservation. Earth filled his mouth and eyes and nose. Natividad was a dead weight above him. Sound threatened to burst his eardrums. He didn't know exactly when he shoved the boy out ahead of him into the tunnel. He crawled out himself in a flaccid, exhausted way. He heard Felipe's voice dimly.

"Damn' *pendejo*, damn' fool . . . !"

He remembered laughing weirdly. Then he let himself sink into unconsciousness without a struggle.

Ⓥ Ⓥ Ⓥ

Felipe was right about the upward slant of the old diggings leading them out. He had revived Chisos Owens and, carrying the boy between them, they staggered up through the terror of that thundering darkness. Hours, days, years—it was all the same. Light reached them from the mouth of the cave finally, and they stumbled toward it with a pathetic eagerness, sagging down in the black brush. Behind them the rumblings died slowly.

The shaft had led them onto the slope far to the

south of the main tunnel. The house lay behind several intervening rises. They worked toward it through a grove of Mexican persimmons and approached a compound that seemed strangely silent. Circling around the mouth of the large mine shaft, they finally stopped at the fringe of juniper to the left of the house, half way up toward the corral. An old woman appeared at the rear door of the building's right wing. She seemed to be crying. Natividad leaped forward, and Owens barely caught him before he was in the open.

"Careful!" Chisos warned, but the boy yanked free of the heavy hands.

"Granny," hissed the boy.

The woman's seamed face turned toward them. She glanced back up toward the cave then walked around the house. She appeared a moment later with an empty bullhide pail and walked away from the adobe wall toward the river that coursed through shadowy motes of cottonwood in the bottom of the valley. Her route was circuitous and carried her past where the three men stood, hidden from above. She set the heavy pail down as if to rest, speaking without looking directly at them.

"*Gracias a Dios*, you are alive," she hissed. "Hawkman thought you had been killed in the cave-in . . . no, don't show yourselves. There are still a couple of guards at the mine."

"The cave-in missed them then?" grunted Chisos.

"It was between you and them," she said. "Hawkman's men all escaped. And Chisos, Elgera is trapped back in the mountains somewhere. She was trying to get through to you when they holed her up. The two men who had followed her didn't have the courage to go in after her by themselves. The one named Tommy came back with a bullet in his

117

shoulder. They left him here. But the rest of them have gone back, Valeur and Hawkman and Bickford and two or three of the A H *vaqueros*. I heard Valeur tell Hawkman they couldn't take any more chances, heard him say they were going to forget she was a woman. Chisos, they've gone to kill Elgera."

VII

Chisos Owens's buckskin was jaded now. Lather caked its flanks thickly. All three men had driven their horses at a cruel run through the heat of noon and afternoon. Granny had saddled the mounts and brought them to the men in the timber. Then she had attracted the attention of the guards at the mine with her cracked wails, while Chisos and the other two circled the house and used the cover of the stream lower down till they were out of sight.

They all carried gum-pitched *morrales* of fiber, full of water. But even that didn't save their horses, the way they had forced them. Owens knew he was two or three hours behind Hawkman. All he could think of was Elgera, and he knew it would have to be a dead run every step of the way if they expected to save her. They were cutting down through a slope of prickly pear when they passed the dead sorrel with the blazed face.

"Hawkman's first casualty," puffed Felipe, "and that's what will be happening to our *caballos* soon if you don't ease up."

"That sorrel's been shot," said Chisos.

"Shot or not, you can't run a horse all day through heat like this," muttered Felipe. "Let him drink and you founder him. Don't give him water and he dries up and blows away beneath you."

Owens bent in his saddle to study the plain trail they were following. "That's Valeur's chestnut . . . couldn't miss a Tennessee Walker in this country. They weren't pushing as hard as we are. Intervals between hoofs aren't as long as ours. Passed here two-three hours ago. That gramma's already beginning to rise up in the tracks."

He put a boot into his buckskin, and the animal lurched forward. Owens's face was caked with alkali. His heavy shoulders were humped beneath the faded jumper in terrible weariness. The heat was draining the men as well as the animals. Natividad almost slid off his horse when they veered at the bottom of the slope.

Chisos reined over, caught the boy's arm, yanking him back into the saddle. They rode on that way, Chisos holding up Natividad. Maybe it was a mile past the dead sorrel that Owens's buckskin began to quiver beneath him. He halted it and slid off, standing there a minute with his big rope-scarred hand on the lathered rump, a certain faint grief entering his glazed eyes. Then he jerked a Barlow knife from his jumper pocket. The muscles across his face tightened until cracks appeared in the thick cage of dust. He took a hoarse breath, jabbed the knife into the buckskin's haunch.

"*Santa Maria*," groaned Felipe weakly. "What good will the death jab do? So you bleed him, and he goes another mile, so what then? So he dies anyway."

"Shut up," said Chisos harshly. "I've had the General six years. Shut up."

A strange expression crossed the Mexican's face. Perhaps he was beginning to realize what a grim thing was driving Chisos Owens. Some hands would rather kill themselves than deliberately ride a horse

119

to death they had owned that long.

Owens climbed back on and leaned forward. What he said into the animal's ear was not audible. The horse twitched a little, staggered into a heavy trot, then a gallop. The other two men followed. They were passing a bunch of clawing agrito when Natividad jerked straight in his saddle, kicking his boots free of the *tapadero* stirrups with a weary curse. He hit the sand to one side of the lurching animal, staggered two or three steps, then went onto his face. The horse went down to its knees before it stopped, then keeled over on its side, put its foam-flecked nose into the sand, and died.

Natividad began to sob from utter exhaustion. "That's all, Chisos. That is the end of it."

Chisos almost fell when he dismounted. He stumbled over to the boy, bent down, and grabbed him by the shirt collar. "Get on my hoss. We aren't through with it yet."

He had Natividad standing on his feet finally and turned him toward the buckskin. Then he stopped. The buckskin was down too, and the blood trickling from the wound he had made was thin and watery. He looked at it dully for a moment, wishing he could feel something. A man should feel something when his horse died like that. Maybe he was too tired for emotion now. He didn't know. Felipe tried to get his mount moving again, but it stood dispiritedly beneath his curses and feeble kicks. Finally he got off, leaning wearily against it.

"This *caballo* is *solado*. No . . . ? *Sí.*"

Natividad sank to the earth again. Lips thin, Chisos went to his dead animal, slipping the *morral* off the saddle horn. He slung the fiber canteen over one shoulder and moved heavily back to the boy, pulling him to his knees, to his feet, shoving him

120

forward.

"Think I'll let you quit now?" he said, and the utter lack of expression in his voice made it more terrible. "Think I pulled you out of the mine to bring you out here and let you die? We've got a long way to go yet. We'll finish this if its on our bellies, see . . .?"

Like drunken men they staggered away from the two dead horses and the one standing on its feet, glazed eyes unseeing. Their footprints left a weaving, meandering trail behind them. They reached a stunted cottonwood. Felipe staggered into it, low branches giving before his weight with a popping sound. He could hardly speak.

"Listen, I know when I'm done. At least let me die in peace. *Por Dios, un hombre* has that much right. *Por Dios.* . . ."

He trailed off, panting, sweat darkening his white silk shirt. Chisos grabbed him, yanked him feebly away from the tree. He bunched the soft white collar of the shirt in one fist, slapped the Mexican's fat face with a callused palm.

"Damn you," he gasped. "I told you how it's going to be. You've got a lot of *pasear* left in you!"

The glaze left Felipe's eyes. He fought feebly. Then he stumbled on around the tree, tearing free of Chisos's grip, going on forward.

"I am beginning to see," he panted. "I am beginning to see why Anse Hawkman should fear you enough to want you killed on sight."

Beating them, kicking them, Owens drove the two men down the valley. Sometimes he didn't feel it when his hand struck Felipe or the boy. His legs were numb and flaccid beneath him. The sun seemed to be inside his head, burning his very brain. Finally Natividad fell on his face in some mesquite. Chisos bent to get hold of his collar. He tried to lift the boy's weight, failed. With a dry sob he let him sink back into the sand.

"Oh, hell," he said, and staggered on past, "oh, hell . . . !"

His tongue was swollen in his mouth. He stopped once to sip at the *morral*, spilled most of the water anyway, and then dropped the bag clumsily. He started to pick it up, knew he would fall if he bent over, and knew he would never get up again if he fell. Felipe must have given up somewhere behind him. He couldn't see the man any more. He went on like a blind man, hands out in front of him, crazy sounds coming from his cracked lips.

Then the shot came to him, small and thin and far away but distinctly a shot. His head jerked up. His glazed eyes went to the narrow cañon that cut into the high cliffs of sandstone. The thing that had driven him this far flamed anew down inside him, blotting out all weariness and thirst and pain, and he began to run in a tottering, stumbling way toward that cañon.

At first he thought it was something wrong with his eyes, the sudden darkness that swept over him. Then he saw that it was a reddish haze emanating from the other end of the notch. Horses stood there, too. And beyond them was a man, squatted down in the purple shadows at the base of the cliff, a rifle across his knees. Chisos's hand brushed absently across his own empty holster.

He began to climb the cliff on that side of the horses, seeking a bench higher up. He must have risen several times his own height when his hand slipped across the shelf formed by the strata of eroded *turfa*. Crawling along the flat on his belly, he passed above the mounts.

Patently Hawkman had taken it easier on his horses. Just as patently he had driven them hard enough to stove them up. And seeing those ruined mounts, Chisos realized how much Anse must have wanted to stop the girl. Or was it Anse? Valeur was here, too.

Cracked lips thinning, Owens moved ahead with a sudden awkward kick of his legs. He could see the end of the cut through the cliff now. It opened out onto a slope grown over with a weird spread of leafless trees, their dead gray branches clawing up to form an insane pattern against the reddish haze that hung over the bowl-shaped valley.

He must have made a small noise, rising up above the man below. The man turned toward him with a grunt. It was Bickford. Most of his heavy-boned face was covered by a white bandage where Chisos's axe had hit him. Bickford had always been a slow-moving, enigmatic man, and Owens had almost expected the lack of surprise or anger or fear in his thick voice.

"Chisos," he said as if they might have been meeting on the street, and his Winchester swung upward in freckled hands.

Owens jumped, and the rifle exploded in his face. His head jerked backward to the stunning blow of the bullet, and he couldn't see Bickford any more, or the haze, or anything.

VIII

Elgera stiffened when the gunshot came to her from the cañon. She stayed that way for a moment, one hand gripped tightly over the upthrust of rock in front of her. She wondered why the shot had sounded from there. Then she sagged back into the pothole. What was the difference? They had come, and they were all around her now, out there in the red fog, spreading through the grove of trees, or they would approach her from all sides. Valeur. Hawkman. Pinky. No telling how many more.

The wind blowing down off the rimrock rattled through the dead trees like mocking laughter. Elgera changed her revolver from one hand to the other so she could wipe sweat from her palm. When she changed it back, the butt was still sticky in her fingers.

Her blonde head bent forward slightly as she tried to pierce the haze. Her circle of vision was growing smaller and smaller as that mist swept in. She wondered dully why she felt no fear. She should. They had come to kill her. It struck her suddenly that maybe she wanted to die. Maybe she wanted that relief from all this exhaustion and thirst and waiting, waiting, waiting. . . .

The crackling sound to her left was louder than that of the wind. She grew rigid, gun swinging that way. Then someone called.

"Valeur?"

Valeur's voice was husky, tense. "Yeah. Anse?"

"Where are you?" said Anse Hawkman.

"How do I know?" snapped Valeur. "Over this way."

Elgera's fingers cramped on the gun butt. Her eyes ached with trying to pierce the dark haze. There was the crackling of dead branches as someone moved through them, then the voices.

"Did you run into that heat?" Anse almost whispered.

"Yeah," grunted Valeur. "Must be what stopped her. She can't get away. All we have to do is find

124

that hole. . . ."

"You're talking too loud," hissed Anse.

"She can't hear us," said Valeur. "Smith said that pothole was over on the other side. He's working in from there. We'll know when we're near if we find her palomino."

"You won't let her get away this time?" said Anse, that high pitch to his voice.

"What about you?" answered Valeur contemptuously. "You've got a gun. What about you not letting her get away?"

"I won't, but. . . ."

"But you hope it's me who comes to her first," said Valeur. "You want her killed, but you don't want to do the dirty work."

"She's a girl. . . ."

"Chisos Owens wasn't a girl," snapped Valeur. "Lucky you let Bick have that crack at him in the cave, or it would have been your face that got smashed. You've just been letting other men do your gunning so long, you've forgotten how yourself. Or can you be afraid, Anse?"

"Afraid!" said Anse shrilly. "You know it isn't that."

"Do I, Anse?" said Valeur. "I think you're afraid of Chisos Owens."

"Damn you, Valeur."

Hawkman's voice cut off to the crackling sound that must have been Jan Valeur crawling away. The girl tried to hold her breath, listening. She couldn't tell if it was the wind now or a man, that eerie popping of the dead trees. It seemed to be all around her. Valeur had said the man named Smith was working in on her from the other side. She turned her head that way, and she drew a choked breath, biting her full underlip.

125

Smith was the chunky little man with the saddle gun who had stayed behind when Tommy had returned to the house for Valeur and Hawkman. He wore a buckskin ducking jacket and patched *armas* for chaps and, when he materialized out of the fog, he was even more surprised to meet Elgera than she was to see him. It gave her the chance to haul her gun up and fire.

Yelling sharply, Smith threw himself to one side, firing a wild shot from the hip. Desperately wanting to keep him in sight, the girl half rose from her protection, jumping over the lip of rock, firing again and again after the dim figure staggering back into the fog and the trees. She heard him cry again, heard a heavier crash of snapping branches. She didn't realize he had quit shooting until her own gun clicked on an empty chamber. In the following silence she began punching madly at the exploded shells. They dropped to her feet with small pattering sounds. She thumbed the first fresh cartridge from the loop in her belt. Maybe she was turning anyway, then; maybe it was the scraping noise of a man's boots on the rocks behind that turned her.

The haze shredded around Anse Hawkman as he stepped into the open. He saw Elgera standing helplessly there with that single fresh shell still held between the thumb and forefinger of her left hand, and the empty gun in the other. A sudden triumph glittered in his cold blue eyes. He brought up his own gun.

Elgera threw her iron from where she held it beside her hip, a scooping underhanded throw, casting her own long slim body after it. The heavy weapon struck Hawkman's gun arm below the elbow, and his own six-shooter blared on an upward cant, the slug whining harmlessly into the smoky

126

sky. Then Elgera's weight struck him and carried him back, and he rolled to the ground beneath her. She felt her nails rake the man's flesh, saw the thin red tracks appear on his weathered cheek. With a bitter curse he pistol-whipped her.

Head rocking to the blow, she felt herself rolling off Anse. She tried to hold him, but the blow had stunned her, and she couldn't control her muscles. A heavy lethargy held her. Unable to rise, she saw the man lurch to one knee, free hand held across his bloody face. His thumb around the hammer of his gun, it made a sharp metallic sound as he cocked it.

In that last moment Elgera didn't know why she should say the man's name because he was somewhere on the outside, far away from this insane place in the Dead Horses where she was going to die. "Chisos," she mumbled, and saw Anse's gun twitch to her.

He stopped like that, with the black bore of his weapon aimed at Elgera's head. He was looking past her toward the trees. His face was dead white. He said the same thing the girl had, only his voice held a sudden shaking fear.

"Chisos . . . ?"

The man came stalking through the dead trees in a hard, swift, bent-forward stride that looked as if it might be hard to stop. The set of his dust-caked face was made more terrible by the red furrow that ran from the corner of his eye back through his hair above the ear, deep and bloody. The Winchester he held across his square belly had B B carved into its stock. He just kept right on coming, levering a shell into the chamber with an ominous snap.

Anse's lips worked around words that wouldn't come out as he tried to jerk his gun toward Chisos. Owens pulled his trigger without any expression and without breaking his stride, and Anse took the bullet where the buckle of his gun belt glittered against his spare middle. He bent over with a hollow cough. His revolver slipped from his hand. He fell on his face.

Elgera rose to one elbow, trying to retain consciousness. Chisos stepped over Anse's body, looking at something beyond Elgera, levering again the .30-.30 with B B on its stock.

Elgera could see Valeur then. He was coming in out of the fog and gathering dusk and dead gray trees, coming in a hard pounding run, that .38 in his hairy fist. The gun flamed. Wood splintered from the stock of the Winchester, deflecting it upward in Chisos's hands. Chisos fired anyway.

Valeur yelled and jerked half way around, .38 leaping from his hand. It didn't stop him. With his bloody hand knocked out to one side that way, he came right on in. His boots made growing sounds in Elgera's ears. Owens was levering another shell into the carbine. Before he could shoot, Valeur's body slammed into him. They went back into a tree with a dull, fleshy thud, limbs snapping and breaking beneath them. Then they rolled to the ground and flopped away into the fog like a couple of big cats, slugging, kicking, cursing.

Elgera got to her hands and knees, head still spinning from Hawkman's blow. Painfully she scooped up Anse's gun. She could still hear them, fighting on the ground, just out of sight back in the haze. She crawled toward the noise.

She thought she would faint for a moment. Her hand went to her blonde hair, came away bloody. She shook her head, and it made her sick. She reached a tree finally, caught a low branch, pulled herself up. It was all she could do to stand there, trying to keep the gun from slipping out of her lax fingers.

The two men came rolling back through the trees. They had the rifle in between them, both with their hands on it, each struggling to get it free of the other. Valeur came on top, and only then did Elgera see how big a man he really was. Owens was larger than average, with a bulk to his solid torso that gave him heft without actually being fat. Somehow, though, he looked small and helpless beneath the swarthy man.

Heavy shoulders bunching, Valeur yanked the .30-.30 upward. With the same movement he smashed the butt end back down into Chisos's belly. Chisos collapsed.

The girl tried to raise her six-gun as Valeur jumped to his feet, reversing the rifle, white teeth bared in a snarl. But a fresh wave of nausea swept her. She saw Owens roll over, one of his hands pawing feebly for the gun barrel as Valeur jerked it around toward him. Then the girl felt herself going over on her face. She couldn't see the men any more. She only heard the shot.

Lying there, half conscious, it was Valeur's bitter curse that raised her head. Somehow Owens had thrown himself at Valeur, knocking the gun aside so that the slug had gone out between them. He was on his knees now, doggedly trying to hold onto the rifle.

Cursing, Valeur jerked it free, clubbed it. Elgera groaned with her inability to move. Pain and lethargy and nausea held her powerless. Chisos launched himself from his knees, bloody face set in an awful mask. Valeur swung with a vicious grunt. The gun caught Owens on his shoulder between the arm he had thrown up to ward off the blow and his neck. The sound of it hitting him sent a fresh wave

129

of sickness through Elgera.

Owens stumbled a little to the side. He didn't go down. He didn't stop.

Valeur took another step backward, rifle swinging again. It slammed into Owens's head. Chisos's hoarse sob held the awful pain of it. His arms pawed out, and he staggered forward with his head down, and the girl thought he was going over on his face for good this time. He didn't.

Something desperate came into Valeur's blazing eyes. With a panting yell, he took another swift step backward, swinging it behind his head for a third murderous blow. That was all.

Stumbling forward blindly like that, arms out in front of him, bloody head down, Owens went into Valeur. They crashed to the ground again, rolling away into the fog, the branches of the dead cottonwood setting up an echoing crackle. Elgera could see the dim movement of them farther on. Valeur still had the rifle. He jammed it upward into Chisos's face.

Elgera saw Owens's head snap back, saw Valeur take that moment to claw at the rifle's lever, cocking it. The sudden movement of Chisos's body cut off whatever happened next.

Elgera heard Valeur gasp. She saw one of his arms thrust out to the side with the rifle. The gun slipped from his grasp. He made a spasmodic series of jerks with his arms and legs. The dull fleshy noise came to the girl for a long time after that before she realized what it was. She saw Chisos's bulk lunge to one side, then the other, straddling Valeur, and each movement was punctuated by the sodden sound.

Slowly she got to her hands and knees. She grabbed hold of the tree again. She stood there a moment, eyes on Chisos Owens, still swerving from

130

one side to the other that way, grimly, silently. Finally she gathered herself and staggered to him, almost falling when she reached out to clutch his shoulder.

"Stop," she panted. "Chisos, stop it. Can't you see it's done now. He's . . . dead!"

Chisos stopped beating Valeur's head against the rocky ground. He straightened, taking his fist out of the man's long black hair. Finally he got to his feet, looking at his hands as if realizing for the first time what he had done. The girl sagged against him, face buried in the dust and blood and sweat of his torn jumper.

"Don't," she sobbed weakly, "don't look like that. He would have killed you. . . ."

"Yeah," said Chisos dazedly. "Yeah. I guess I went sort of loco. It was a long ride up here. I had plenty of time to think about what they were going to do to you. I guess I went sort of loco."

She might have asked him to explain the miracle of his coming to her call like that, but somehow it could wait. She only wanted to feel his arms slipping around her, to know it was all over. Then she stiffened.

"Chisos! There's another one. Pink . . . ?"

"Pinky," said the pudgy little Mexican who had walked in out of the fog, "sends you his regrets. He will not be coming this evening."

The girl turned toward him, eyes widening a little. The fat man smiled blandly, looked at the rocky formation by his feet, kicked at it.

"Volcanic *turfa*," he said. "Irregular masses of igneous rock permeated with vitreous matter and encased in black scriaceous crust of basic lava. Placed with some force against a man's head, it renders him *non compos mentis*, as it were. I found

131

Pinky wandering around in the fog. I placed it against his head with some force."

"I thought I left you on the other side of the notch," said Chisos dully.

"The shots spurred me on, as they did you," said the Mexican. "I came to the *morral* of water you had dropped. It revived me. Farther on I found Bickford. You left him in poor condition, Chisos."

He chuckled as Owens passed a hand across that furrow in his head, muttering. "Bick's shot caught me here. Knocked me out for a minute. But I was already going down on top of him. I came to in time."

"Apparently," laughed the Mexican, turning to sniff at the haze. "Oxidation of ferruginous constituents. Causes the red color. We stand in an extinct crater, *señor y señorita*. I wager it is rather hot farther on, where the shell is thinnest. I never expected to see the Lost Santiago, either. One finds many strange things in the Dead Horses."

He caught the girl's eyes on the briefcase under his arm and smiled. She spoke hesitantly.

"Who are you?"

"I found my case in the saddle bags on Valeur's chestnut, where I presumed it would be," said the Mexican. "You could call me Felipe, if you chose, and that would be my name, or you could call me Amole, or Juan, and that would be my name, yet none of them would quite be my name, either, if you see what I mean. *Porque*"—he flourished one of the gilt-edged diplomas from the brown case—"as it says here, I am Ignacio Juan y Felipe del Amole Avarillo, mining engineer *extraordinario*, archeologist *magnífico*, consultant on business matters and affairs of the heart, or whatever you happen to require at the moment."

"I might've known," grunted Chisos.

"*Sí*, and so might have Bickford, except that neither one of you knew me," said Felipe. "You see, they found out about me in the first place when Hopwell's letter was sent to me. They read the letter before sending it on. Thus must they have intercepted my letter back to Hopwell in which I identified myself by this briefcase I always carry. It was the only way Bickford knew me. The night was black as a *negro* bull. They met me on the road to Alpine beside the cottonwood grove north of town, knocking me from my horse. Recognizing caution as the better part of valor, I escaped into the grove. I hadn't recognized any of them nor any of them me. That is why I could go to Alpine and wait, *señor*. Everything comes to him who waits. No . . . ? *Sí!*"

"If you are Avarillo, you're a little late," said the girl, looking up at Chisos Owens, "and somehow I can't seem to care much."

"Late?"

"Thomas was Hawkman's lawyer," she said. "He had the deed . . . I saw him sign it and date it as of this month in our own living room. They registered their transfer. The Santiago is now a part of the A H spread. I'm glad Father never had to see that."

"He's . . . ?"

"Dead," said Elgera. "We took him to the hospital at Marathon about six months ago. He was an old man. They couldn't do anything for him."

Felipe began to chuckle. Chisos looked at him angrily, growling. "What's so funny?"

"Six months ago he died," said Avarillo, "and she saw Thomas sign and date the quit-claim as of this month. A fine lawyer that Thomas. Didn't he know your father was dead?"

"I only got as far as taking Father to the hospital

133

when Valeur interrupted," said Elgera. "I guess he was in a hurry to get the deed. He was an impatient man, anyway."

"You have the death certificate?" asked the Mexican and, when she nodded, he began to chuckle again. "Then your valley is most certainly not a part of the A H. As in the case of Oliver versus Lynn, Emmet and Emmet, volume three, page twenty-seven, the delivery of a deed after the grantor's death is not effective. Thomas rendered the quit-claim invalid himself when he dated it. You have your proof in the death certificate."

Perhaps Chisos had seen too much already for more than the slight surprise that showed through the dust and blood caking his face. "You . . . ?"

"Oh, *sí, sí*," chuckled Felipe, taking out a black *cigarro*. "Did you think I would pass up the overcrowded practice of law. I was an *abogado* in Mexico City for a time. As I say, whatever you might require. Mining, archeology, affairs of the heart. . . ."

"Yes," said Elgera, looking up at Chisos, "affairs of the heart."

But even Avarillo's talents in such matters failed when it came to Chisos Owens. Using Hawkman's horses, they returned to the valley, picking up Natividad there beyond the notch. The boy was delirious but began to recuperate soon. The guards Anse had left at the cave were glad enough to leave when they learned that Hawkman was dead. Chisos let them go, knowing there would be no more trouble from that direction. He stayed at the Santiago a week or so, helping the Douglases get back to normal. Then Elgera began to notice the small, restless signs in him.

It was early morning when the three of them

stood beneath the portal that formed the roof of the flagstone porch, Elgera, Chisos, Felipe. Chisos spoke uncomfortably.

"It's like I told you before, Elgera. It's hard to explain. Maybe it sounds loco to you. But if I stayed here, I'd either be living off you or working for you. I won't be a kept man. And do you think I could hire on like an ordinary thirty-and-found 'puncher when I feel like I do about you. If I had anything to offer, I'd ask you to come away with me. I haven't even got a hoss now. Thomas has power of attorney for Anse. He's no cattleman, and maybe he'll open up things outside again. Maybe I'll be able to get my Smoky Blue back. If I had that. . . ."

"I understand," she said, trying to keep the tears back. "Maybe this just isn't the time."

"There'll be a time," he murmured, "sooner or later. Meanwhile you're in good hands with Felipe. And if there's anything he doesn't know about, just call me again. *Adiós*."

Elgera and the Mexican stood there, watching the blocky man ride up the hill on the gelding the girl had given him from her remuda. Avarillo took his *cigarro* out with a flourish. "*Sí*," he said, "*adiós* . . . which is only a corruption of 'go with God' and doesn't literally mean good bye at all."

The girl smiled wistfully. "*Adiós*, then, Chisos Owens."

THE SECRET OF THE SANTIAGO

I

The angry flush in *Señorita* Scorpion's golden-tan face turned her cheek to a darkly etched line, startling against the gleaming blondeness of her long hair. She stood looking out the window of the big room, slim hands clenched tightly against the soft buckskin of her Cheyenne skirt. Basket-stamped Hyer boots covered her bare legs halfway to the knee, spike heels accentuating the long slim line of her rigid body. The exasperated rise and fall of her bosom was apparent beneath her white camisa. Sun streaming in from the outside caught the dangerous flash in her wide blue eyes as she turned sharply to the man sitting by the fireplace.

"I never heard anything so fantastic," she snapped. "How can you possibly be any relation to me, how can you have any claim on the Santiago Mine? The Douglases have been in this valley . . . !"

The man held up a thin, imperious hand. "Spare me the details, please, Miss Douglas. I know the story well enough . . . how Don Simeón Santiago and George Douglas discovered this valley and the Santiago Mine in Sixteen Eighty-One. How, a year after they began working the mine, a band of Comanches and Apaches raided the valley and cut off its only access to the outer world, trapping Douglas inside. It only seems rather far-fetched to me that Douglas and his descendants would be able to live here for two hundred years without finding their way out again."

Elgera drew a sharp breath, fists clenching. "That mine shaft through the mountains is the only way in

136

or out of the Santiago Valley . . . the shaft the Indians caved in behind them on their way out after the raid. And you saw the mountains beyond that. You know you'd never have gotten through them alive to the shaft itself if my brother hadn't brought you. That's why we were never able to get out . . . the Dead Horses. They're all around us, and the Douglases who tried to go over them never reached the outside. . . . and never came back. It was only seventeen years ago that my own father succeeded in digging the shaft through again and got on through the Dead Horses alive. Seventeen years! And yet you sit there and claim to be a Douglas."

The man, who had given his name as Harold Bruce-Douglas, leaned back in the ponderous hand-carved armchair, stretching patent leather boots languidly toward the crackling flames in the stone fireplace. He turned his narrow head toward Elgera slightly, and again she was struck by the supercilious curl of his thin lips, the inbred arrogance in his aquiline beak of a nose. He threw aside the heavy lapel of a blue greatcoat, reached a slender hand beneath it, drawing forth a small gilt box. Elgera had never seen a man take snuff before. Bruce-Douglas pinched it testily between a pale thumb and forefinger, tilted his close-cropped head back slightly. He snapped the box shut and thrust it beneath his coat again. Then he took out an embroidered silk handkerchief, voice condescending.

"My dear girl, your vaunted ancestor, George Douglas, was over thirty years old when he was captured by the Spaniards in the Caribbean and subsequently ended up in this valley in Sixteen Eighty-One, as Don Simeón Santiago's slave. Thirty years old, I say, and he left a goodly family in England when he decided to go free-booting"—the

137

man dabbed at his nose with the kerchief—"yes, a goodly family. A wife and two sons, as I recall. Sons who had sons and who handed the name down unto me. Now, the very fact that George Douglas's first wife was living undivorced in England while he was begetting children by another woman in this valley renders invalid whatever claim you, as a descendant of that second union, have on the estate, namely the Santiago Valley and the Santiago Mine."

The girl stepped toward him abruptly. "You . . . !"

"Elgera, Elgera," said Avarillo, catching her arm. "Let us hear the *hombre* out." He turned to Bruce-Douglas. "You must handle our *chiquita* gently, *señor*. She is not the demure type, if you understand what I mean. No . . . ? *Sí*."

He chuckled until his gross belly quivered against the broad red sash bound around it. He was the mining engineer Elgera had brought down from Alpine to work her Santiago, Felipe Avarillo, a pudgy barrel of a Mexican with big sad bloodshot eyes that always reminded her of a hound dog's. His fat hams took all the slack in his gray whipcord jodhpurs, and his post-oak calves strained a pair of English riding boots till their seams looked ready to burst. Elgera shook his heavy hand off.

"I hope you don't think you can just come in here and take the valley," she told the other man. "In the first place, proof. . . ."

"What I prove to you, or what I don't," said Bruce-Douglas indifferently, "has no significance. My lawyer is already entering my claim to the Santiago in Texas courts, and it will be established soon enough. However, I have brought with me a small portion of the total evidence that validates said claim. I see you have the old pistol case on the mantle. It has one weapon in it."

138

The flush left *Señorita* Scorpion's face suddenly. Her eyes shifted to the leather box on the hand-hewn mantelpiece. How could he know there was only one gun? Only members of their immediate family even knew what the case contained. Bruce-Douglas caught her eye, inclined his thin head imperiously toward the mantle. Frowning, Elgera moved around him. The skin of her slim hand made a golden-tan glow against the battered black leather as she opened the lid of the case. A single dueling pistol lay against the purple satin inside, a large G D inscribed on the golden plate over the gun's old-fashioned firing pan. There was a place for the second gun below it, empty.

"You know where it came from, of course," said Bruce-Douglas.

"George Douglas brought it with him when he came here in Sixteen Eighty-One," said the girl, watching the Englishman narrowly.

The skin was drawn across his bony forehead like transparent parchment, with a tiny network of blue veins visible beneath. His eyes were the gray-blue of shadowed ice, and for a moment the girl saw something almost feral in their depths. She drew away slightly.

"Have you ever wondered what happened to the other gun?"

"This is the only one we've ever had," she said.

"It is an Adams dueling piece, my dear, made by that famous gunsmith in London about Sixteen Seventy," said Bruce-Douglas, reaching beneath his greatcoat again. "George Douglas valued the guns highly. He left one of them with his first wife in England, took one to the New World with him."

Elgera's glance was drawn to the hand he took from beneath his coat. It held a dueling piece with G

D inscribed on the golden plate above its old-fashioned firing pan. Avarillo's riding boots made a swift scuffle on the earthen floor.

"*Con su permiso*," he said, reaching for the gun.

Bruce-Douglas handed it to him disdainfully. The fat Mexican examined the weapon, muttering to himself.

"Adams, you say, Sixteen Seventy? The same firm that made the self-cocker in Eighteen Fifty-Two?" asked Avarillo.

Douglas shrugged, watching the fire. "Perhaps."

Elgera shook her blonde head angrily. "Do you think I'd hand over the Santiago just because you have a gun like the one I have?"

Bruce-Douglas leaned back, thin lips curling superciliously. "Hardly, hardly. As I said before, my lawyer is handling everything, and actually I am under no compulsion to prove anything. However . . . what about the secret of the Santiago?"

The dull metallic thud turned Elgera sharply toward Avarillo. The fat Mexican stood there with pudgy hands empty, the gun he had dropped lying at his feet. He had turned pale beneath the natural coffee color of his moon face. His inevitable black cigar dangled slackly from one side of his mouth. Finally he tore his wide eyes from Bruce-Douglas, clamped his lips shut on the *cigarro*, bent to pick up the gun. He handed it back to the Englishman, muttering a garbled apology.

"What is it?" demanded Elgera. "The secret of the Santiago?"

Avarillo made a helpless gesture with his plump hands. "*Dios*, Elgera. I didn't think, that is, I didn't know. . . ."

Bruce-Douglas's thin laugh was unbelieving. "Miss Douglas, are you trying to tell me you don't

140

know the secret? Are you trying to tell me you don't know what my knowledge of it signifies?"

Avarillo took a vicious puff of his cigar. "How ... ?"

"How did I know?" supplied the Englishman. "Isn't it logical that the true heir to the lost Santiago should know the secret?"

"What are you talking about," cried the girl. "Avarillo, what is it?"

Avarillo's eyes dropped before hers, and he made that helpless gesture with his hand. "I don't know, Elgera. I didn't think anybody else in the world knew about the secret. I don't know."

She would have said something else, but someone came across the porch outside in a hard-heeled walk, shoving open the big front door. Natividad Douglas stood there a moment, lighted by the Texas sun slanting in through the jagged red peaks of the Dead Horses. Elgera's older brother, tall and lanky, wore reddish charro leggin's. He came on in, removing a black soft brim from his dark hair.

"We've got the mules all packed for Alpine," he said, glancing at the Englishman, "but the men. . . ."

Elgera turned to him, frowning. "Why do we have so much trouble with them? Avarillo, you said you picked good men."

Avarillo was still watching Bruce-Douglas. "Better not go up there, Elgera. They aren't in any mood. . . ."

"It's my mine," she snapped, glancing pointedly at Bruce-Douglas, "and I'm settling this once and for all."

Behind the hall door was her big Army Model Colt hanging on a peg. She slipped it around her slim waist, notched the cartridge belt up to its last hole, jammed the heavy gun down until it hung snugly against the curve of her thigh. Natividad held out his hand protestingly.

"Elgera!"

"You stay here and see that Mister Bruce-Douglas has whatever he needs," said Elgera to her brother. "That train's going to Alpine if I have to ride it myself!"

Ⓥ Ⓥ Ⓥ

The Dead Horses rose barren and forbidding on every side of the Santiago Valley, waterless slopes shadowed by the gaunt skeleton trees, dry river courses marked by the bones of men who had died trying to penetrate the unknown mountains. The Santiago was the only spot in the whole range with water enough to support animals and people. The sprawling adobe ranch house had been built by Don Simeón when he first arrived in 1681, the wings of its U stretching back on either side of a flagstone *placeta* where a pair of greening willows dropped their shade over a red-roofed well. The scrub oak grew upslope behind the house to the mouth of the shaft which led through the heart of the mountain for many miles, dug there by the Indians many centuries before.

"What is this secret?" Elgera asked Avarillo as they climbed the hill. "I've never seen you so shocked before. What is the significance of his knowing it? Does it mean he is the heir of George Douglas?"

Avarillo shrugged, puffing like a windsucker from the climb. "It might. I didn't think there were three men in the world who knew about the secret of the Santiago. You know there are a thousand and one legends about your fabulous mine, Elgera. As a mining engineer I thought I had heard of them all.

142

But some years ago a blind priest down at Monclava let slip something about the secret. He didn't want to talk, and I didn't question him directly. All I found out was that there is a secret."

"Then you don't know what it is?" she said.

He shook his head. "Only of its existence. *Dios*, it isn't enough we have this trouble with the diggings. Now somebody has to show up claiming them."

"What trouble?" *Señorita* Scorpion asked. "What's got into the men?"

"Have you ever noticed how each level of the mine only goes back into the earth so far then stops dead? It looked as if Santiago sunk them that far, then quit and punched the vertical shaft down another few feet, and started digging back on another level. He did that with each level. We are on the seventh level now, and we have dug back about as far as Santiago's first six went."

"But the ore you took up assayed true." She frowned.

They skirted the split-rail corral and went on up through a clearing of curly gramma. "*Sí*, true, but nothing like the fabled riches Don Simeón Santiago sent out. The first load we took to Alpine assayed some twenty dollars the ton. The next fifteen. The third, nine. Gato's men are miners, Elgera. They have worked on veins that pinched out before. Perhaps this vein will get better. They do, sometimes. But I keep asking myself why Don Simeón and George Douglas only dug back so far and no farther. The men are beginning to ask that, too."

"Do you need to ask that any more?" said the huge Mexican standing between two scrub oaks at the edge of the clearing.

Elgera turned sharply, realizing the miners had

143

come down through the trees from where the string of mules stood loaded by the mine above. Gato was the one who had spoken. He was called Cat because of his claim that he could see in the dark. His eyes did look feline, somehow, gleaming opaque and milky from beneath a heavy black brow, pupils oblong rather than round. He wore tremendous mustaches that hung long and greasy over the brutal jut of his unshaven chin. The girl took in the pair of black-handled Colts strapped about his thick hips.

"Like Avarillo says," growled Gato, "we have worked veins that pinched out before, *señorita*. We would like our pay now."

The girl clenched her fists. "Your contract isn't up. You'll get paid when you deliver that load of ore to Alpine."

Gato grinned balefully. "We will get paid when we deliver the worthless ore to Alpine, did you hear that, *compadres*?"

The dozen Mexican peons began to move restlessly behind him. The one on his right was Enrique, great bull-shoulders straining at his dirty white shirt with the bulged knotty muscle that comes to a man who swings a pick for his living. His callused hands held a heavy pick-axe almost tenderly, and the way his flat-nosed face was scarred made Elgera think he had used the axe for more than mining, against other men who used theirs the same way, and whose faces were scarred like that.

Gato stopped grinning. "I said we would like our pay now. You keep your money in the house, *señorita*, no? Who gets it from there . . . you or us?"

Señorita Scorpion flushed, lips opening to say something. She saw the men behind Gato begin to shift. Enrique moved to one side, caressing his axe. The girl realized their intent, and suddenly a strange excitement swept the anger from her. Sunlight caught the gleaming ripple of blonde hair as she threw her head back, and there was something wild in her ringing laugh.

"Gato," she called, spreading her legs, "if you think you'd like to try and get the money in my house, go ahead. I swear I'll shoot the first man who takes another step down that hill!"

Enrique stopped moving to her side for a moment, scarred face surprised. Gato's grin faded. There was a certain hesitancy in his milky eyes as they swung down to Elgera's Army Colt. Then he laughed, too.

"Down at Boquillos they say you can throw a gun faster than the *Caballero Negro* himself. I don't think so. I don't think any *muchacha* could be that *maravillosa*."

Enrique began moving aside once more. She couldn't keep both him and Gato in her line of vision now. Avarillo took his *cigarro* out.

"*Dios*, Gato, you wouldn't do anything with a woman . . . ?"

"I'm taking a step down the hill," grinned Gato, took the step, and pulled at both his guns.

The girl knew what a mistake it would be to divide her attention. Ignoring Enrique, her whole concentration was on Gato, and her reaction was instinctive. She didn't know she'd drawn until the gun bucked upward in her hand. Gato's left hand weapon slipped back into its holster as he let go to claw at his right shoulder, and his other six-gun dropped to the ground from the spasmodically stiffening fingers of his right hand. He reeled back with more surprise on his face than pain.

"¡*Dios*!" he cried. "You've killed me with your damned speed."

Enrique had been too far to the side of Elgera for

145

her to see him move. She heard the pounding thud of his feet. She was thumbing desperately at her hammer and whirling toward the man with the scarred face as he charged down on her with that axe above his head.

"*Santiago*, you black *borrachón*," bellowed someone. "Saint James and clear out of Spain!"

The yell ended in a prodigious grunt as another bulk hurtled in between Elgera and Enrique. The girl saw Enrique fly into the air suddenly, axe jumping from his hands. He came down in a big arc with the momentum of his own rush, striking the ground with a solid thud, lying still after that. Avarillo stood with his post-oak legs spread wide in the position he had assumed to meet Enrique's rush and throw him over one fat shoulder that way. The men in the crowd behind the wounded Gato were still shifting, and one of them had a gun out.

"No," said Elgera.

The peon looked at her blankly, then he let his revolver drop to his side. Gato stood there, looking from his own six-shooter on the ground to the Army Colt in Elgera's hand.

"*Dios*," he said huskily. "*Dios.* . . ."

"I'll shoot the first of you to move a finger," Elgera said.

Avarillo chuckled, flourished ashes from his *cigarro*. "She throws it around pretty fast, Gato. No . . . ? *Sí*. Did you think those were idle rumors about her in Boquillos?"

Blood was beginning to seep through the fingers Gato held tightly around his wounded right arm. He shook his head dazedly. "*Por supuesto*, not a woman, not a woman. . . ."

"She isn't a woman," laughed Avarillo. "She's a wildcat."

"I'm riding the pack train with you," said *Señorita* Scorpion flatly. "And what I said still goes . . . you get paid when you deliver that ore safely to Alpine!"

II

The double-rigged Porter saddle creaked a little as Chisos Owens idly swung off his big claybank and stood there a moment, letting the sleepy afternoon sound of Alpine creep in through the double doors of Si Samson's Livery Stable. Chisos's blue eyes had a squinted look, and beneath the brow of the Texas-creased Stetson the strong flat planes of his face were caked thickly with the dust of a long ride behind him. He wore a faded denim jumper, and his ponderous Bisley .44 hung against the slick leather of old apron chaps, its holster scarred and stiff with little use.

Samson came from the gloom at the rear, a bent oldster with a mop of white hair that stood up like the roached mane of an Army jack. Owens slapped the claybank's hot flank.

"Give you double to take special care of her, *Si*. I pushed it all the way from Rio."

"Sure thing, Chisos," grinned Samson. "By the by, the Douglas gal's in town with a load of her ore."

Owens stiffened perceptibly, then he grinned almost wistfully. It seemed a long time since he had seen her. They had been drawn to one another from the first, Elgera and Chisos, and each succeeding meeting had strengthened that bond.

Owens caught Si watching him and realized he had been reminiscing. His grin turned wry, and he

147

touched the brim of his hat, turning out into Main Street. It was a broad, wheel-rutted way, running north and south through Alpine with the S. P. cattle chutes and brick depot squatting at its upper end along the tracks.

Tawny dust puffed up beneath Owens's boots as he crossed toward the line of cow ponies at the hitch rack in front of the Alpine Lodge, the long porch now shaded by a wooden overhang that slanted down from the bland row of windows on its second floor. Chisos bent forward a little to walk—a square, heavy man who was neither graceful nor awkward in his movements, whose every deliberate step seemed to hold an intrinsic purpose within itself.

The boards rattled beneath his weight as he mounted the sidewalk and went on up the front steps and into the Alpine Lodge. The clerk behind the desk was as drab and faded as the pink carpets on the floor of the lobby. Owens got a dim impression of glasses and a bald pate when he swiveled the dog-eared register. He found the name he was looking for, and his lips thinned distastefully; then he saw another name below it.

"Miss Douglas in?"

The clerk shook his gleaming head. "Went out with her engineer. Mentioned the assayer's office."

Owens nodded and turned to the stairway that climbed the back wall above the desk to the second floor. Going up the stairs, he turned right at the head, halted before a dirty white door with 205 in tarnished metal letters on its casing. It was the room registered to Carry Tuttle, and Carry Tuttle was the name Clay Thomas had said he would use. The door opened to Chisos's knock, and he walked in and stopped with his legs spread a little, trying to hide the dislike from his voice.

148

"It had better be good, Clay. I started from the Rio as soon as your *cholo* boy brought the note, and it was a long ride."

Thomas almost slammed the door shut, turning the key in its lock with shaking fingers. When Anse Hawkman had owned everything from Persimmon Gap on down to the Rio Grande, Clay Thomas had been Anse's lawyer. He might have been tall once. He looked shriveled and old now somehow, his black frock coat hanging slack from stooped shoulders, his legs bent slightly at the knees in what looked like a habitual cringe. His face was seamed and furrowed like an old satchel, gaunt hollows beneath his bony cheeks, watery eyes trying to hide in deep sockets.

"Don't say it that way, Chisos," quavered the man, turning from the door and clutching at Owens's arm with a claw-like hand. "It's all over now. Anse is dead. I'm disbarred. It's all done."

"What else did you expect?" asked Owens, distaste in his tone as he shrugged the hand off. "Did you think they'd let you keep your power of attorney over the A H when they found you'd stolen every acre of it? You stole Delcazar's Rosillos, Clay, and just as good as stole my Smoky Blue. I'm glad you tried to grab the Santiago. I'm glad Anse saw it squatting there right in the middle of the Dead Horses and had to try and get it. The Santiago finished him proper, didn't it?"

"You finished him, Chisos," said Thomas. "The girl couldn't have done anything without you. That's why I asked you here. You're the only man in the Big Bend who can save me."

Late afternoon sunlight was dying in the room, and Owens turned toward the lamp on the round, marble-topped table, fishing in his hip pocket for a

149

match. "What do you mean . . . save you?"

Thomas clutched his arm again. "Don't strike a light, Chisos. They'd kill me if they knew I was here with you. That's why I had to meet you at Alpine, why I registered under another name. They'd kill me if they found me, Chisos!"

Owens noticed the green shades had been lowered. He turned to Thomas. "Kill you? Who?"

A wild light had come into Thomas's eyes. He spoke swiftly, gripping Owens's arm with a growing desperation. "It's the Santiago again, Chisos. It'll always be the Santiago. You know what happens when something as rich and famous as that is discovered. Elgera won't ever be safe with it, Chisos. There'll always be someone trying to get it from her. Anse was the biggest man in the Bend, but he was willing to stake all he had on getting the Santiago. And now it's the secret, Chisos, the secret of the Santiago. I've got a third of it in my wallet, see, a third. That's what they're after. They'll kill me for it."

He was trembling, and there was a shrill hysteria in his voice. Owens grabbed him by the shoulders. "Third of what? Quit puling like a sick dogie, Clay. Who's going to kill you?"

Thomas panted, collar dark with sweat. "Remember how I got hold of Delcazar's Rosillos spread for Anse?"

"Del thought his old Spanish grant was good," said Owens disgustedly. "Never took out homestead papers."

Clay nodded, almost eagerly. "That's right, that's right. Del never filed on his land. Anse hired him for fall roundup, kept him away from the Rosillos long enough for one of our A H hands to squat there and take out homestead papers. There wasn't anything

150

Del could do when he got back. His family had their papers down in Mexico City. That old Spanish *sitio* didn't hold water, but I went down there to make sure the grant was clear. That's where I found this third of the *derrotero*, among those papers. Delcazar was descended from Pio Delcazar, captain of Don Simeón Santiago's muleteers in Sixteen Eighty-One. That's how they got this piece of the *derrotero*, see, handed down from Pio. They didn't know what it was. They couldn't read. But I can. It's a third of it, see, this piece of the *derrotero*'s a third of it."

"Third of what?" Owens almost yelled.

"Third of the secret," babbled Thomas. "*Derrotero*. Third of the secret of the Santiago. They know they can't do anything without the whole. That's why they're after me. They know I have a third. They think the girl's got a third, too. . . ."

Owens grabbed him, face twisting. "The girl?"

Clay Thomas cringed beneath his grip. "Yes, Elgera Douglas. That's why I called you, Chisos. I knew you'd do anything to save her. I'll give you my third of the *derrotero* and tell you all I know if you'll only help me, Chisos, if you'll only take me down to your Smoky Blue. . . ."

He broke down, sagging across Owens's arm till his face was on the table, sobbing uncontrollably. Chisos tried to lift him. Finally, supporting the man with one hand, he reached around behind him and got a chair and lowered Thomas into it.

"I'm an old man, Chisos," babbled Thomas, clinging to him. "You're the only one can save me now. I've got no place to go. If anybody connected with the old A H showed up in Boquillos now, his life wouldn't be worth a plugged *peso*. Nowhere to go, Chisos, and they'll kill me. If you only knew what kind they were, Chisos. Hawkman's games

151

were penny ante beside this."

Over the man's hysterical babbling Owens caught a slight scraping noise behind him. He was turning when the room suddenly became lighter. Whirling on around, Chisos saw that the shade had been shoved aside and that the last fading afternoon light was streaming into the room. He was pawing for his Bisley when the gun blasted from the window.

He threw himself aside with the terrific thunder of that single shot filling the room. He heard Clay Thomas scream. Chisos had his .44 out by then. He snapped a shot at the bulk of a man skylighted against the open window. The curtain flapped back into place, and there was a sharp sliding sound. Owens scrambled around the table and lurched to claw the shade aside. A shed roof slanted down into the narrow alley behind the Alpine. He heard the diminishing pound of feet from down there. Impulsively he raised a boot to climb out. Then he halted, turned back. "Thomas?" he called. "Thomas?"

Ⓥ Ⓥ Ⓥ

The Mescal Saloon squatted in ugly iniquity on the northwest corner of Main and Second. From Second Street a covered stairway led up the west side of the Mescal to the assayer's office on the top floor. *Señorita* Scorpion was coming down the stairs when the first shot drummed out from across the way. She clattered on down the shaky steps, Colt flopping against the big silver *conchas* sewn down the seams of the buckskin *charro* leggin's she had worn for the long ride north from the Santiago.

Men were already shoving through the batwings of the Mescal by the time she had reached the sidewalk. Si Samson legged it from his livery stable

152

at the intersection of Main and Second, shouting something.

The Alpine Lodge stood directly across Second from the stairway Elgera had taken down, its side toward her, its front facing the livery stable across Main. A narrow alley separated the lodge from the Alamo Saddlery just behind it on Second. Charlie Done came out of the saddlery and turned up the sidewalk at a run, and the second shot crashed over the other sounds. Charlie crossed the mouth of the alley in time to collide with a man plunging from its shadowed darkness—a squat little man with greasy black hair done up in a queue, and a six-gun stuck nakedly through the waistband of his *chivarras* in the middle of his belly.

"Thomas has just been shot," he yelled. "Chisos Owens just shot Clay Thomas in the Alpine."

"Chisos!" gasped the girl.

Sheriff Hagar clattered onto the walk from his office on the same side of Second as the Mescal and out into the street. Elgera was running then, shouting over her shoulder at Avarillo where he stood by her line of loaded mules at the curb.

"Stay there and watch the mules . . . and Bruce-Douglas!"

She passed the man who had run into the street from the alley and reached the opposite walk before the sheriff caught up with her. In the two years Johnny Hagar had held office fame for his inimitable style with the twin, ivory-handled Peacemakers bobbing at his hips had spread far beyond the confines of Brewster County where he held jurisdiction. He was a tall young man in his mid-twenties with black hair close-cropped beneath the jaunty line of his center-creased John B. Stetson. Even in high-heeled Justins his long-legged run held

153

a certain easy grace. Elgera caught the reckless smile spreading his mouth as he came up beside her.

"What's that about Chisos Owens?" he shouted.

She shook her head, not wanting to answer. There was already a crowd gathered on the sidewalk and porch of the hotel, blocking the way in like a mill of thirsty steers. But Nevada Wallace had come across from Samson's Livery and reached the porch about the time Elgera and Johnny Hagar did. Nevada was one of the deputy sheriffs and, though Hagar was six feet or more, the deputy topped him by a big head. He had to send to St. Louis for custom-made shirts because no store in Alpine had ready-mades large enough to fit him. His tan cowhide vest had an extra piece fitted into the back so he wouldn't split it across the shoulders every time he bent over or reached for something. He went through the crowd like a man swimming the breast-stroke, making a broad lane for Elgera and Hagar to follow through. The bald clerk stood in the middle of the lobby.

"Shooting," he gulped. "Shooting upstairs."

"Yeah?" grinned Hagar and went on by.

He left Nevada on the second floor at the head of the stairs to keep the crowd down in the lobby. Elgera saw George Kaye come across the pink carpet below. He was Hagar's other deputy, a lanky boy from Kentucky. Then she had gone on down the hall after the sheriff. A derby-hatted whiskey drummer stood discreetly in the open door of 203. Other men stood farther down the hall. None of them had made a move toward the closed door. Hagar banged on 205.

"Owens, you in there?"

The voice came muffled. "Lighting the lamp. Minute."

Elgera felt her breath coming faster as she heard

154

the dull metallic sound from within the room then the thud of footsteps. A key rattled in the lock, the door opened, and he stood there, a big heavy-bodied man blocking off whatever was in the room.

"Chisos . . . ?" almost whispered Elgera.

He looked past Hagar to the girl. A rope-scarred hand raised in some small, nameless gesture. Hagar nodded his head forward, and Owens moved back into the room without speaking, still looking at the girl. Elgera saw the Bisley lying on the table beside the oil lamp and then the body of Clay Thomas sprawled grotesquely over the chair he had knocked down when he had fallen.

The sight of death drew Hagar's lips back against his teeth. "Well . . . and Clay never packed an iron."

Patently Chisos Owens realized how it looked.

"You know Chisos isn't that kind," said the girl hotly, stepping around the sheriff.

"I know what kind Chisos is," said Hagar. "I know that next to Anse Hawkman he hated Clay Thomas worse than any man in the world. Remember they took his Smoky Blue, Elgera."

"Hagar," said Owens heavily, "I'm not going to argue."

A grim purpose slid into his weathered face. He seemed to settle forward slightly. A dogged line entered the hunch of his big shoulders. The signs were easily readable. Most men who knew Chisos Owens wouldn't have been able to go on smiling. Johnny Hagar knew Owens. He kept on smiling.

"I'm not going to argue, either," said the sheriff. "Let me see your gun."

Chisos picked up his Bisley. He didn't hand it to Hagar. "It's got one bullet gone, if that's what you want to know."

"I heard two shots," said the girl.

"I didn't," said Hagar. "I asked for your gun, Chisos."

Owens fist clenched around the gun, and he hardly moved his lips when he spoke. "I know what's on your mind, Hagar. Do you think I'll be taken in for a killing I didn't do? Do you think I could prove my innocence behind your bars?"

Si Samson appeared at the door, a sour looking man in a black fustian behind him. Samson spoke to Hagar. "Coroner's here."

Hagar didn't seem to hear him—he was still watching Owens. "I've got to hold you, Chisos. It's what they call circumstantial evidence. Everybody knows how you hated Clay. One slug gone from your gun, one slug through him. Give me your gun and come easy. That's the way it has to be."

"Don't be a fool, Hagar," snapped the girl. "That man who ran from the alley. What about him?"

"There were lots of men running around," said Hagar. "Give me your gun, Chisos."

Owens shifted the Bisley until it bore on Hagar. "If you want my gun, come and get it."

It must have struck Si Samson then just what he had stepped into. He took a stumbling pace backward into the coroner.

"Judas!" he said.

Hagar laughed easily. "I'll come and get it all right, Chisos. Think you have what it takes to shoot me cold like that?"

"Maybe not," said Owens and holstered the gun. "Try it now."

Elgera turned pale. She knew Chisos was no gunman. He had always been the first to admit that. Hagar's brilliant skill was recognized throughout the Big Bend. And there was Chisos Owens facing him like that.

156

Hagar's eyes dropped to the battered .44 hanging so indifferently at Owens's hip. The momentary expression that came into the sheriff's face might have been admiration.

"You don't want it that way, do you?"

"I told you," said Owens with a heavy deliberation.

Gunman or not Owens wasn't the kind to pull his .44 without using it. Hagar lived by the same code. The girl could see the tacit understanding that had settled between the two men now. It was in the way Hagar's lips pulled back flat against his teeth still in that grin, in the way Chisos took a careful breath and leaned forward a little—the next move by either man would start both of them for their guns.

"Johnny!" cried the girl. "Chisos. Don't! I won't let you do it, Johnny. I won't let you take him . . . !"

"I'm coming, Chisos," said Johnny Hagar.

He was still grinning when he shifted his boots on the carpet. It snapped both men into movement. But Elgera moved too. With a wild cry she sprang toward Hagar, her big Army Colt flashing upward in her hand. From the corner of her eye she saw how clumsy Owens's draw was. Ahead of her she caught the glint of Hagar's Peacemakers leaping out of leather. Then she felt the solid shock of her blow striking him and saw his hands stiffen spasmodically on his guns.

Hagar's sick grunt was lost in the detonation of his right Peacemaker. It sent a futile slug into the door. Then he was lying in a heap at Elgera's feet. She stood there above him, panting, eyes flashing. Chisos Owens didn't even have his Bisley out. He was bent forward, with it half drawn, surprise just leaving his face.

The girl grabbed him and shoved him over Hagar

and out the door. The coroner made a jerky move down the hall then stopped, mouth open. Si Samson was backed up against the opposite wall. He grinned at them as they ran by. The girl and Owens were half way to the stairs when Hagar lurched out of the door behind them, holding his head in one hand, a Peacemaker in the other.

"Nevada's down there," he shouted. "You'll never get through him. Nevada, stop 'em. Stop Chisos Owens!"

Then Elgera saw why Hagar hadn't shot. Nevada Wallace had come into the hallway off the stairs where Hagar had left him and would have been in the line of fire. His gigantic bulk filled the whole hall, and he pulled his gun, bellowing.

"Stop, Chisos. I'll shoot."

Georgie Kaye, Hagar's other deputy, came pounding up behind Nevada.

"Chisos," choked Elgera hopelessly, because she was still running behind him and she saw how completely the two huge deputies blocked the hall, and she didn't think even Chisos Owens could get through a giant like Nevada Wallace.

But Owens just bent forward a little in his stride, his denim jumper flapping away from his square block of a torso. He didn't even go for his gun, and he shouted only once.

"Get out of my way, Nevada!"

"I'll shoot, damn you!"

But he couldn't shoot for fear of hitting Hagar and the others in the hall farther down. With a yell he raised his gun, and Chisos crashed into him, knocking him back into Kaye.

Elgera ran head-on into all three of them, expecting to be stopped abruptly. To her surprise she felt herself stumbling on forward. Owens's legs were driving into the carpet so hard his boots ripped the rug with each pounding step, and his right arm was working back and forth like a piston. Every time it jerked forward, Nevada gave a sick gasp.

Stumbling back behind Nevada, Kaye raised his gun to slash at Owens. The girl struck at him over Owens's shoulder with her Army Colt. His face twisted with pain, and he reeled backward. Nevada tried to hit Owens with his gun. Chisos reached up his big knuckled fist, grabbed the giant's wrist, and kept on slugging him in the belly that way, driving forward inexorably. Nevada's feet made a final desperate scuffle against the floor as he tried to set himself and stop Chisos. Then he collapsed backward and fell. As he went down, Owens rammed a shoulder against him, knocking him on into Kaye. Both the men stumbled sideways and crashed into the wall.

Chisos pulled Elgera roughly over the kicking feet of the two men and around the corner of the stairs. Hagar stumbled across Nevada as he came running after them, cursing.

Pulled on down the stairs by Chisos, Elgera had to keep going at a headlong run or fall on her face. Nevada and Kaye had been quieting the crowd in the lobby below. One or two townsmen stood on the stairway, turned up toward the sounds of the fight. A man shouted and threw himself aside as Owens and the girl pounded down the stairs.

"It's Chisos," one of the crowd shouted, and a pathway melted for them toward the door.

Hagar clattered into view at the head of the stairs behind and still couldn't fire for fear of hitting someone. Then Elgera and Chisos were out of the front door and across the porch and down the steps.

"The palomino," panted the girl.

Owens was ahead of her, and he cut toward the hitch rack at the corner where Elgera's Morgan palomino stood. He ducked beneath the rack and knocked the palomino's reins loose and the reins of a *trigueño* horse. A man ran out onto the porch of the Alpine Lodge, yelling.

Elgera jumped the rack from the high curb, caught her reins up, carried them back over the palomino's head as she vaulted into the saddle with her free hand slapping the horn for leverage. She wheeled the startled horse in a full circle before she could drive it into the open. Then she whirled it to follow Owens on the *trigueño* south on Main. She had a fleeting glimpse of Avarillo standing in the middle of Second as she swept past the intersection.

Señorita Scorpion felt a sudden savage joy in their escape. The swift tattoo of drumming hoofs and the wind whipping through her long blonde hair filled the girl with a heady exhilaration—and she threw her head back to let her laugh echo down Main Street behind her, infinitely feminine, wildly triumphant.

III

Felipe Avarillo stood in the middle of Second, watching the dust settle into the wheel ruts of Main after Elgera had passed. Sheriff Hagar appeared at the corner of the hotel, having difficulty mounting a strange horse. Avarillo felt a hand on his sleeve.

"You're not just going to stand here," said Bruce-Douglas. "You're not going to let them go without you?"

Avarillo chuckled complacently. "You mean I'm not going to let them go without us, don't you?

Señor Bruce-Douglas, that was Chisos Owens with Elgera. If you think you can follow him, go ahead."

"Chisos Owens?" said the Englishman. "What do you mean?"

Avarillo took his time about answering. He removed his inevitable *cigarro*, blew a smoke ring. Bruce-Douglas had insisted on accompanying them north to Alpine. Avarillo had no particular liking for the man. He twirled his cigar in fat fingers, studying it.

"I said what do you mean?"

No, reflected Avarillo, he had no particular liking. In fact, he felt a certain aversion. *Sí*, an aversion. He took a slow puff on his smoke.

"What I mean," he said finally, "is that there isn't an Indian in Texas you could hire to track Chisos Owens. That is what I mean."

Hagar had managed to mount the horse now. He gigged it across Second, shaking his head groggily, bent forward in the saddle. Suddenly he wheeled it back and turned to look for a long moment at Avarillo and the Englishman. Then he wheeled it again and booted its flank. The horse broke into a gallop down Main after Chisos and the girl.

Avarillo stood there a few moments before he sensed that Bruce-Douglas was no longer by his side and realized the man had been gone since Hagar had halted and looked at them. Avarillo turned to see the Englishman back by the lead mule at the other end of the pack train, talking with Gato and his miners. There was something tense in the way Bruce-Douglas stood that started the fat Mexican back toward him. Avarillo got close enough to hear Bruce-Douglas speaking. The man's voice was no longer testy or disdaining. It held a thin, feral menace in its cold tones. It stopped Avarillo in his tracks.

"You played the fool with Elgera back at the Santiago once already, Gato," said Bruce-Douglas, "and once is enough, I think. You'll put that pack saddle back on the mule."

Avarillo could see the *aparejo* lying on the ground beside the lead animal. Enrique was still bent over its hitches, his axe lying on the ground, his scarred face turned to watch the Englishman. Gato stood a little to one side of him, and he made an abrupt gesture with his hand, speaking viciously.

"We haven't got any money yet or anything else. We're taking what we can get right now, *Señor* Bruce-Douglas. We're taking the mules. They'll bring ten *pesos* apiece at the border, and that's. . . ."

"Put the pack saddle back on the mule," said Bruce-Douglas without raising his voice.

Avarillo moved sideways and forward until he was almost at the curb and could see Bruce-Douglas's face. Avarillo stopped again there. The perpetual smile faded from his moon face. His *cigarro* sagged, forgotten in one corner of his mouth.

The Englishman stood bent forward a little with both hands in the pockets of his blue greatcoat. His thin lips were compressed until the flesh about them was white. He was looking at Gato with a terrible intensity. His eyes, still the chill blue of shadowed ice, were as indefinable as they was deadly.

For a long moment there was no sound. Gato and Bruce-Douglas seemed locked in some silent struggle. Suddenly Gato's eyes fell and he turned, snarling at Enrique.

"*Pongase el aparejo en el burro!*"

Enrique looked at him blankly. Then he stopped to heave the pack saddle on the flop-eared jack again. Avarillo became aware that his cigar had

162

collected a long ash. With a sudden motion he took it out, tapped it.

"You seem to have some hold over Gato, *señor*," he said.

Bruce-Douglas turned toward him sharply, as if coming out of a daze. He shrugged, and Avarillo could see the effort it took for him to make his voice indifferent.

"My property after all, you know. Just protecting my interests."

"*Sí*," chuckled Avarillo, "*sí*. I'm glad you feel that way. You can take care of the pack train for me."

"I thought you said you weren't going to follow Chisos Owens."

"That is right," said Avarillo. "It is also right that I don't think you know what the secret of the Santiago is. You know of its existence perhaps, but not what it is."

"I don't care much," said Bruce-Douglas, "what you think I know or don't know."

Avarillo went on as if he hadn't heard. "I do not know what the secret is either. However, when there are things to be found out, there are usually places at which one can do the finding out, if you understand what I mean. No . . . ? *Sí*."

Bruce-Douglas seemed to bend forward. "Monclava?"

Avarillo laughed softly. "You seem to know, *señor*."

"You mentioned it to Elgera," muttered the Englishman.

"Did I now?" said Avarillo. "Did I? *Bueno*. When Spain owned this country, Monclava was the capital of the combined provinces of Tejas and Coahuila. All the official business of the province went through there, including the gold shipments from the northern mines, of which the Santiago was one. *Sí*, when Mexico broke away from Spain, the official documents of the old Spanish government were handed over to the Church. I have had access to the archives at the *Capilla del Santo* down at Monclava. Perhaps I missed something that I shouldn't have missed. Perhaps it would behoove me to seek access again."

"I'll get my horse," said Bruce-Douglas.

Avarillo turned to him in mock surprise. "But, *señor*, you already know the secret."

"I'll get my horse."

Avarillo studied his *cigarro*, laughing in that soft way. "It is summer, *señor*. Why do you wear such a large coat?"

"My health requires it," replied the Englishman testily.

"And the snuff, does your health require that?" asked Avarillo, still looking at his cigar—then he turned to the man. "No, I don't think you are as anemic as you appear, *señor*. In fact, I think you are a man who could do a lot to get what he wants and to go where he wants. Perhaps it would be foolish to antagonize you unnecessarily, No . . . ? *Sí*. If you wish to accompany me to Monclava, that is your affair. *Pues*, you'd better fill up your snuff box. It is a long ride."

Ⓥ Ⓥ Ⓥ

The day after Chisos and Elgera had escaped, Sheriff John Hagar came wearily back into Alpine and left the horse he had ridden into the ground at Si Samson's Livery Stable. He got a breakfast of ham and eggs at the Mescal. While he was eating, his two deputies came in.

164

Hagar took his coffee in a gulp, clapped the cup onto the table. "He and the gal headed into the Del Nortes. From there on it was like trying to follow a bald eagle. No wonder you can't hire the Indians to track Chisos Owens. He led me the wildest trail I ever want to ride. Finally I lost his sign completely."

"I thought you was a better tracker than that," grumbled Nevada.

Hagar glanced at him sharply, then he grinned and pointed his finger at the tremendous deputy. "Whenever you start talking like that, just remember you were the ranny who couldn't stop Chisos Owens, Nevada. I would have stacked you against ten Brahman bulls in a horse-high corral. I thought there wasn't a man in the world could throw you. Just remember sometimes. Chisos Owens did."

Nevada sunk his massive head into his chest, growling suddenly. Kaye laughed softly, turned to Hagar.

"You ain't going out again?"

Hagar took a last bit of ham, shoved his chair back. "Think I'll let 'em get away with that? I had to come back for a fresh horse and some grub, that's all. There's other ways of trailing a man besides the prints he leaves. What kind of horse did you say Owens took?"

"Coroner's horse," said Kaye. "The brown kind the Mexicans call a *trigueño*."

"He'll have to switch it somewhere," said Hagar. "It isn't a range horse like that gal's palomino."

"But those are his hills down there, the Chisos, the Santiagos," said Nevada. "People couldn't find the Lost Santiago Mine for two hundred years, and it was standing still. Chisos Owens isn't going to let any ground get warm beneath his hocks."

Hagar laughed, and it sounded reckless. "I won't

165

give him a chance to set his hocks down, much less warm sandy ground with them. If he murdered Clay Thomas, I'll get him for it. That's my job, isn't it?"

"That part is," said Nevada. "The girl?"

"Why not?" said Hagar.

Kaye stood up, punched Hagar playfully in the shoulder. "Better not let the county board hear that one. They didn't hire you to chase a blonde *bandida* all over Texas."

"I'm chasing a murderer," said Hagar. "Can I help it if he took a pretty girl along? While we're talking about Elgera, did you nab her bunch like I told you to?"

Kaye shook his head. "Time we got around to it, Avarillo and the Englishman had vamoosed. They left the jackasses at Si's livery. That Gato and his *amigos* had taken a *pasear* too."

Hagar shook his head disappointedly. "I wanted a talk with the Englishman. Bruce-Douglas. Name's familiar from someplace. Face too."

Kaye was fishing something from his pocket. "Couldn't be this *hombre*?"

He handed a crumpled reward dodger to Hagar. There was no picture. There never had been one of the *Caballero Negro*. There was not much description either. The people who might have gotten a good look at him were generally found in no condition to do any describing. The single paragraph on the paper said he wore black clothes and rode a black stallion, a full Arabian.

"Got it on the morning train from Austin," said Kaye. "His latest was over at Marathon, and they're hot to have him caught."

"The *Caballero Negro*," read Hagar. "The Black Horseman wanted for bank robbery and murder in Marathon, Texas, June third, Eighteen Ninety-Four;

166

wanted for train robbery in Austin, January tenth, Eighteen Ninety-Four; wanted for murder in Tucson. . . ." Hagar stuffed it in his pocket, grinned. "Gets around, doesn't he? Wonder what brings him down this way?"

Ⓥ Ⓥ Ⓥ

Hagar got his own horse, now fresh, and bacon and flour and coffee. He didn't mean to come back till the chase was over, one way or the other. He struck the Comanche Trail on the second day out, riding toward the lower Big Bend where Chisos Owens's Smoky Blue spread was.

When Geronimo had been defeated and gathered in, Army life had become tame for Johnny Hagar. Once his enlistment was up, he took his discharge papers and began hunting the excitement that had lured him over the next hill since he was old enough to ride a horse and carry a gun. Brewster County was in the wildest, toughest, deadliest section of Texas, and two predecessors had died with their boots on in office. The good citizens of Brewster were hard pressed to find a man to replace the last deceased sheriff when Johnny Hagar hit town. On his second day there a pair of drunken gunnies had begun tearing the Mescal apart, and Hagar had handled them with his usual inimitable style, and that was all it took to put him behind Brewster County's five-pointed star.

His center-creased Stetson was set at a jaunty angle on his bandaged head. There was a rakish swagger to his long figure, swaying in the saddle. He couldn't help thinking of the girl and remembering how he had run out of the Alpine Lodge to hear that ringing, taunting laugh echo down Main behind her as she rode out of town. Some said it was that laugh which had first drawn Chisos Owens into the unknown Dead Horses after Elgera. Hagar didn't doubt it. Her wildness drew him too—like a magnet. Suddenly a reckless grin spread his lips, and he began humming "Stable Call."

Oh go to the stable, all you who are able,
And give your poor horses some hay and some corn.
For if you don't do it, the captain will know it. . . .

He rode a weary mount into Ramón Delcazar's spread on the east fringe of the Rosillos Basin. Ramón, a young Mexican who wore his white cotton shirt tails outside his buckskin leggin's and a pair of forty-fives buckled on around that, came out of his two-room mud *jacal* and stood watching Hagar dismount.

"See you still pack those irons, Ramón."

The boy shrugged almost sullenly. "Habit I picked up when Anse Hawkman was grabbing things down here."

"You worked for Anse, didn't you?"

"*Sí*," said Ramón bitterly. "Many *pobres* down this way thought the old Spanish land grants, the old *sitios*, were all they needed for title to their spreads. Like me and my father, they didn't file any homestead papers. That's how Clay Thomas got hold of more than one spread for Hawkman. After I lost the Rosillos, it was work for the A H or buck it. There was only one man who ever bucked it and stayed alive."

"Chisos Owens?" asked Hagar, and he was looking at the horses in the ocotillo corral behind the house. There was a *bayo coyote* in it, with a black stripe down its back, and a gray mare.

168

"*Sí*, Chisos Owens," said Ramón. "And I am not Chisos Owens. That is why I worked for Anse Hawkman. Is it Chisos you are hunting?"

Hagar glanced at him then grinned. "That's right. You're a pretty good *amigo* of his. How about it?"

The boy rubbed a dark hand across his leggin's. "I heard Chisos is accused of murdering Clay Thomas. He wouldn't do anything like that, Hagar. If Thomas is dead, it will make everybody in this part of the Big Bend that much happier, but Chisos wouldn't do it. Like you say, I'm a pretty good *amigo* of his. We're all pretty good *amigos* of his down here. It's his country. How about that?"

Hagar was still grinning. "I didn't expect you to answer, Ramón. I won't ask you to. Prospector up by Nine Point Mesa said he thought there was a powerful lot of *pasear* going on down here during last week. All south, he said. What's down south, Ramón? Boquillos?"

"Mariscal," continued Ramón indifferently, going on south, "Santa Helena. . . ."

"Monclava," said Hagar

There were other towns on down, but he stopped at that, because he had been watching the ocotillo corral all the time, and the mare and the other horses had shifted so that he could see the one standing behind them that he hadn't spotted before. It was a brown animal. It was a *trigueño*.

IV

Monclava was across the Rio Grande and on down past the purple bulk of the Sierra Mojada, its huddled cluster of tawny adobe *jacales* flanking a

169

dusty main street that lead to the ancient *Capilla del Santo*—Chapel of the Saint. Chisos Owens had tried to make Elgera leave him once they were out of Alpine, but she refused to do so until she had helped him prove his innocence in Thomas's murder. Chisos told her why he had taken so long to open the door, that he had been hunting for Thomas's wallet. He had found it, but neither the girl nor Chisos could find anything in the pockets that could be connected with the Santiago.

Elgera had heard Avarillo tell how the *presidio* at Monclava had been the capital of the province when Spain had ruled Tejas, and how the gold shipments had gone through there. The official documents had all been given into the keeping of the Church when Mexico overthrew Spain, and Avarillo had found much of his amazing knowledge concerning the history of the Santiago in the archives of the *Capilla del Santo*. Patently, Thomas's death was mixed up somehow with the mine, and south of the Rio was out of Sheriff Johnny Hagar's official jurisdiction. Monclava was the logical destination for Chisos and the girl.

With more than two weeks of the weary trail behind them, they ate breakfast at the ramshackle *posada* that passed for Monclava's inn, left their horses to be fed by the sleepy hosteler, and went across the sunlit plaza and down the winding cart road to the chapel at the edge of town. Framed by tall poplars, the ancient doorway of oak was sunken deeply into a recess formed by massive adobe buttresses. A niche on the right hand contained a tarnished bronze bell. Chisos gave it a shove, and its brazen clang shook the sleepy silence. Elgera glanced backward down the cart road.

"Nervous?" he asked.

"I can't get over the feeling we're followed," she said.

"That's natural," he laughed, "for a couple of fugitives."

A sudden violent screech stiffened Elgera—she whirled, hand grabbing at her gun. Then she leaned back against the adobe, laughing shakily. The noise had come from a creaking *carretta* being hauled into the plaza by a ponderous speckled bull. The cart's great solid wheels squeaked raucously on dry axles, and a dozing peon sat on top of the onions piled high in the bed. A couple of bawling children ran across the street; a hen clucked, scratching the yellow earth. Elgera turned back to the door, relaxing a little.

Then the heavy hand-carved portal of ancient oak was swung open on its beaten iron hasps, and a lay brother stood there, tall and gaunt in a simple cassock of brown wool. There was something ethereal about him, as if he could release his earthly bonds almost at will. He was completely bald, and the faint glow emanating from his dome-like skull seemed to come from within. His bloodless lips hardly moved when he spoke. His voice held the dry, sibilant rattle of a wind through the summer aspens.

"*Los bendiciones de Dios en usted, niños mío,*" he said.

Owens cleared his throat. "We. . . ."

"Ah," the man held up a pale hand. "*Americanos.* You will pardon me, *señor*. I thought you were one of my flock. You are welcome to our humble *capilla*."

The Franciscan wore smoked glasses, and Elgera suddenly realized that he was blind. Ushering them in, he allowed his hand to brush the girl slightly. It was thin and spidery, that hand, with soft flesh lying

171

in slack pink folds. It revolted the girl strangely.

"*Perdón*," murmured the brother, "but touch, you see, is my substitute."

Coming in from the outside, the interior had been only a myriad of candles winking in a velvet gloom for Elgera, but now her eyes were becoming accustomed to the cloistered darkness. She could make out the hand-hewn corbels supporting the *viga* poles that formed the beams and rafters for the steeply slanted roof. Light came meagerly through the leaded, stained glass of the slot-like windows, casting pale stripes across the earthen floor in front of the girl. In the shadowed niches beneath the windows were many ancient *bultos*, statuettes of saints that might have been carved two centuries before by some reverent peon. Gradually the girl became aware of the other man in the room, silhouetted by the candles set beneath the high back of the altar.

"You have come a long way," the blind brother was saying. "The smell of dust is still heavy on your clothes."

"*Sí*," said the man by the altar. "All the way from Alpine. You should have given them a more royal welcome, Brother Katopaxi. It is not often that such personages as Chisos Owens and Elgera Douglas honor Monclava."

The girl's voice was high. "Avarillo!"

"*Buenos días, mi compadres*," chuckled the fat Mexican. "You spent too much time running around in the Del Nortes trying to throw Sheriff Hagar off your trail. Bruce-Douglas and I beat you here by a *día*. Such an interesting place, too. Belongs to one of the oldest dioceses in the Americas . . . the sacristy is part of the ancient *parroquia* in the original monastery which was founded in Sixteen Hundred.

172

¿Correcto, Hermano Katopaxi?"

The blind man's voice was no more than a whisper. "*Sí, señor*, that is correct."

"What did you find?" asked the girl impatiently.

"*Sí*," chuckled the fat Mexican. "Founded in Sixteen Hundred. The archives contain such fascinating documents. Ancient land grants from the King of Spain, a fine old map of Tejas. Brother Katopaxi was kind enough to help us in our perusal. We have been supping in the *padre*'s garden while I studied at my leisure. If you would care to join me in a bite of tortilla, and a sip of *pulque*. . . ."

Chuckling secretively, he led them out into the flagstone garden. Beneath a pair of weeping willows a large oak table was set with clay *ollas* of grape wine and a big wooden bowl of steaming tortillas.

There were a few pieces of ancient parchment to one side, and a pile of stiff sheepskins on the white cotton cloth. The sun fell warmly over the thick adobe wall, but the man sitting languidly on one of the peg-legged benches had the collar of his blue greatcoat pulled up around his narrow chin. His thin face betrayed no surprise at the sight of Elgera.

"It looks," said Bruce-Douglas casually, "as if we all had the identical idea."

"*Sí, sí*," grinned Avarillo, walking over to the table, putting one foot on the bench, and reaching for the parchments. "And now, *señores y señorita*, from the innumerable documents and papers in the archives we have sifted out a few that might be indicative, if you understand what I mean. This one, for instance, was among the *papeles* from the *presidio*, transcribed by a government clerk. It is dated July the Fourth, Sixteen Hundred and Eighty-One. '*Recibimiendo este día, veinte cargas del oro desde la Mina Santiago. . . .*'"

"English, please," said Bruce-Douglas testily.

Avarillo shrugged, again chuckling. "'Received this day, twenty *cargas*' . . . a *carga* is a mule load, understand? . . . 'twenty *cargas* of gold from the Santiago Mine, each *carga* consisting of twelve round bars bullion, each bar measuring one *metro* long, one *decimetro* in diameter. . . .'"

Owens's voice was impatient. "We already know Santiago shipped his gold through here . . . it was a government depot."

"*Paciencia*," said Avarillo, holding up a fat hand, "patience. If you will allow me, I will read from another paper. In the Sixteen Hundreds, understand, the Spaniards had many other mines north of the Rio Grande besides the Santiago. This second document is another receipt transcribed by a clerk, recording a shipment from one of the fourteen San Saba diggings. *Ahora* I will read: 'March Tenth, Sixteen Eighty-Three . . . received this day, twenty-two *cargas* of gold, each *carga* consisting of six square bars bullion, each bar measuring two *metros* long, one and one half *decimetros* in diameter.'"

Avarillo stopped, looked up inquiringly. Bruce-Douglas made a bored gesture with one slender hand. "From that, I take it, we are to gather that Santiago's gold came in round bars and the San Saba's gold in square ones. Brilliant, Avarillo, positively brilliant."

Avarillo chuckled. "You have made the correct deduction, but you fail to draw the correct conclusion from it. The standard mold set by royal decree at that time was for square bars, two *metros* long, one and one half *decimetros* thick. All the shipments from the other mines are in bars of that size and shape. Yet, without fail, the receipts for bullion from the Santiago register shipments of

174

round bars."

"Really," said Bruce-Douglas. "Could it just be conceivable that Don Simeón Santiago was using a different mold?"

"No," said Elgera, shaking her head, trying to form something in her mind now. "No. Don Simeón was *adelantado*, entrusted with the visitation of mines in New Spain. He, of all men, would have the proper equipment, the standard molds. No, it's something else."

Avarillo flourished ashes from his *cigarro*, poked it at the girl with a grin. "You are beginning to understand, aren't you, *chiquita*? I will give you aid. When I was working for your mine, Elgera, I found a large boulder about a quarter mile above the mouth of the main shaft, hidden in a thick clump of *chapote* trees. Did you ever see it?"

The girl was frowning. "No."

"I didn't think so," said Avarillo. "It was almost impossible to penetrate the brush under those persimmons. It looked as if nobody had been there for a long time. The boulder was hollowed out on top as are *metates* the peon women use to grind their maize in. But this was no *metate*. The hollowed-out portion was blackened as by the smoke of many fires. The dirt around its foot did not contain signs of grain . . . it was hard and slick like a slag heap. I did not attach much importance to it at the time. *Pues*, now . . . !"

"A smelter," said the girl excitedly. "The Indians had worked the mine for centuries before Don Santiago found it. That boulder must have been the smelter they refined the ore in. And the round bars, Avarillo, I've seen gold molded like that before. The Indians used hollow canes from a cane brake when they hadn't anything better. It's an old way. They

175

poured the refined molten gold into a section of cane. When it cooled, they broke off the cane. It left a round bar."

She was breathing faster because she was beginning to sense what it meant. Watching her, Avarillo chuckled.

"You have arrived, *señorita*, you have arrived," he said. "Do you wonder now, Elgera, why the tunnels Don Simeón dug from that vertical shaft only went back so far, no farther? Don Simeón found out the same thing we did. The veins pinched out too soon for any use. The mountains had been worked clean of paying ore long before Santiago discovered the mine. He wasn't getting his gold from the Santiago Mine at all!"

For a long moment the little garden was silent. *Señorita* Scorpion noticed dully how Bruce-Douglas had leaned forward suddenly, unable to keep his surprise from his face. Brother Katopaxi's spidery hand was running up and down the slim gold chain that held a cross around his neck. Finally Elgera spoke.

"Then . . . how . . . where . . . ?"

Avarillo took his foot off the bench and plumped himself down, reaching for an *olla* of wine. "In the old days Coronado and Pizarro and Cortez were all hunting it. Call it the Seven Cities of Cibola of the Gran Quivira, or the Treasure of the Incas, call it whatever you like. It is all the same thing. Gold. The Spaniards who found the New World knew the Indians possessed great riches. They saw irrefutable evidence of that. But few ever found those riches. Perhaps Don Simeón was luckier. The mine had obviously been worked out long before he discovered it . . . yet he sent gold through Monclava as fast as Pio Delcazar could drive his mule trains,

176

gold enough to be the basis for the fable for the richest mine in the Southwest. Round bars of it, *señores y señorita*, one *metro* long!"

"You are redundantly expository," said Bruce-Douglas, having recovered his composure. "What you are saying, in so many words, is that the Indians who worked the mine prior to Santiago's discovery of it refined their ore and molded it into round bars and stored it somewhere, and that Don Simeón found where they had stored it. All right. Where?"

Laughing, Avarillo poured grape *pulque* from the clay jug. "I admit I am a remarkable man, *señores y señorita*, but not that remarkable. We knew the secret of the Santiago existed before, but not what it was. Now, we know what it is, but not where. The third part is going to be the hardest, I think."

"The whole thing seems divided into thirds," muttered Elgera. "How about the *derrotero*, Chisos? Don't you think it's time?"

Chisos shrugged, taking Clay Thomas's black wallet from beneath his shirt. He put it on the table and told Avarillo how the lawyer had come to him with it.

"He babbled something about a *derrotero*," said the heavy man. "We couldn't find anything that looked like a third of the secret, or a *derrotero*, whatever that is."

Avarillo took the wallet with an air of suppressed excitement. He dumped the contents on the table, sorting through them. "A *derrotero*, Chisos, literally means a route. But in the old days it meant a map or chart. Don't you see the possibility therein . . . a map . . . ?" He picked up a bunch of cards, shook his head, scanned an old will and testament of some long-deceased peon, shook his head again. Then he fingered the wallet. "I see you slit the lining. This is a Mexican *hato*, this wallet, Chisos. Clay probably picked it up in Mexico City. You said he was there. No . . . ? *Sí*. It contains all the love of intrigue so characteristic of a Latin. One lining? Pah. Two, or three, or five. *Sí* . . . !"

The knife that had suddenly appeared in his corpulent hand might have come from his broad red sash. Elgera had seen other surprising things come from it. He did something with his thumb on the golden-chased shaft. A gleaming blade leapt into view. Then he was touching the point to the wallet. The outside which Chisos had already cut away gaped open. Then the blade slipped lengthwise beneath it, and another layer of soft leather suddenly dropped away from the blade. Avarillo slipped an exploring finger in. A smile spread his fat face. He took out a thin piece of ancient yellowed parchment almost reverently.

Elgera bent over his shoulder, spelling out parts of words at the bottom of the paper. "*A el.* . . . *ondido de Indios.* . . . *iago Mina.* . . ."

"It is only a part, you see," chuckled Avarillo. "One third of a *derrotero*."

Elgera pulled away suddenly as a pale bloodless hand slipped down beside her on the table. It was Brother Katopaxi's. There was something almost ghastly in the way his bony fingers groped blindly until they encountered the jagged edge of the paper. She saw his hand tremble slightly. He reached inside his cassock and pulled out a buckskin *maleta*. From this pouch he removed another piece of paper. His voice was hardly audible.

"Would this fit, *señores*?"

Avarillo accepted the second piece. The girl knew it would fit before he put it down. The two jagged edges came together, forming the sides and bottom

178

of a large square, leaving a large gap torn out at the top in the form of a rough triangle.

"*Dios* is kind," said the blind brother. "Do you know how many years I have been waiting here with that piece of paper, *señores*? When I was young and still had the blessing of sight, I was called to give benediction to a peon near Saltillo, Pedro Tovar, dying of the plague. He told me he had been the personal *mozo* to Don Rodriguez Santiago, the last of the Santiagos whose ancestor discovered the Santiago Mine. When Mexico overthrew Spain, remember, the ruling classes lost everything. Don Rodriguez was reduced to a penniless wanderer. The only one of his myriad of retainers who stayed with him was this Pedro Tovar. When Don Rodriguez died, he had nothing to give the faithful Pedro but the sword of his house and this piece of parchment."

With the two pieces together like that the words took form, and Avarillo read them. "*El derrotero del tesoro escondido de los Indios Santiagos.*"

"The chart of the hidden treasure of the Santiago Indians," Elgera said breathlessly.

"According to this Pedro Tovar," said Katopaxi, looking blindly straight ahead, "the piece of paper I gave you was sent from the Santiago Mine in Sixteen Eighty-One by Don Simeón Santiago, carried to his son in Mexico by a faithful Tlascan slave. The Tlascan died from the hardships of the journey before the mine was lost. And when Don Simeón and his Santiago Mine disappeared as suddenly, the only clue to its whereabouts was this third of the *derrotero*. Don Simeón's son never found the mine, and the piece of the map was handed down in the Santiago family until it reached Don Rodriguez who gave it to Pedro Tovar, who in turn gave it to the Church on his deathbed. I knew the other portions of the chart would come, if I but had patience. If you find the *tesoro*, *señores*, you will see that the Church gets its share . . . ?"

"*Naturalmente*," said Avarillo, "*naturalmente*."

A strange, secretive smile caught at Katopaxi's bloodless lips for a moment, and his hand seemed to run up and down the chain around his neck a little faster. Elgera couldn't help shivering a little. She looked up—sunlight fell across the wall and lighted her face warmly. Still she felt cold.

Chisos Owens put a blunt finger on a spot at the bottom of the page marked with an X bearing the name, Monclava. Avarillo nodded and began tracing a dotted line that ran from the spot marked Monclava on up the page.

"Zaragosa," he said, "that was a *posada* on the old trail from Tejas. Farther on, the Comanche Crossing . . . we are at the Rio Grande now. The line turns east up the Rio to Boquillos. A turn northward from that town, and we have another landmark. *Los Dos Dedos de Dios* . . . The Two Fingers of God. And finally, *La Resaca Espantosa*. . . ."

He trailed off as his fat finger had reached the jagged edge of the paper. Elgera looked at the last spot.

"*La Resaca Espantosa*," she muttered. "The Haunted Swamp? I never heard of that, but if you turned northward from Boquillos like this, you'd be . . . ."

"Right in the Dead Horse Mountains," finished Avarillo, then he shrugged. "Why not, Elgera? The Indians wouldn't have gone too far away from the Santiago Valley to store their treasure. *Quién sabe*, if we had the other third of this *derrotero*, it might lead us right back to your house."

The *padres* kept Indian *mozos* to serve the

Church, and the one who slipped in from the garden door was dressed in white doeskin leggin's and a hand-tooled vest of calfskin over the smooth bronze slope of his shoulders. He whispered something to Katopaxi.

"Someone is outside who would like to see you," said the blind brother, turning to the group.

"Really," said Bruce-Douglas indifferently.

"*¿Quién es?*" asked Avarillo.

"He says," answered Katopaxi, "that he is Sheriff John Hagar."

"Yes," said the lean young man who had stepped through the garden door, "Sheriff John Hagar."

Elgera whirled about the same time Chisos did, and both of them started to do the same thing. Then they stopped, and let their hands fall away from their guns. Johnny Hagar stood with his Justins spread apart on the flagstones and his John B. shoved back on his close-cropped hair and his two ivory-handled Peacemakers steady in his fists. He moved forward in that lithe, effortless walk.

"I spotted your *trigueño* at Delcazar's."

"Did you?" said Chisos. "It wasn't any range hoss. The palomino's the only one lasted down here."

"You should've left that with Del, too," said Hagar. "Nobody could miss that animal in a thousand miles . . . no, don't move any more . . . every Mex I asked had seen it go by. Unbuckle your gun, Chisos. If you try anything funny, I'll shoot you in the legs and take you back behind my saddle like a sick dogie."

"Before we go any farther with this little drama, you might disburden yourself of your own weapons, Mister Hagar," said Bruce-Douglas's arrogant voice, whirling Elgera toward him.

181

The Englishman still sat at the table, face depicting utter boredom. His pale hand rested on the cloth. It held the dueling pistol with G D inscribed in the plate over its old-fashioned firing pan.

Elgera didn't see Hagar shoot because she was still turned toward Bruce-Douglas. She heard the deafening sound and saw pain twist the Englishman's face as his hand jumped upward suddenly, Adams pistol flying from smashed fingers.

But it had taken Hagar's attention for that instant and, as the Adams hit the flagstones with a dull, metallic sound, Chisos threw himself at the sheriff. The girl whirled back and jumped Hagar, too. The young man's other Peacemaker bellowed. Then Chisos struck him, and Elgera struck him, and Avarillo's resilient bulk smashed in behind her, and all four of them went to the ground in a kicking, cursing, slugging mass.

Elgera saw Avarillo's English riding boot come from somewhere and catch Hagar neatly across the right wrist, knocking his gun from that hand. The girl had his other arm, and she rolled on it so her body pinned his forearm against the ground. She caught the hand, twisted viciously. Hagar cried out, let go of that Peacemaker. Elgera got to her knees, grabbing the gun.

With her weight off his arm, Hagar rolled over and jammed a shoulder into Owens, shoving him sideways. Then the sheriff got to his hands and knees and threw Owens clear off him and rose, whirling to grapple with the heavy man before he could get fully erect.

Elgera jumped them, clawed at Hagar. The sheriff jerked his arm back to slug Chisos, and his elbow struck the girl in the stomach. Breath knocked out of her, she clung grimly to his shoulder, trying to pull

182

him off Owens. She raised the Peacemaker to hit him.

"Elgera," gasped Chisos, rearing up beneath Hagar, "not that way. . . ."

Fat arms were suddenly around Elgera, yanking her off of Hagar, and Avarillo's chuckle was bland in her ear. "*Señorita*, that would not be ethical. Let them fight it out, man to man, now. Let it be fair. This has been coming a long time and might as well be settled once and for all. No . . . ? *Sí*."

She sagged in his grip, realizing he was right. It had been coming a long time, and it had to do with more than the issues involved in Clay Thomas's murder. Owens was battling to stay free and prove his innocence, and Hagar was fighting for his duty to return Owens—but both of them went at it with a terrible savagery that came from something deeper, something far more primitive, something that needed no words to bring them together fighting like this whenever they met. Elgera had sensed what it was back in the room at Alpine. She could see it plainer now. There was an eager ferocity in the way they met, like two wild stallions battling over a mare.

Hagar's lean frame was lighter by twenty pounds, and Elgera knew Owens, and she expected the sheriff to be completely outmatched. What he lacked in bulk, however, he made up with skill. For a long terrible time the two of them stood there slugging it out, and Hagar's feet moved in a swift, skilled shuffle, too fast for Elgera to follow, and his bony fists landed three blows for every one Owens got in.

The flat-lipped grin spread on Hagar's mouth as he danced in and out, not allowing Owens to set himself, cutting the bigger man's face to ribbons. He ducked in and rolled his right into Owens's square belly and his left into Owens's face and danced out

183

again.

Chisos tried to spread his legs, and that dogged hump came into his shoulders. But Hagar moved in again before Owens could get his balance, pounding the man's face with a tattoo of lefts, jumping back before Owens could strike. Again, Hagar weaved in, grinning. Then, while he was bent low in there, Elgera saw him jerk suddenly, saw the sudden look of pain that had crossed his face. She knew Chisos had landed a blow.

Quickly Hagar retreated, covering up, head ducked into his shoulders, elbows hugged in tight. It gave Owens his chance. His square torso bent forward a bit, and he spread his legs and started moving forward, and the girl had seen it like that before.

"*Nombre de Dios,*" muttered the blind priest, his head moving helplessly from side to side. "Stop this, my sons. . . ."

Hagar had recovered. The grin was back as he stepped in again, hooking a sharp right over Owens's heart. Chisos grunted sickly. He bent forward a little farther. His boot made a relentless scraping thud against the flagstones, coming on.

Johnny Hagar warded off his left and ducked in under his right to smash a straight arm low full into Chisos's mouth. Owens gasped and spat blood but didn't stop.

The girl couldn't help her choked cry: "Chisos . . . !"

Desperately Hagar struck Owens again, trying to stop him, but an adamant cast had settled into the flat planes of Owens's bloody face. He slogged into Hagar, moving with his heavy deliberation that was neither graceful nor awkward. His square torso jerked from one side to the other as he threw his patient, driving blows.

Hagar danced in and pounded three lefts into Owens's face and countered Owens's swing and threw a right into the heavy man's stomach. Then Elgera saw the sheriff's body jerk again and saw the agony twist his face suddenly. The pale, set look hadn't left him when he danced backward this time, hugging his elbows in, shaking his head, blinking his eyes.

"Let me go!" sobbed Elgera, fighting Avarillo's fat arms. "They'll kill each other. Let me go!"

"*Sí*," said Avarillo, holding her without much apparent effort. "They'll probably kill each other, but you can't stop them. That is Johnny Hagar and Chisos Owens, Elgera, and nobody could stop them now, I think."

The grin was fixed and ghastly on Hagar's face. There was a desperation in the way he slashed back in, bending forward and driving his swift blows from clear down at his boots. The grunting sounds of pain Owens made were hardly human. He leaned forward to take the blows and kept on walking, and his boots still moved across the flagstones with that inexorable scraping thud, and nothing Hagar could do would stop him.

Hagar blocked one, sunk his fist into Owens's belly. He rolled another off his shoulder, came in with an uppercut that jerked Owens's head back with a snapping sound. He drove a third back into Owens's belly that doubled the big man over. And with that last one, he dropped his guard. Before he could step back, Owens caught him. Elgera saw Hagar stiffen suddenly, and his spasmodic grunt slapped against the garden wall.

He staggered back, trying to cover up. Owens was still almost doubled-up as he plodded into Hagar, and his head went against the man's hugged-in elbows. One of his big rope-scarred fists smashed up from below and knocked the elbows apart and ripped Hagar's shirt from waist to neck as it howled on up to crash into his chin.

Hagar's head snapped up. Owens's own head was against the sheriff's body now, and he kept on hitting from there. His right fist thudded into Hagar's belly with a sickening, fleshy sound. Hagar stiffened. Owens slugged him in the ribs. Hagar spun half way around, tottering there. Owens slugged him again, and Hagar jerked around the other way. Again. Again. Again.

Hagar went over on his back, stiff as a board and stretched his length on the flagstones. Owens stumbled on over his body, hands pawing out, and for a moment, Elgera thought he would fall too. Then he caught himself and turned around. He stood there a moment. He drew a hoarse, sobbing breath and then held it, waiting. Avarillo's arms slackened, and the girl bent forward, lips open slightly, waiting.

But Hagar didn't move. He lay there with his shirt almost ripped off, blood leaking from one corner of his split lips, one eye closed and beginning to swell already. There were big, red, beefy spots on his lean torso as if he had been slapped with the flat of a board. His breathing was hardly audible. He didn't move.

Finally Owens dabbed at his battered face. He began walking around in little circles, one hand held out in front of him. His face was even worse than Hagar's. His brow was laid open from one temple to the other, bleeding profusely, and his cheeks were lacerated and torn until they looked like fresh hamburger. He was bleeding at the mouth too. He spat out a tooth and kept dabbing feebly at his eye

186

that way, walking around in circles. Elgera realized he couldn't see, and she broke free of Avarillo with a sharp cry, running to Chisos. She caught his arm and led him to the bench.

"I didn't think," he gasped, sagging to the seat, "I didn't think there was a man that tough in Texas."

He put his head into his arms and drew a great, sobbing breath, shaking and quivering like a wind-broken horse. The Indian *mozo* had brought in a silver bowl of warm water and some clean cotton. Elgera went to Hagar, knelt beside him.

"Oh, Chisos," she said, "did you have to do it this way?"

From the corner of her eye she saw Avarillo pick up the Adams dueling pistol which Hagar had shot from Bruce-Douglas's hand. The fat Mexican started to slip it into the voluminous folds of his amazing sash. Bruce-Douglas walked over with one hand inside his coat. He held out his other hand.

"What did you expect to do with it against Hagar's guns, anyway?" grinned Avarillo. "You know it won't work." He handed back the pistol.

Elgera's head raised sharply, and for a moment she forgot the sheriff's wounds. She had wondered what it was Bruce-Douglas hid beneath his affected hauteur. She knew now. Owens and Hagar weren't the only deadly men in that little garden.

Hagar regained consciousness finally, and they half carried him to the bench. Brother Katopaxi had ordered the *mozo* to boil some live-oak bark and mix it with pounded charcoal and maize. From this the brother made poultices. He put some on Bruce-Douglas's hand and sewed a piece of bullhide around it. Then he applied it to the other men's faces, holding a poultice on Chisos's wrecked brow by a strip of cotton around his forehead, bandaging

187

them in other places where it was possible. Speaking with difficulty through mashed lips, Owens told Hagar about the *derrotero* and showed him how the route on the map led back to Boquillos and on to the *Resaca Espantosa*.

"Clay Thomas's murder is hitched up with the secret of the Santiago, somehow," said Chisos. "And we have two-thirds of the secret. Find that other third, and where it leads, and we're just as likely to find out who shot Clay. I'll give you your choice, Hagar. You can come with us and give me your word you'll let me have a chance to clear myself. Or I can take your guns and your horse and leave you stranded here. This is out of your jurisdiction. You aren't known down here. It'd take you a long time to get back."

Hagar shook his head groggily. He looked around at the girl. Suddenly she saw him grin.

"All right," he said, "I give you my word I'll let you try and clear yourself."

Chisos gave him back the Peacemakers—then he stood up. "The way I feel now, you'll probably have to tie me on Del's horse, but we might as well hit for Boquillos."

"What good will that do?" asked Bruce-Douglas. "We have only two-thirds of the map. Perhaps you think you'll get the other piece by asking the first peon you see in Boquillos to hand it over."

Avarillo's chuckle was sly. "*Pues*, it might be almost that easy. I think we better go to Boquillos, all right."

The *mozo* had brought their horses from the *posada*. Though Owens and Hagar could hardly stand up, they insisted on starting at once. The girl helped Chisos into his saddle and mounted her palomino, kneeing it in close so she could catch

Chisos's arm. Avarillo hoisted Hagar onto his horse. The girl watched the fat Mexican narrowly, almost angrily.

"*Vaya con Dios.*"

Katopaxi's dry rattle whirled *Señorita* Scorpion. He stood in the small arched doorway piercing the wall, his spidery hand running up and down the slender chain supporting his cross. Elgera murmured good bye—then a strange expression came into her face, almost a fear, and she gigged her palomino forward suddenly to touch Chisos. She caught his arm.

"Did you see that brother," she asked in a strained voice.

Chisos was trying very hard not to be sick. He swayed forward in the saddle, one rope-scarred fist gripping the horn tightly. "Katopaxi? What about him?"

"The cross he wears around his neck," said Elgera. "It was hanging upside down!"

V

When Anse Hawkman had controlled all the land from the Rio Grande north to Persimmon Gap, he had made his headquarters at the border town of Boquillos. But the A H empire had crumbled into the dust now, and Boquillos was already slipping back into the obscurity and peace it had known before Anse had put his greedy hands on it. With the long ride from Monclava behind them, Elgera and the four men entered Boquillos from the west, turning into the main street which had been known as Pasadizo Hawkman. They passed the big adobe *cantina* Anse had run. Elgera glanced for a long moment at the idlers by the hitch rack in front of the saloon and under the cottonwoods at the corner of the building. Chisos Owens rubbed his healing face gently, grinning.

"You won't find any A H hands," he said. "They mostly drifted up to Alpine and Marathon, where the air's a little healthier for the men who worked for Anse."

They passed the adobe stables across from the *cantina*, a large squat building with the *viga* poles that formed rafters extending out through the yellow walls and casting an uneven shadow pattern across them. Under two persimmon trees in front the gnarled smithy was shoeing a huge black horse. A heavy-set Mexican rose from where he had been hunkered down against the water hut. Elgera reined in her palomino.

"Gato!"

The man known as Cat came on from the cool shade into the bright sunlight and shoved his roll-brim sombrero back and stood squinting up at them, grinning maliciously.

"You left Alpine in a big hurry," he said. "You forgot to pay us. Perhaps you would like to do that now."

Avarillo bent forward in his saddle as fast as his prodigious girth would allow and spoke ironically. "*Muy afortunado*, Gato, that you just happened to be here when we rode by, most fortunate."

Gato glanced at him. "This is my town, *Señor* Avarillo. Why shouldn't I be here?"

From the corner of her eye Elgera caught the shift of men across the street. Enrique had come down the alley between the *cantina* and the adobe hovel next door. His scarred face was turned toward the riders, and he shifted the inevitable pick-axe from his

190

shoulder to across his belly where he held it with both hands.

"You know you'd have gotten paid by going back to the Santiago," snapped the girl. "My brother's there."

"Go back through those Dead Horses?" grinned Gato. "Even I couldn't find my way through them to the mine shaft, *señorita*. You Douglases are the only ones who could ever follow that trail. A man would be a fool to try it alone."

"Chisos did," said the girl.

Gato looked at Owens, spat. "Sometimes I think maybe he is not all man, like the Indians say. We would like our money now, *señorita*."

One of the idlers in front of the *cantina* turned and called softly through the open door. A man appeared there then, moving out. Elgera spoke angrily.

"You know I don't carry that much money around in my saddle bags, Gato. I can't pay you now."

Gato moved toward her. "Can't you? Can't you, *señorita*?"

A Quill was a pure-blooded Indian of Mexico. The man who had come from the door of the *cantina* was a Quill. He was short and squat with his greasy black hair done up in a queue and buckskin *chivarras* for leggin's. He had his hand on the butt of a gun stuck through the waistband of his trousers in the very middle of his belly. Elgera couldn't help wondering where she had seen him before. Then Gato reached up and grabbed the cheek piece on her bridle. The palomino jerked its head up. Gato pulled it down with a brutal grunt.

"Can't you *señorita*?" he repeated. "My town. Can't you pay me now?"

"Gato," shouted Hagar, wheeling his horse trying

to get around Chisos.

Owens tried to turn his animal, too, and got in the sheriff's way. Bruce-Douglas spurred his animal in between them and to the head of the palomino, turning until he was broadside there. He bent forward as if to speak, but *Señorita* Scorpion had already turned in her saddle and dropped one hand to the cantle near enough to the butt of her big Army Colt. Facing Gato that way, there was a wild look in her flashing eyes.

"I don't have to remind you what happened before, do I, Gato?" she said. "We're just passing through Boquillos. You'll get paid, and you know it. Right now, we're just passing through. Better let us."

The baleful grin slipped off Gato's dark face. For a moment his strange, opaque eyes met Elgera's, then they dropped to her hand where it rested so near her gun. Enrique had come around behind the palomino, hefting his axe. The Quill followed him, face impassive. Another man was walking across from the *cantina*, shifting a holstered gun around in front of him a little.

Bruce-Douglas was leaning forward that way, and his voice wasn't arrogant now or testy or supercilious. It was strangely flat and cold.

"Gato. What are you doing?"

The Mexican's head turned toward him momentarily. For a moment their glances locked. Elgera could see how the Englishman's thin lips were compressed until the flesh showed white around them. His eyes were as cold as his voice.

Gato's own eyes dropped before them suddenly. He looked at the girl's hand again. The palomino's head jerked up as he let go of the cheek piece. A dull flush crept into his thick neck as he took a step back, raising his eyes again to Elgera.

Avarillo suddenly took his *cigarro* from his mouth and laughed. "*Sí*, Gato, Elgera doesn't have to remind you of what happened before, does she? You remember well enough. *Caracoles*."

But Elgera was watching the Englishman, and she was wondering if Gato had taken his hand off because of her. . . . or because of Harold Bruce-Douglas.

She wheeled her palomino away and broke into a canter up the street. Bruce-Douglas was next after her, then Hagar. They were close enough for the girl to hear what they said when the sheriff caught up with the Englishman. Hagar spoke first.

"What did you mean by that back there?"

The Englishman sounded supremely bored. "By what?"

"You asked Gato what he was doing?"

"Could you suggest," asked Bruce-Douglas, "a better way of finding out?"

Hagar was unperturbed. "It meant more than it sounded like. When did you meet Gato?"

"Really now," said Bruce-Douglas. "Really."

Elgera knew Hagar was grinning without turning to look at him. She dropped her palomino back beside them.

"You ride like Army," Hagar told the Englishman.

Bruce-Douglas took his snuff box out, pinching the powder disdainfully between thumb and forefinger. The way he tilted his head back was eloquent. He put the box back, dabbing his nose with the silk handkerchief.

"Posting, old boy," he condescended. "Posting."

Hagar shook his head. "That isn't posting . . . not the way they do in England, anyway. You ride like Army. I was in the Army, Douglas. I'll remember

193

sometime."

Ⓥ Ⓥ Ⓥ Ⓥ Ⓥ

Hawkman had built a two-story frame hotel on the south side of the little plaza, and they decided to rest a day there. Elgera took a front lower, overlooking the sunlit square. She had finished bathing and was combing her long, gleaming hair by the cracked mirror over the rickety bed table when someone rapped on her door. Hagar came in to her call.

"Thought you'd be about ready," he said, rubbing a freshly-shaved jaw. "Want to eat?"

She nodded, buckling on her gun. "Why do you think Avarillo was so insistent we come to Boquillos?"

"Don't know exactly," said Hagar. "Now he's talking about heading on up to the *Resaca Espantosa* marked on that *derrotero*. I think he knows a lot he doesn't tell."

"Maybe we shouldn't have let him keep those two pieces of the *derrotero*," she said, frowning.

Hagar shrugged, coming closer, and he was grinning, and it wasn't so brash now, somehow. "Elgera, how do you feel about Chisos?"

She drew a breath. "I like him very much."

"I heard it was more than that. I heard he was sweet on you," said Hagar—and her fingers were suddenly caught up in his strong hand. "You know it wouldn't work that way, Elgera. It would be like hitching a Thoroughbred with a plow horse."

"I wouldn't say that," said Chisos Owens from the open door.

Hagar let go of Elgera's hand and turned. They stood looking at each other for a moment, the two

194

men. Owens shoulders stooped forward a little as he moved on into the room.

"You got your cows in the wrong pasture, Hagar," he said heavily.

"I didn't see any fence around it," answered the sheriff.

"I figure you're the kind who'd climb over the fence if there was one," said Owens.

The girl was looking from one to the other, and was aware of what it was that had lain between them all along. Her lips twisted a little. She had known it for some time, really. She had just been reluctant to admit it. She had sensed it lying between them there at the Alpine Lodge, had seen it at Monclava. It was a new thing to her but not really a new thing. It was as old as Adam and Eve.

"This is what the fight was about at Monclava then?" she said in a low voice.

"I came to take Chisos back for a murder," grinned Hagar.

"You know what I mean," said the girl.

Hagar's grin faded slightly. "Yeah, I know what you mean. I came to take Chisos back, but the fight wasn't really about that. She's right, isn't she, Chisos? This is what the fight was about."

"I guess so," said Owens.

"You know so," said Hagar.

Owens bent forward a little. Hagar's grin spread again, but his lips had flattened against his teeth. The girl stepped between them swiftly.

"Didn't you settle it once?" she said. "Don't start in again."

"We didn't settle anything," said Hagar.

"So you're just going to keep on fighting every time you meet," said the girl hotly. "If you do it that way, I promise I won't have anything more to do with either of you. Now, are we going out and eat like intelligent adults, or am I saddling up for the Santiago?"

Hagar seemed to relax, and Owens shrugged, and Elgera turned to smile at the sheriff. "That's better. Avarillo has the map . . . I think you'd better get him and Bruce-Douglas, Johnny."

Hagar left reluctantly. Owens turned to Elgera, speaking slowly. "He was right, in a way, Elgera. It'd be like hitching a Thoroughbred to a plow horse. But that's the kind I am. I can't help it. You know how I've felt about you all along."

She patted his thick forearm. "Don't talk that way. I know."

"And Hagar . . . ?"

"A young man who can be very nice or very deadly, and who can smile just as pleasantly when he is being beaten to a pulp as when he's making love," she said.

"He means more to you than that," Owens grumbled. "But I guess I'm acting like a kid."

"Both of you are," she laughed. "Maybe that's why I like you."

Hagar came back down the hall and into the room. "Not in their rooms. Funny, too. Douglas was in our room when I left."

"Avarillo shared mine," said Owens. "He was in, too."

Elgera saw something cross his face then. Her hand slipped off his arm as he turned to walk toward the window. He put his hands on the sill and bent to look out toward the hitch rack in the plaza. *Señorita* Scorpion saw his callused fingers tighten on the sill.

"Avarillo's horse is gone," he said. "So's Bruce-Douglas's. They're both gone."

196

The *Sierra del Caballo Muerto* rose, jagged and mysterious, northward from Boquillos, and their very name bespoke the death that lay in their unknown vastness. There was not enough water in the Mountains of the Dead Horse to maintain human life. A few stands of skeleton timber clung to the barren slopes and rattled in the wind and mocked the three riders heading down the dark cañon that led deeper into the terrible range. Shadowy mesquite squirmed down the barrancas, and the prickly pear sought fissures in the rocks as if hiding from the malignant spirit that hovered over the whole region.

The golden coat of Elgera's palomino was turned gray with dust. She sat the horse with a dull weariness, legs slack against sweat-darkened stirrup leathers, both hands holding the pommel of her three-quarter rig. Behind the cantle were slung a pair of Army canteens, the water sloshing in them continually with a hollow, tinny sound, reminding Elgera of how little was left. Three days of the grueling ride had passed beneath their horses' plodding hoofs, yet Hagar still rode with that insouciance in the easy slouch of his long body, his grin splitting an unshaven chin. He hummed idly at his "Stable Call."

Oh go to the stable, all you who are able,
And give your poor horses some hay and some corn.
For if you don't. . . .

He sat erect suddenly, snapping his fingers. "That's where he was. Troop A of the Fourth. I knew I'd remember it."

"Who was in Troop A?" asked Elgera uncaringly.

"Bruce-Douglas," said Hagar. "Corporal Bruce-Douglas. Court-martialed in 'Ninety-One for letting one of Geronimo's Apaches escape while we were taking them to Florida."

Elgera turned farther toward him, eyes darkening. "Then he isn't an Englishman. He isn't. . . ."

Hagar shrugged. "Might be English, all right. Might even be the rightful heir to your mine. I don't know. I do know he was in the Fourth, though. Drummed out for letting that Indian get away. That was about a year before my own discharge."

Owens halted the horse he had taken from Delcazar. Ahead the cañon spread out. Flanking it on either slope, two spires of reddish sandstone stood in fantastically eroded majesty.

"*Los Dos Dedos de Dios*," said Hagar.

"The Two Fingers of God?" Elgera asked.

Chisos nodded. "We made our mistake in letting Avarillo keep the map. But I remember the route we traced down there at Monclava. You been wondering why I cut back and forth so much? From Boquillos, remember, the dotted line turned north to the *Resaca Espantosa* . . . the Haunted Swamp. That was the last spot for a distance, and if we could find them, we could find the swamp, and if these ain't the fingers, I'm not a Texican."

Hagar spat. "Swamp! We've come a hundred miles without seeing enough water to wet a sidewinder's last rattle."

"He's right," said the girl. "In four hundred years the Santiago's the only place in the Dead Horses where men have found water like that."

Owens hiked a boot over his saddle horn, reaching for the makings in his jumper pocket. "Right. So, if there is a swamp, it must be fairly near the Santiago. And like Avarillo says, the Indians wouldn't go very far away from the valley to store their gold . . . no farther than the length of time the water they could carry would last. Which brings us to what?"

Hagar wasn't enthusiastic. "The gold and the swamp are close to each other."

Owens rolled himself a wheatstraw, thick fingers amazingly deft. "Once more. The gold and the swamp and the Santiago are close to each other."

Hagar slapped his canteen. It emitted a hollow sound. "If you're wrong about the swamp, we'll be slitting our own throats by going ahead. As it is, we'll be lucky to make it back out. And even supposing there is a swamp, if you miss it by one hair, you might as well miss it entirely."

Chisos glanced at Elgera. Elgera looked at Johnny. Hagar grinned, gigged his horse.

"All right," he said. "I don't have a back door, anyway."

As they rode on toward the *Dedos de Dios*, Elgera noticed how Chisos kept bending from side to side in the saddle. Finally, in the shadow cast by the twin spires of sandstone, he halted. They were standing beside a hollow sink, its clay bottom slick and hard, criss-crossed by deep cracks and fissures. Elgera thought the mesquite here seemed darker than the growth they had been passing. Owens climbed from his horse. He dropped the stub of his cigarette, grinding it out with a heel.

"We'll stop here."

Night fell slowly through the blinding heat of the afternoon. Finally the shadows had turned to darkness. A lizard made a sibilant scraping sound in the silence. The thirsty horses fiddled nervously. Then the moon yellowed the blackness, casting an eerie light over the weird peaks surrounding them.

And Elgera saw why Chisos had stopped here.

The bottom of the sink was wet already. The horses bent weary necks to muzzle the dampness eagerly. Owens grunted in a satisfied way.

"If there's water at all, it seeps up this way at night," he said. "The mesquite looked healthier than most we passed. It's usually the sign. Let's go."

From the sink led several gullies. Owens took each one in turn, following it a few yards, squatting down to feel the earth with his hands. Finally he came back and picked up his reins and led them into the gully which turned northward between the needles of sandstone. Elgera followed, leading her palomino. At first her boots made a soft shuffling in the damp sand. Then they began passing through slush, and farther on the slush turned to ooze that popped and sucked with each step. The mesquite on the banks of the gully gave way to intermittent hummocks of toboso grass that sighed eerily in the light breeze. Elgera's hand tightened on her reins. Ahead of her Chisos swung aboard his horse, and Elgera could see why—the animal was sloshing through muddy water to its knees. Elgera mounted, turning to see Johnny coming up behind her, and behind him the *Dedos de Dios* towering into an ominous sky. Then from ahead came the unmistakable boom of a bull frog.

As they moved forward more slowly now, a strange sibilance entered Elgera's consciousness, an insidious rattling, not as loud as the croaking of the frog yet more intense. She wiped a perspiring palm against her *charro* leggin's, unable to recognize the sound. The first spread of cane brake rose against the low moon in a tall, ghostly pattern, rattling incessantly in the breeze. And she remembered the round bars which might have been molded in canes

200

from a brake like this.

"*La Resaca Espantosa*," said Chisos. "The Haunted Swamp."

Elgera's palomino started at a sudden movement on the bank of the gully above. Johnny's voice rang sharply from behind.

"Watch it. Elgera, watch it . . . !"

The thunder of a shot cut him off. The palomino reared, squealing. Fighting it around, Elgera could see Hagar bent forward in his saddle. He held his right shoulder with his left hand. His right holster was empty, and his right hand.

"Please don't continue acting so foolish," said someone from the bank. "We really don't want to kill you."

VI

The flickering camp fire turned Elgera's blonde hair to a ruddy cascade where she sat with her back against the gnarled bole of a post oak. Beside her Johnny Hagar lay full length on the soggy ground, his reckless grin forced against the pain of his wounded shoulder, hands bound behind him, ankles tied together. Chisos Owens was at Elgera's other side, rawhide lashings gathering his denim jumper into folds about his blocky torso. She could hear his heavy breathing and an occasional grunt. Already he was beginning to strain at his bonds.

Bruce-Douglas stood farther out, firelight throwing sinister shadows across his thin face. It had been the Englishman and Gato and Gato's men on the bank of the gully. Under the threat of their guns Elgera and Chisos and Johnny Hagar had been disarmed then taken across the bog and through the cane brake to this clearing of salt grass and post oaks. The Englishman was toying with the Adams dueling pistol he carried with him, studying the G D inscribed over the pan, apparently enjoying the strain which the lengthening silence caused Elgera and the others. His thin smile was turned toward the man lying at his feet. It had surprised Elgera at first. She had thought all along that Avarillo had conspired with Bruce-Douglas, had left Boquillos willingly.

There was nothing willing about the corpulent Mexican, lying there with his arms spread-eagled by the stakes they had thrust into the ground and to which they had tied his hands. He lay so that his bare feet would have been in the fire if his legs hadn't been curled up beneath him. The reddened, blistered look to those feet held its own grim significance. Bruce-Douglas caught Elgera's horrified eyes on them.

"This little exercise on his pedal extremities isn't the only persuasion we have tried," he said. "Gato worked all the way up from Boquillos, but so far his handicraft has failed miserably. We thought, like you Elgera, that Avarillo knew more about that third piece of the *derrotero* than he told us at Monclava. We spirited him out of the Hawkman Hotel while Chisos and Johnny were in your room."

"I am dying, *señores*," panted Avarillo. "Tender me one more *cigarro* before I pass on. Just one. It's all I ask."

"We'll give you something more *caliente* than a *cigarro*," grunted Gato viciously.

He wasn't the Gato Elgera had known now. His magnificent black Arabian stood tethered apart from the other horses, Spanish rig the same color as the animal, heavy with silver-plating. His big Colts were

202

thonged low around the legs of shiny black *mitaja* leggin's. His white shirt had been replaced by a black one, and over that he wore a black *charro* jacket hemmed in gold.

Elgera hadn't been surprised, somehow, at Gato's being the *Caballero Negro*. What had caused her real shock was to see the blind man, Brother Katopaxi, and his Indian *mozo* from Monclava. Katopaxi stood just outside the circle of firelight, one bloodless hand running up and down the slender chain holding his inverted cross, like a spider on its web. The husky, sibilant rattle of his voice held a sinister note for the girl now.

"Why not give our dying *hermano* this last consideration?" he said mockingly. "We are all *hermanos* in the sight of our Majesty. Give him a *cigarro*, Gato, my son."

Gato squatted beside Avarillo, shoving his tremendous black sombrero back on his head. He took two cigars from the pocket of Avarillo's silk shirt, lit them in the fire. He jammed one in the fat Mexican's mouth, put the other into his own. Avarillo sucked gratefully on the smoke. Finally he spoke.

"Why do you always play with that Rodriguez, *Señor* Bruce-Douglas?"

Elgera saw the surprise in the Englishman's face for that instant; then he covered it with a careful indifference. "The gun is an Adams. London, you know, Sixteen Seventies"

"No," said Avarillo. "It is a Rodriguez made in Toledo by the Rodriguez brothers, much later than your Sixteen Seventy."

Hagar was watching the Englishman, and maybe he had caught that momentary surprise, and maybe he saw the game. "Perhaps he's right, Corporal Douglas."

Bruce-Douglas turned toward him sharply. Then he tilted his head back slightly. "Really, gentlemen. Really!"

"Then you aren't English," said Elgera swiftly. "You aren't . . . !"

"I'm not descended from your infamous George Douglas, if that's what you were going to say," shrugged the man resignedly. "And as far as the other . . . I owe no special allegiance to any one country. I was born in the Bahamas. I was sent to Eton. Served in the French Foreign Legion as well as your stupid U. S. Cavalry. What would that make me?"

"Do you really want us to tell you," chuckled Avarillo, then he grimaced with pain. "Where did you get the dueling pistol, *señor*, where did you really get the Rodriguez?"

Bruce-Douglas condescended. "On a detail transferring some of Geronimo's chaps to Florida. One of the Indians promised to give me the key to the secret of the Santiago. That was before the outside world had become aware of the Santiago. Naturally I thought the secret was the knowledge of its whereabouts. I helped him get away. This dueling pistol was all I got for my trouble. The Indian said it was a tribal fetish . . . said it had been taken by one of his ancestors who raided the Santiago Mine over two hundred years ago. Said Don Simeón Santiago ran out of the house with this gun when he heard the Indians. It misfired. He threw it into a Comanche's face. The bounder then killed Don Simeón and took the gun as well as his hair. That is how the Indian I helped escape came by it. He traded with the Comanche."

"Why the Adams business then?" asked the girl.

"I claimed it as an Adams only to enhance my

rôle as the Bruce-Douglas recently from England who was the legal heir to George Douglas's estate," said Bruce-Douglas. "I had found out by then that the gun was no key to the secret . . . had found out, in fact, what the secret really was. We had one third of it. We thought, naturally, that Elgera would have a third, being George Douglas's descendant."

"We?"

"Gato, Katopaxi, and I," smiled the Englishman thinly. "I was drummed out of the service for letting the Indian escape. The gun wasn't what I'd expected, but it had whetted my curiosity. Eventually I drifted to Mexico City, hunting some other clue to the secret. There I found out that in the *Capilla del Santo* were all the old official documents of the Spanish government during the time Santiago had shipped his gold through Monclava. It was how Katopaxi and I met. He had that third of the *derrotero* he got from Pedro Tovar. And when he saw the dueling piece. . . ."

"Saw!" cried the girl.

Bruce-Douglas glanced at Katopaxi, and his laugh held a thinly veiled contempt. "Our bogus Franciscan is a complete hypocrite, being neither a priest nor blind. Gato is his son. Long ago Katopaxi became too decrepit for the kind of life led by the *Caballero Negro*. He took the cloth as an easier way to spend his last years. It has proven very beneficial to all."

"But the cross, the friars . . . ?"

"Do you think I let them see my cross?" cackled the old man. "No, my dear, for ten years I have been the blind Brother Katopaxi, tending his flock of ignorant peons, waiting for the riches of the Santiago to come to me. It was in my first year at Monclava, you see, that Pedro Tovar called me for benediction and gave his third of the *derrotero* to the Church. I knew what that piece of parchment meant. I knew I only had to be patient, and I would get the treasure men have been hunting for two hundred years. Soon I heard the Santiago had been found again, owned by a half-wild girl descended from George Douglas. When Bruce-Douglas came to the Monclava with the dueling pistol and the same name as the girl, it gave me the idea. Gato wanted to try and find the girl's portion of the *derrotero* by means of force. The other way was more intelligent, don't you think?"

"Not especially," said the girl. "You didn't get anything."

"If you had possessed a third of the chart," said Bruce-Douglas coldly, "I would have found it, believe me."

"What does it matter?" laughed Katopaxi shrilly. "You have been delivered into our hands by his Satanic Majesty. . . ."

"*Dios*, a devil worshipper!" gasped Avarillo. "Cross me, quick, somebody cross me!"

Gato's laugh was ugly. Elgera shifted her bound wrists uncomfortably behind her. The hemp was rasping them. Hemp? Yes, not rawhide. Chisos and Johnny had been tied with rawhide dallies, but Gato had used a spare piece of rope on the girl. She caught the sudden bright glow of Avarillo's *cigarro*.

"It was you following Clay Thomas, then," said Owens.

The firelight caught opaquely green in Gato's eyes as he turned toward Owens. "When Clay Thomas got Delcazar's spread for Anse, he went to Mexico City for the papers they had with a law firm there and to clear the old Spanish grant. I have connections down there. Clay had been in Mexico

206

City about a week when I heard that he was pestering the government officials for the old maps of the border states."

"*Sí*," hissed Katopaxi. "We knew that Ramón Delcazar was descended from Pio Delcazar, *capitán* of Don Santiago's muleteers in Sixteen Eighty-One. It wasn't hard for us to guess what Clay Thomas had found among the Delcazar's papers that made him so suddenly interested in old maps. We tried to get him in Mexico City, but he got away."

Enrique had come with Gato. He stopped at the fringe of the light, scarred face fantastic in the glow of red flames, axe over his shoulder. Another man had come with the *Caballero Negro*, too. He was the Quill who had walked across the street there in Boquillos when Gato had stopped Elgera. A squat little man in his buckskin *chivarras*, greasy black hair queued, gun stuck nakedly through his waistband in the middle of his belly. His appearance had stuck a familiar chord in Elgera at Boquillos. She knew why, now.

Gato caught her intent gaze on the Quill, and laughed. "*Sí, señorita*, that is Torres. Torres is the man you saw run from the alley behind the Alpine Lodge, remember? As my *padre* says, we missed Clay Thomas in Mexico City. While Enrique and I hired on as miners to Avarillo, we sent Torres to floor Thomas and get what he had. Torres didn't know Chisos Owens was in that room at Alpine. I'm afraid it surprised him a little. He really shouldn't have run until he got the *derrotero*, should he?"

"I told you, Johnny," said the girl grimly.

She saw Hagar's face turn toward Owens a moment. The sheriff grinned suddenly; Owens grinned. Gato suddenly squatted again beside Avarillo and grabbed a leg, snarling.

"I'm tired of this talk. I'll give you something more *caliente* than that *cigarro* if you don't tell us where that last piece is!"

"Gato!" said Bruce-Douglas imperiously. "I think we have a superior stimulus, now that everyone has arrived. I wondered why our fat Mexican had been so obdurate about telling. Perhaps I see. . . ." He turned to Elgera. "You're such a fascinating creature, Elgera, you draw men like moths to a flame. Other than his amplified waistline and his amazingly diversified accomplishments, Avarillo isn't much different from other men, is he? Perhaps he's undergone our tender ministrations so stoically because of an unavowed devotion to you. Yes, I think that might be it."

Still holding the dueling piece in one hand, he bent to the fire. Grasping the unburned end of a glowing stake in his free hand, he straightened and moved toward the girl. Her breath gagged in her throat suddenly. There was a sharp ripping sound to her left. She saw Chisos's jumper had torn across the bulge of his muscles humped up on either side of his big neck as he writhed madly at his bonds.

"*Por Dios*," gasped Avarillo. "Not that, Douglas . . . !"

Bruce-Douglas bent almost languidly. Elgera drew back from the growing heat as the brand was brought closer to her face by that slim pale hand. She could see the strange, feral light in the Englishman's icy eyes. She jerked spasmodically as a burning ash fell on her leg.

"You have but a moment, Avarillo," said Bruce-Douglas in that bored voice. "Such a lovely soft face, too. The other third of the *derrotero*, please."

Avarillo made a choked sound. With a sudden hoarse roar Chisos Owens jerked onto his knees and

208

drove upward and threw himself on Bruce-Douglas, bound hand and foot as he was. With Owens's big head in his stomach, Bruce-Douglas grunted sickly and went over backward, burning stick flying from his hand.

Gato let go of Avarillo's leg and jumped erect, pawing for one of his guns. Avarillo snaked out one of his burned feet and slammed Gato across the back of his knees with a post-oak calf. Gato's legs snapped shut like a pair of hinges, and he stumbled forward, falling to his hands and knees as his gun went off into the ground. The Quill named Torres tried to get around from behind Katopaxi, but the old man got in his way, shouting maledictions in Spanish.

Owens rolled on over the Englishman and flopped onto his knees again and then onto his tied feet, throwing himself forward toward the horses before he fell onto his face once more.

"Stop him," yelled Bruce-Douglas, rolling onto his belly.

Hemp, hemp, hemp. It ran through the girl's mind as she rolled toward Avarillo. Torres shoved Katopaxi so hard the old man fell, and then the Quill was free to snap a shot at Owens. But the big man had already jerked to his feet again, and the slug kicked up dirt behind him as he heaved his tied body in another prodigious jumping hop toward the horses. Enrique was running toward him with the axe upraised. Bruce-Douglas was on his knees. He still held the dueling pistol, his free hand fumbling beneath his coat for something.

"Stop him, you fools!" he called.

Sheriff Hagar's lean body suddenly flopped into the Englishman, knocking him over again. Elgera was half lying on Avarillo now, her bound hands by

209

his head.

"Hemp on my hands," she panted. "Your *cigarro*, quick."

He had a nimble wit, Avarillo, and he needed no more than that. She stiffened with the pain as the glowing cigar was jammed against the rope on her wrists. Gato was running after Owens and so was Enrique and Torres, and they were all getting in each other's way. Hagar's body had rolled on over Bruce-Douglas and right into the fire. Owens took a last heaving jump and crashed in among the horses, sending them into a kicking, squealing, whinnying mill.

Hagar bounced around on his back in the fire, kicking embers and burning wood and coals every which way. Gato turned back toward him with a shout, pointing his gun at the sheriff. But the fire was scattered already, and the moon hadn't yet risen above the tall cane, and the darkness that settled over the clearing so suddenly was solid and intense after the ruddy glare of the flames.

Writhing with the pain of the burning cigar, Elgera saw Gato's gun stab at the gloom. A horse must have broken free. It galloped across the clearing. Someone shouted, stumbling out of the animal's way and toward Elgera. She was sobbing now, but she could smell the rope beginning to burn. Two more horses came thundering across the soggy grass. Then the man coming toward her stumbled over her leg.

Elgera caught the shadowy movement that might have been his hand, and she knew she had to do it now. Throwing herself upward with a savage cry, she wrenched desperately at her bindings. She felt the burned rope around her wrists give, then break. She went into the man with her freed arms jerking around in front. The thick wool of Bruce-Douglas's greatcoat was suffocating against her nose and mouth.

She caught him around the legs. As he fell, he slashed at her viciously with a gun. She stopped his arm coming down, let go his legs to grab the weapon, and twist it from his hand. Then they hit the ground, and she rolled free of him. More horses clattered across the clearing, and one of them galloped between Bruce-Douglas and Elgera. She got to her knees but couldn't see the Englishman now. She heard someone fighting on the other side of the clearing.

"Gato!" shouted the man.

Elgera turned toward the noise, tripped, and fell over a body. She still held the gun she had taken from Bruce-Douglas. She raised it to strike.

"Elgera," panted Johnny Hagar.

She halted, the gun above her head. Then she was tearing at his bonds, feeling him stiffen with the pain of burns he had taken in the fire. Finally she had him free.

"*Caracoles*," shouted Avarillo, "either give me another *cigarro*, or untie my hands, somebody."

She found him and yanked up the stakes holding his hands spread-eagled. A shot bellowed, another.

"Gato?" yelled that man across the way again.

She realized Chisos was over there somewhere and once more scrambled to her feet and turned that way, running. Suddenly she slid off the solid ground into the mud. Floundering around, she half fell into the canes. She held the gun in one hand, pawing with her other, trying to feel her way back to the clearing. The canes kept rattling against her. She thought she had become turned around. She whirled the other way, plunging through the rattling madness. Panic caught at her when she didn't emerge. She turned back, panting. It took her that long to realize what had happened. She couldn't hear the sounds from the clearing. No sounds. Nothing.

Then the sibilant rattle of canes caused her to turn around. Her voice sounded small. "Avarillo?"

"Really now," said someone. "Really!"

VII

Just before Hagar had scattered the fire and thrown everything into darkness, Owens had cast himself in among the horses with Gato's bullets kicking up mud behind him. Still tearing at his bonds, Owens heaved up under the stake ropes, tearing the stakes from the ground and freeing the animals. He got to his knees, tearing bloody wrists finally from loosened bindings. He was stooping to untie his feet when Gato dodged in through the frenzied horses. He jerked his gun up. Elgera's palomino wheeled to gallop away, and its rump knocked the weapon aside. Chisos threw himself at the man, catching the gun and twisting it out between them before it went off again.

"¡*Cabrón*!" snarled Gato, fighting for balance.

Someone else came running in, shouting: "Gato!"

Owens bellied up to Gato, holding the right hand gun in one fist. Gato tried to pull away and free his left arm from between their bodies so he could draw his other gun. He got the arm out. Chisos slugged him in the face. The man coming in heard Gato's grunt and fired twice into the sound.

"Stop that, you *necio*!" Gato swore. "It's me. You'll hit me."

"Gato?" yelled the man again.

Gato had his other gun half way out now. Owens turned suddenly and rammed a hip into the man's belly and grabbed that right-hand gun with both big hands, twisting viciously. Gato screamed and let go. Chisos bent low and slugged him; at the same time he pushed him back into the other man. Both Gato and the man who had run in among the horses went to the ground in a kicking heap. Avarillo's fat mare ran in between Owens and them. By the time it had passed, one of the men had regained his feet and was farther away. Chisos jumped past the mare's flying hind hoofs and slugged the second man with Gato's gun as he tried to rise. He sank back with a groan. Owens bent to feel his face. No mustaches.

He turned toward the other figure, farther across the clearing. He made the man out dimly in the dark, bent over, apparently reloading.

The man straightened suddenly, shouting. "Do you know why they call me Cat, you *borrachón*? They call me the *Caballero Negro* because I ride a black horse and wear black clothes. But I like Cat better. I can see in the dark, *Señor* Chisos Owens. Come on and get me. I can see you. Come on!"

He fired, and the slug clipped at Owens's jumper. He began to move forward, lips pulled back in a half grin, half snarl. He couldn't see Gato very well, and he knew it would be useless to fire until he had a better target. His feet made a solid, dogged sound against the soggy salt grass.

"¡*Asno, burro, diablo!*" bellowed Gato and fired with each word.

Owens was bent forward in that slogging advance, and the first bullet caught his arm from wrist to elbow, jerking it up, and still he didn't fire. The second one took a hunk from his neck, and he felt the hot pump of blood out over his collar. He

213

was almost running when the third one burned through his side and threw him half way around. He lurched on forward, twisted sideways like that, almost falling until he finally squared himself. And still he didn't fire. His boots made that inexorable pound against the wet ground.

"¡*Madre de Dios*!" almost screamed the man who could see in the dark and pulled on his last shot.

Owens didn't even know if that final one had hit him, and he didn't care if the flame of the shot blinded him for that instant, because he had caught the dark suit of Gato over his sights, and he squeezed his trigger on a sure thing and kept squeezing out one deliberate shot after another as he ran on into the man.

Ⓥ Ⓥ Ⓥ

The clearing was ominously quiet when Johnny Hagar clawed his way up out of the muck surrounding it, dragging Katopaxi's servant, running from the stampeding horse. The Indian had bowled Hagar over, and both men had rolled off the ground into the bog.

Hagar didn't know how long it had lasted in there in the mud. He only knew everything had stopped out in the open when he finished it with that last blow. He had broken his hand on the blow, too. And everything had stopped in the open.

He wouldn't have bothered taking the Indian out, but the man had confiscated Hagar's Peacemakers when Gato had stopped them in the gully. Hagar wanted guns.

He had them unbuckled off the man and was strapping the belt around his hips when the silence and the darkness were suddenly filled with the pound of someone's feet.

"Hagar!" a man shouted.

The sheriff whirled. The man coming at him wasn't the one who had shouted. It was Enrique. Moonlight sifted through the canes now and yellowed the man's twisted, scarred face and flashed on the great pick axe he swung above his head. Hagar wasn't fully turned, and he knew anything he did would be futile, and he had time for nothing but the thought that this was it—this was it!

Then a great, square-bodied bulk hurtled out of nowhere and blocked Enrique off from Hagar's sight and knocked him aside as he went into Hagar. Hagar stumbled back, Enrique's axe falling on one side of him, Enrique and the other man going to the other side. And the sheriff saw who had shouted then.

Chisos Owens came up on top of Enrique as they rolled and stopped their momentum by spraddling out his legs. Enrique clawed at his mouth, gouged at his eye with a thumb. Owens raised up and drew a great rope-scarred fist back. Terror was in Enrique's widening eyes. He tried to jerk aside, voice breaking.

"¡Dios!"

Chisos lay there a long moment after the blow. Finally he got to his hands and knees over the limp Mexican.

"That axe would've been in my skull right now," grinned Hagar. "I thought you were my rival?"

"You've got it twisted," groaned Owens. "You're my rival. But not that way."

"Gato?" asked Hagar

Owens nodded his head across the clearing. "Taken care of."

Hagar saw the blood soaking Owens's jumper then and got to him, attempting to help him off the unconscious Enrique. Then he stopped trying to help him, stood straight again, and turned toward the canes rattling at the edge of the clearing.

"Gato?" asked the man who had just come out of the brake.

It was the Quill who had murdered Clay Thomas. It was Torres. The moon had risen above the tops of the canes now, and it caught the glint of Torres's gun stuck nakedly through his waistband in the middle of his belly. His hand hung stiffly over it.

"No, Torres," said Hagar, and his body bent in a lithe crouch, and the moonlight glinted on his guns, too. "No, not Gato."

"Oh," said Torres.

Hagar's hands curled slightly. Pain shot through the one he had broken hitting the *mozo*. There was a reckless grin on his face. His voice was almost amiable.

"You've got an even go, Torres. Shall we count it off?"

There was no expression in Torres's voice. "You count it off?"

Hagar's grin spread. "I'll count to three. Have your go at the last one or anything in between. All right? *Uno* . . . !"

Torres stiffened a little there at the edge of solid ground. Hagar was still grinning. The slight bend in his body was easy.

"*Dos* . . . !"

Owens's labored breathing stopped suddenly as he caught and held his breath.

"*Tres!*"

Torres dove, and Hagar dove, and the thunder of their guns rolled on through the *Resaca*, and the canes answered in ghostly response.

Elgera stood stiffly there in the darkness after Bruce-Douglas had answered. She still held the dueling pistol she had torn from him back at the clearing. The weight of it in her hand only accentuated her feeling of helplessness. From the first she had sensed the corrosive menace hovering beneath the man's affected arrogance. She remembered now the strange control he had over Gato, remembered how coldly he had faced Hagar's fabulous Peacemakers back there at Monclava— with this same useless dueling pistol.

"Perhaps I should have done this like Gato wanted to at first," called Bruce-Douglas thinly. "But killing a woman is a sordid business. Such a beautiful woman, too."

The soft, popping gurgle of mud around the man's feet came to her. She felt a little vein begin to pound in her throat. He had been fishing for something beneath his coat back there in the clearing when Chisos knocked him over—he had another gun.

Fighting panic, Elgera stooped, feeling around for the clumps of toboso grass growing in the muck. She felt the thick growth, grasped a handful of it, pulled. The clump came up with a dripping gob of mud at its roots. She swung her arm in an arc, and the mud-weighted toboso slapped into the bog far to her right.

She heard a sudden rattle in the canes, as if a man had turned sharply in them. "Elgera?"

She didn't answer. She was seeking another clump of grass. She pulled it up, throwing it far to her other side this time. Again there was that sudden rattle in the brake—as a man would make turning sharply toward the sound of the grass striking the swamp.

"Elgera?"

She thought his voice sounded higher this time. Sweating, trying to keep her breathing silent, she pulled up another bunch.

"It's no use moving. Elgera," he called. "No use trying to get away. I have a gun. I know you haven't. I'm going to kill you, Elgera. No use trying to get away."

It sounded as if he were trying to convince himself more than her. Suddenly she wanted to laugh because she knew he was afraid, too. She threw the next hunk of grass far to the right and lurched forward under cover of its sound. There was that rattle in the canes ahead of her, then a gun blared, stabbing toward the noise of that last toboso grass falling into the swamp.

The flame revealed his position. It was a shock to realize how close he stood. She began pulling fanatically at the grass now, throwing clump after clump all around her, lurching forward.

"Elgera," he called shrilly. "Elgera!"

He fired to her right, to her left, to her right again as each chunk of grass struck. She threw a final bunch, waited till his gun flamed that way, leaped into the canes at him.

Brake slopping at her face and rattling against her body, she struck Bruce-Douglas. She beat at his pale thin face with the dueling pistol. She caught his gun and twisted it away as they both fell into the mud. The strength in her grasp must have surprised him, for that instant there was no resistance in his wrist as she twisted it. Then his arm stiffened, and his body arched against her. The gun exploded between them.

She felt the hot burn of powder against her ribs. Bruce-Douglas remained stiff like that for another moment. Then he collapsed in the *Resaca*.

Dazedly she got up off him, ooze dripping from her *charro* leggin's. She saw how the gun was twisted in on his own body. She felt nauseated and had to force herself to stoop and fumble beneath his blue greatcoat for the two pieces of the *derrotero* he had taken from Avarillo. Someone came stumbling through the bog. A man called her name. It was Johnny Hagar.

Together they found their way back to the clearing where Chisos Owens sat propped up against a tree. Enrique was tied up and so was the Indian *mozo*, and the fire was beginning to blaze again.

"Avarillo?" she asked.

"*Madre de Dios*," said an amiable voice from the edge of the cane brake, "this mud feels so good on my feet I hate to leave it."

The moon was above the cane. Its light fell on the familiar corpulence of Felipe Avarillo at the fringe of the brake and on the glittering object he held in one fat hand. It was a cross on a golden chain. It hung upright.

He chuckled. "I see you still have the dueling piece."

The girl looked at the gun she held gripped in one hand, realizing only then how tightly her fingers were cramped around its ancient butt. Avarillo came reluctantly from the *Resaca*.

"The politics of New Spain in Sixteen Eighty-One were so rotten," he began, "that any man, finding such riches as the Santiago boasted, would be the first prey of every greedy government official in the province and would undoubtedly be ruined in the mad scramble to get his discovery. How deep a secret Don Simeón wanted to keep his find is evidenced by the manner in which he cut this map into three parts, each part going to a man he trusted implicitly. One to Pio Delcazar, *capitán* of his muleteers, the second sent by a faithful Tlascan to Don Simeón's son in Mexico.

"The third . . . ?" began Hagar.

"*Sí*, the third," chuckled Avarillo. "This dueling piece, as you know, is not an Adams, but a Rodriguez, made by those famous brothers in Toledo. At Monclava there is a transcript of an order sent by Don Simeón Santiago from the mine to Rodriguez for that pair of gold mounted dueling pieces inscribed with G D on the firing pan. What else could they be but a gift from Don Simeón to George Douglas? Undoubtedly Douglas had by that time won Don Simeón's friendship by his invaluable service in the mine. And if Santiago thought enough of Douglas to give him such a handsome gift, wouldn't he go a little farther and trust his friend with the third portion of the *derrotero*?"

The girl raised the pistol, and Avarillo saw the look in her eyes and chuckled again. "*Sí*, Elgera, why do you think it misfired when Don Simeón ran out of the house and shot at the Indian. Douglas, you remember, escaped the massacre because he was in the bottom level of the mine where the Comanches couldn't find him. Would he take such a valuable pair of guns down there? No. Perhaps they were on the very mantle that holds the one pistol you retained. Don Simeón grabs the first weapon at hand when the Indians come. Unfortunately for him he should take the gun in which Douglas had hidden his part of the map. Why do you think I tried to get the *pistola* down at Monclava when Bruce-Douglas had it shot from his hand? In the butt, Elgera, rolled up in the butt."

The girl smashed the handle against a rock, felt

the dry harsh paper rolled there in the hollow frame. It tore as she pulled it out. She took the other pieces of the map, fitted them all together on the ground.

"The secret of the Santiago," grinned Avarillo, "and Bruce-Douglas had it all the time and didn't know it."

Ⓥ Ⓥ Ⓥ

Chisos Owens's neck wound was superficial, as was the wound down his forearm. They tied his ribs tightly in torn strips of his own ducking jacket so the ride wouldn't jar the bullet hole through his side. They filled their canteens with boiled water from the *Resaca*. And with their two bound prisoners they set out next morning to follow the last leg of the route marked on the third portion of the *derrotero*. As Chisos said, the *Resaca Espantosa* wasn't very far from the Santiago Valley, and it was still afternoon of the same day when they topped the last ridge and looked down into the green valley with the Rio Santiago rising from underground at its northern end.

"What did I tell you?" chuckled Avarillo. "This is the way Santiago shipped his gold down to Monclava, instead of out through the mine that way. We took the back door into your valley, Elgera."

She shook her head, unbelieving. "For two hundred years the Douglases have thought that route through the mine was the only way out."

"Natural enough," said Chisos, "when the map to the other route was scattered all over Texas and half of Mexico."

Elgera's people welcomed them joyously and, as soon as they were fed and rested, they followed the secret to its end. The mouth of the main shaft was clearly marked on the third piece of ancient parchment. From that the dotted line led straight back up the mountains, measuring off five hundred *pasos*. Five hundred double steps back of the shaft took them to the grove of *chapote* trees and the huge boulder which Avarillo had found there before—the boulder which the Indians had used to refine their ore in, the dirt around its foot slick and hard.

From this rock directions on the *derrotero* led them ten *pasos* north, where the growth of *chapote* and mesquite was so thick they had to hack their way through with machetes and shovels. Avarillo was in the lead, and suddenly Elgera saw his feet kick up into the air as he burst through the stubborn brush.

"*Caracoles*, there is a hole here," he cursed—then he stopped a moment and, when it came again, his voice sounded strangely hollow. "This is it, *señores y señorita*, the *tesoro*. Bring your *entraña*, Natividad. It is one of the old shafts dug by the Indians."

Natividad lit one of his buckthorn torches and preceded Elgera into the tunnel. Chisos had insisted on coming, and the girl and Johnny helped him down. Natividad's light fell across Avarillo, standing farther down. In front of the Mexican was a pile of what looked like the rawhide kiaks use to pack ore on the *burros*. Avarillo stooped and grabbed a hitch on one, tugged at it.

"Received this day," chuckled Avarillo, "one round bullion bar, one *metro* long, one *decimetro* in diameter. And a thousand more where that came from. You're *una rica*, Elgera!"

The girl looked at the round golden bar a long time without speaking, unable to believe it somehow. Finally she smiled at Avarillo dazedly.

222

"We're all rich, you mean. Whatever it is, we'll divide it evenly."

Avarillo flourished his *cigarro*, grinning. "*Bueno, bueno*. I always wanted to be a fat old miser. I guess that settles about everything."

"There's a lot that isn't settled," grinned Chisos.

The sheriff nodded. "How about it, Elgera? Was Chisos right down there at Boquillos. Did I put my cows in the wrong pasture?"

"You can't ask me to decide that now," she smiled. "Give me time to get over all this first. Then maybe . . . ?"

Her blonde hair rippled suddenly as *Señorita* Scorpion threw back her head, and there was something wild in her laugh, and the three men looked at each other as if they knew how long it would be before any of them ever tamed a girl like that.

Les Savage, Jr. was an extremely gifted writer who was born in Alhambra, California, but grew up in Los Angeles. His first published story was *Bullets and Bullwhips* accepted by the prestigious Street and Smith's *Western Story Magazine*. Almost ninety more magazine stories all set on the American frontier followed, many of them published in Fiction House magazines such as *Frontier Stories* and *Lariat Story Magazine* where Savage became a superstar with his name on many covers. His first novel, *Treasure of the Brasada*, appeared in 1947, the first of twenty-four published novels to appear in the next decade. Due to his preference for historical accuracy, Savage often ran into problems with book editors in the 1950s who were concerned about marriages between his protagonists and women of different races—a commonplace on the real frontier but not in much Western fiction in that decade. As a result of the censorship imposed on many of his works, only now have they been fully restored by returning to the author's original manuscripts. *Table Rock*, Savage's last book, was even suppressed by his agent in part because of its depiction of Chinese on the frontier. It has now been published as he wrote it by Walker and Company in the United States and Robert Hale, Ltd. in the United Kingdom. Savage died young, at thirty-five, from complications arising out of hereditary diabetes and elevated cholesterol. However, his considerable legacy lives after him, there to reach a new generation of readers. His reputation as one of the finest authors of Western and frontier fiction continues and is winning new legions of admirers, both in the United States and abroad. Such noteworthy titles as *Silver Street Woman*, *Outlaw Thickets*, *Return to Warbow*, *The Trail*, and *Beyond Wind River* have become classics of Western fiction. His most recently-published books are *Copper Bluffs* (1995), *The Legend of Señorita Scorpion* (1997), *Fire Dance at Spider Rock* (1995), *Medicine Wheel* (1996), *Coffin Gap* (1997), *Phantoms in the Night* (1998), and *The Bloody Quarter* (1999).